3 1

D0441980

Honor's Quest

3 9075 03187941 1

KRISTEN HEITZMANN

◆◆◆◆◆◆◆◆◆◆◆◆◆◆◆◆◆◆◆◆◆◆◆◆◆◆

Honor's Quest

BETHANY HOUSE PUBLISHERS
MINNEAPOLIS, MINNESOTA 55438

Honor's Quest
Copyright © 1998
Kristen Heitzmann

Cover illustration by Joe Nordstrom
Cover design by Dan Thornberg

All rights reserved. No part of this publication may be reproduced, stored in a retrieval system, or transmitted in any form or by any means—electronic, mechanical, photocopying, recording, or otherwise—without the prior written permission of the publisher and copyright owners.

Published by Bethany House Publishers
11400 Hampshire Avenue South
Bloomington, Minnesota 55438
www.bethanyhouse.com

Bethany House Publishers is a Division of
Baker Book House Company, Grand Rapids, Michigan.

Printed in the United States of America

Library of Congress Cataloging-in-Publication Data

Heitzmann, Kristen.
    Honor's quest / by Kristen Heitzmann.
        p.   cm. — (Rocky Mountain legacy ; 3)
    ISBN 0–7642–2033–0
    I. Title. II. Series.
III. Series: Heitzmann, Kristen. Rocky Mountain legacy ; 3.
PS3558.E468 H67   1999
813'.54—dc21   99–6536
                                                                     CIP

To Devin
As you grow into manhood
may you become the man of honor
God created you to be

. . . whatever is true, whatever is noble,
whatever is right, whatever is pure,
whatever is admirable—
if anything is excellent or praiseworthy—
think about those things

PHILIPPIANS 4:8

Rocky Mountain Legacy

◆◆◆◆◆◆◆◆◆◆◆◆◆

Honor's Pledge
Honor's Price
Honor's Quest
Honor's Disguise
Honor's Reward

Diamond of the Rockies

◆◆◆◆◆◆◆◆◆◆◆◆◆

The Rose Legacy
Sweet Boundless
The Tender Vine

◆◆◆◆◆◆◆◆◆◆◆◆◆

Halos
A Rush of Wings
The Still of Night
Twilight

www.kristenheitzmann.com

KRISTEN HEITZMANN is the acclaimed author of novels, including the 2003 Christy Award finalist, *The Tender Vine*, and *A Rush of Wings*. An artist and music minister, Kristen makes her home, with her husband and four children, in the foothills of the Colorado Mountains.

Part One

One

Ragged scraps of cloud hung beneath the edge of blue nubby mountains like gauze torn from a blanket of gray. The keen December air held an expectant breath as Abbie stepped out and drew it into her lungs. She watched a black-capped chickadee puff itself on the bare cottonwood beside the ice-edged stream, then took the bucket and headed for the pump.

Monte's plan for indoor plumbing was only talk now, with the financial struggles that seemed to mount daily. Her heart ached that her own foolishness had put them in jeopardy. Monte blamed it on a kind heart and a stubborn streak, but she knew it was just plain ignorance.

Abbie hung the bucket and gripped the pump handle. The cold of the metal penetrated her beige kid glove. She'd thought all her schooling, her voracious reading, and the woodcraft Blake had taught her would set her up fine for life. Marriage to Montgomery Farrel had proved her wrong.

She worked the handle until the water gushed, then kept it smoothly coming. When the rush nearly reached the brim, she released the handle and lifted the bucket from the hook. She didn't need indoor plumbing and spigots that ran hot and cold. She'd bathe in a mountain stream if only Monte wouldn't worry.

He tried to hide it, except in those honest moments when they held each other in the dark. Then he admitted his fears. Had he not lived through ruin enough with the war that destroyed his father's southern plantation?

He had established himself so solidly here in the Colorado

11

Territory. But his brother-in-law had turned things upside down, and, man of honor that he was, Monte vouched for Kendal's debts. Abbie wished she'd known and understood.

But she hadn't. She had foolishly sacrificed valuable stock certificates held in her name. That she had thought to help Kendal, that the venture turned out fraudulent, that those certificates were now held by a self-satisfied banker, were all due to her ignorance.

Monte's sister, Frances, was right. There was more to being a lady than she would ever know. Abbie held the bucket with both hands and started for the house. She was too headstrong, too impetuous, too—

A hand snaked from the shrubs and clamped her mouth as a cold knife touched her throat. Her heart thundered in her chest and she felt her pulse against the blade's edge. She tensed to swing the bucket into her assailant, but with a swift glance at the hand on her mouth, she went immediately still.

Taut brown fingers trapped her breath with her voice. One move and the Indian knife would not only open her throat, but relieve her of her hair, as well. She forced her nerves to calm and stood straight.

Any show of fear could endanger her. She thought of all the tales she had scorned, all her brave declarations that the Indians were not to be feared but respected. Now with her life at the tip of an Indian blade, she resisted the surging terror.

She waited. Almost imperceptibly, the hand loosened; the knife left her throat. Still, she did not move or turn.

The man's breath warmed her ear as he spoke very low. "Wise One."

Abbie spun, sloshing water down her skirt. Its icy jolt was nothing compared to her sudden relief. "Gray Wolf!"

He snatched her into the cedars and gripped her mouth again. What was he doing? Why would he threaten her with a knife after once saving her life? Had he lost his mind?

"No speak." His face was hard and firm. He looked every inch Comanche. Though their worlds touched at strange, unexpected times, she could not assume she knew him.

She nodded.

Gray Wolf raised his head, listening. A second later, Abbie heard the approaching hooves. They were far but moving fast and coming their way. Gray Wolf stiffened. It seemed his every sinew tensed, as a buck ready to spring, and she realized it was fear driving his actions. Did he think she would betray him?

He flinched when she touched his arm. She pointed to the door, then started for it. She could scarcely hear him follow but felt him there. She pulled open the door to the back room. The kettle was steaming on the small stove for her bath. She left the door open behind her and set the bucket on the floor beside the tub, then removed the kettle from the heat.

The light dimmed as Gray Wolf filled the doorway, then stepped inside. She walked slowly to the door and closed and latched it behind him. His scent filled the small enclosure, an aroma of sweat and something musky from the small pelts that hung at his belt beneath the black woolen coat. He stood like a caged animal.

"It's all right," she whispered, then walked to the door connecting to the kitchen. She pressed her ear to the wood. Pearl's humming was interrupted. Abbie caught Monte's voice but not his words.

"She's havin' her bath, Mastuh Monte."

His steps approached the door. Abbie motioned Gray Wolf into the corner. He pressed in among the brooms and carpet beaters.

Monte tapped the door. "Abbie?"

She reached into the tub and sloshed the water. "What is it, Monte?"

"There's a posse here looking for an Indian brave."

"What on earth for?"

"I don't have the details, Abbie. Have you latched the door behind you? They found his horse in our pasture."

"The door is latched." Abbie prayed he'd ask no more. She wouldn't lie to him, but she wasn't sure how he'd take her hiding

Gray Wolf from the law, and she owed Gray Wolf a debt greater than Monte's honor.

"I don't want you out there until this is settled. Have you water enough?"

She smiled. "Yes, plenty."

"Marshal Davis and the men are searching the grounds."

"I won't go out, Monte." Nor, she realized, would they come in. Not if they thought she was bathing. She relaxed as his steps faded and Pearl took up her humming again. The smell of grits and hot cakes sizzling in pork fat seeped into the room. Gray Wolf had not moved.

Abbie crept to his corner. "Gray Wolf, why are they looking for you?"

"White man's lies."

"What have you done?"

"My brothers are dead."

Abbie pictured the young braves who had hunted with Gray Wolf. The same men who, with Gray Wolf, had slain Buck Hollister and the other outlaws and rescued her. They had given her life and freedom. Could she now do less for Gray Wolf, whatever his crime?

She heard voices outside and spun as the door latch was shaken. It held firmly, and the voices passed on. She turned back. "You'll be safe here, for now at least. Do you understand?"

He nodded once.

"Turn to the wall . . . please."

He stared at her a moment, then obeyed, arms crossed at his chest, back straight. She poured the hot water from the kettle into the bath with the cold from the bucket, then doused her head and scrubbed her hair clean. Once she caught him glancing over his shoulder, but he didn't repeat it.

She toweled her hair and twisted its thick length at the nape of her neck, then pinned it there. She approached Gray Wolf. "I'm finished now. I'll bring you food." She went through the door to the kitchen.

Pearl turned from the stove. "Breakfast is ready, Mizz Abbie.

I fed de marshal's men, but they's plenty more."

"Thank you, Pearl."

Monte stood when she entered the dining room. His white pleated shirt, gray vest, and trousers were immaculate, and his dark hair waved back from his face and fell in unruly curls to the back of his collar. His brown eyes were as warm as boiled molasses as he pulled the chair and seated her, then kissed the crown of her head. "Mmm. You smell sweet."

"I should. It's the honeysuckle rinse you bought me."

He brushed her shoulders with his hand as he sat. She thrilled at his touch and wished nothing distracted her from his company. But Gray Wolf waited, and she hadn't any idea how to broach his presence to Monte. Pearl brought the hot cakes and grits and a bowl of stewed apples.

Monte blessed the food, then glanced at Abbie. "Bit of excitement this morning. You heard nothing when you were at the pump?"

Abbie dropped her eyes to the hot cakes and cut. "How well does one hear Indian braves, Monte? You know the skill with which they move."

"It's not a good sign that he left his horse in our pasture. How far can he go on foot?"

"A good distance if he has a mind to. Did they find any sign of him?"

"No. But that doesn't mean he isn't hiding near." Monte reached for the small, cut glass pitcher that held the pure maple syrup, freighted west from the Vermont forests.

Abbie could hardly taste the sweetness she usually savored. "What is he accused of?"

"Murder."

"Of course."

Monte raised a dark eyebrow at her tone. "Meaning?"

"What's the whole story?"

"Four men are dead. The Dillon brothers, Mag French, and his son Travis. It seems they were liquored up; maybe they meant to have some fun. Ethan Thomas heard the commotion out behind his place and saw the brave escape on horseback. The description matches the horse found in our pasture."

Abbie bristled. "Four men to one. That hardly sounds like murder."

"There were three other braves."

"What happened to them?"

"Killed." Monte wiped syrup from his lips with the fine linen napkin.

Abbie controlled the anger in her voice. "You said four men dead. Did the marshal forget to count the braves?"

Monte set down his fork. "Forgive me, Abbie. I spoke without thinking. I'm only repeating what the marshal said."

"I know that. But don't you see, Monte? Just as you took it for granted and didn't look past the loss of settlers' lives, so will others. What chance has that brave?"

"He'll receive a trial, same as any man."

"The same as any man? Can you really believe that?"

"Abbie . . ."

"You know what Mag French and his son were like. The Dillons were little better. Who exactly do you think started the fight?" She was losing control of her emotions.

"It doesn't matter who started it. The fact is—"

"They'll hang him."

Monte made a sound of exasperation. "Abbie, there has to be some order."

"If it were Mag French who escaped with four braves dead, would they hang him?"

Monte folded the linen napkin and laid it beside his plate. He released a long breath. "Likely not."

"So much for order."

Monte narrowed his eyes. "Abbie . . ."

"It's Gray Wolf, Monte. It's Gray Wolf they're hunting."

He rested his hands on the table edge and stared. Abbie held his eyes steadily. He must understand. She couldn't bear to defy him.

"Where is he?" Monte's voice was low.

"In the back room."

"He was with you while you washed?"

"I wasn't in the tub, Monte. I . . ."

"Deceived me." His tone was flat, and she sensed his impending anger.

"Only until the posse left. I couldn't risk . . ."

"Trusting me."

"No, I . . ." Abbie stammered.

Monte pushed away from the table and stood.

Abbie sprang to her feet. "Please. Hear me out. I didn't want to compromise you. Could you have looked Marshal Davis in the eye and told him Gray Wolf was not here?"

He turned. "Could you?"

"I owe him my life. Would you not have lied to a Yankee soldier to protect those in your care?"

"Gray Wolf is in your care?"

"Would I be here today but for him?"

He rubbed a hand over his eyes. "Abbie . . ."

"He is not guilty of murder."

Monte paced across the room and back. "Even if that's so, what do you propose we do?"

"Give him a horse and food. Let him make his way back."

"They have the ranch surrounded."

For a moment she felt what Gray Wolf must feel. His enemies closing in, his safety in the hands of one who could so easily betray him. What chance would he have? "Then let me get him through."

"No."

"Please, Monte."

He leaned his head back, then slowly lowered it. "How?"

"I can head for Pa's in the wagon."

"That's crazy, Abbie."

"They won't suspect if it's me alone."

"They'll think I've lost my mind letting you out. Besides, Gray Wolf won't agree to it."

"I think he will."

Monte ran his hand through his hair. "Abbie, it's not right."

"Is it any less right than what Mag French did to Gray Wolf's brothers? He defended himself, Monte. But will anyone believe that?"

He crossed to her. "I'll take him, then."

"He won't trust you. He came to me, and it's my debt to repay. Besides, I have a better chance." She smiled. "Being a lady and all."

He took her shoulders and drew her close. "I won't have it."

"I'm safe with him." *As safe as anyone could be with a brave like Gray Wolf.*

"You don't know that."

She wrapped her arms around his waist, sensing him weaken. He closed her in a tight embrace. "He's Comanche, Abbie."

"I know." She stretched up and kissed him. "I'll feed him first. You choose the horse."

"That hurts."

"He'll treat it right."

"Hah."

"At any rate, it's necessary." She pulled away. "Tie the horse to the back. I'll say I'm taking it to Pa's, and I'll cut through his homestead to make it true."

"You think of everything. God help me if it's ever me you try your wiles on."

She swirled her skirts in her wake.

"Abbie."

She glanced back over her shoulder.

"No one else is to know."

She nodded.

Gray Wolf ate ravenously. Abbie watched him as she filled a bag with foodstuffs. He ate as though it were his last meal. She prayed it would not be so. She had secreted the cold beef and oatmeal muffins from the kitchen with Pearl none the wiser. Monte's honor depended on her secrecy.

Though she had no doubt that God understood what she did, men were another matter. And whereas she might be forgiven as sentimental and emotional, Monte would not be. A tap on the door told her he had the wagon ready. Gray Wolf looked up from his plate.

"Gray Wolf, I'm going to hide you in the wagon and drive you past the men looking for you. Do you understand?"

He pushed the last piece of muffin into his mouth and stood. He was not tall, but every inch of him was lean and muscular. His chest muscles bulged in the buckskin shirt as he drew himself up. "You hide me."

"Yes. Under the tarp in the bed of the wagon. Monte has loaded it with other things to help with the disguise. He has a horse for you, as well."

"Why you do this?"

"Did you want to kill those men?"

"Yes."

"I mean before they set on you, did you plan to hurt them?"

He stood stoically without speaking.

"The law doesn't always reflect the truth, but truth still matters."

"We were to hunt. White man's settlements drive away the game. Comanche go hungry. Mountains hold the secret places. We came to hunt. We came in peace."

"Then I will get you through to go back to your people."

"My people are no more."

Abbie stared at him. "There must be . . ."

"Those on government land. They are not my people. They do not live free. They live . . . white man's ways."

She felt his emotion like a force—pride, regret, anger. She felt her own shame. "I am sorry, Gray Wolf."

"You." He touched her forehead as he had once before. "Wise one."

She felt the sting of tears. There was nothing more she could do. He had to make his own way. Maybe he would. Or maybe he would end up on the reservation. At least he would be alive. "We must go now."

She cracked the door open and saw Monte standing at the

head of the wagon. The horse tied to the back was young and strong, if not of the finest lineage. She bit her lip in gratitude. Monte would not count that loss lightly if only for the horse's sake. But perhaps Gray Wolf would be more careful than was usual for his people. He could not so easily replace the beast as in years past.

She opened the door and stepped out. "All clear?" she murmured and dropped the sack of food into the back.

Monte joined her. "I believe so." He helped her raise the tarp and Gray Wolf slipped beneath. "I certainly hope you know what you're doing."

"Thank you, Monte . . . for understanding."

"It's honor, Abbie. You owe a debt."

She smiled up at him. That, he understood. *Honor.* Was there ever such a taskmaster beneath God himself?

He kissed her briefly. "Be careful. If you're caught, act feather-brained . . . if you can." His mouth quirked.

Abbie giggled. "I'll give such a performance, Carolina Diamond would be green."

Monte lifted her to the seat. "Abbie, this is not a lark."

She saw his concern and looked suitably subdued. He pressed her hand but said no more. Abbie took up the reins. She was hardly past her yard and into the open country between Monte's ranch and her pa's when two men stepped out from the scrub oaks, one of them large and lumbering.

She reined in. "Marshal Davis."

He removed his hat and held it to his chest. "Mornin', Mrs. Farrel."

"Almost noon. Any sign of your fugitive?"

"No, ma'am." He glanced at the wagon bed. "Is your business pressing? I don't feel too safe with you traveling alone. I'm surprised Mr. Farrel . . ."

"I'm heading to my pa's. It's not far."

"It's a good step yet."

"I've things to deliver that won't keep. Pa's birthday is to-

morrow next." It was, but how that had come to her only the good
Lord knew.

"I still wouldn't—"

"Mr. Farrel was satisfied with your search, and I have my pis-
tol." Of anyone, Marshal Davis should know she could shoot. She
shuddered at the memory of his questions the morning after she
had killed the young rustler.

He hesitated. "I'd send an escort, but..."

"There's no need, though I thank you for the thought."

"Yes, ma'am." He replaced his hat. He looked more bearish
than ever when he lumbered back to the bushes.

Abbie slapped the reins. He hadn't even asked about the extra
horse. But she'd tip the corner of Pa's homestead anyway, just for
good measure. She brought the wagon up the foothills as far as
she could manage on the rough terrain.

Though this wasn't the native home of the Comanches, Gray
Wolf knew these hills. He'd hunted them with his brothers when
hard times forced them north. He'd come to know the mountains
and surrounding hills as he'd known the plains. She reined in and
climbed down.

Gray Wolf raised the tarp. He leaped down from the wagon
bed and stood poised on the balls of his feet. The breath of wind
caught his crow black hair as he gripped his knife and scoured
the scrub oaks and ponderosas.

She made no move until she saw his muscles slacken. Then
she went to the horse and untied its rope. It was unsaddled, and
Monte had not included a saddle in the wagon bed. No matter.
Gray Wolf would ride bareback.

He took the rope and looked hard at her, his eyes burning
with sudden intensity. He reached out and took her arm, his grip
firm and insistent. "Wise One, come."

Abbie's heart jumped to her throat. She shook her head. "No."

"Gray Wolf squaw." He held himself up, straight and powerful, and his grip tightened.

She met his eyes and the fear left her. He'd been the leader of
his clan, respected and feared. Now he was alone. Her heart

squeezed in pity for him, but she didn't show it.

She raised her chin. "I'm honored, Gray Wolf, but I have a husband already. My husband gave you this horse." She'd remind him of his debt. "In thanks for your saving my life." That made them even.

He stood silent, then released her arm and stepped back. She thought he would speak, but always what passed between them in silence was stronger. He took the leather thong strung with animal claws from his neck. She was certain it was strong medicine, but he held it out to her.

She took it from his hand. "Thank you."

With a swift motion he swung to the horse's back and kicked in his heels. The animal leaped upward through the trees, its muscled flanks rippling and its breath white. She watched until he was out of sight, then clutched the animal claws in her palm. *God-speed, Gray Wolf. May your paths lead to peace.*

She turned the wagon down the mountain and headed back. She saw no sign of Marshal Davis as she drove. He must have changed his position. It was too much to hope they'd called off the search, but she was glad now to have it concentrated on her property. Gray Wolf would vanish into the mountains.

Perhaps one day she would see him again, but likely not. She thought of him riding alone and sighed. Not that she would ever consider going with him. She might know how to track and fish with a spear and other things that hardly behooved a lady, but her world and Gray Wolf's would never blend. And she was already married to the man she loved.

She would certainly not mention Gray Wolf's offer to Monte. How he would scowl! She glanced back over her shoulder and smiled. Then again, maybe she would.

Two

Abbie looked down at the elegant pink stone, white-gabled, pillared house. Her home. The house, yard, and outbuildings had a settled graciousness that both welcomed and unnerved her. It was Monte's grace, Monte's heritage she saw. Her spirit was in the land, the wide open range ahead, and the wild, rugged mountains behind her.

As she neared the house, she saw Sterling Davis ride away. He was not part of the searchers, she was certain. He worked with Pa and ran the telegraph. He must have brought news, urgent news if it came by telegraph.

She quickened her pace, left the horse and wagon at the stable, and hurried inside. She stopped at the door to the library. Monte stood in the center of the Aubusson rug, his face ashen. He held the telegram but stared at the wall.

She rushed in. "Monte, what is it?"

He turned. His dark eyes looked deep and hollow. His voice seemed to come from a great depth. "It's Frances. She . . . died of pneumonia."

She felt the breath leave her. "Oh, Monte." She gripped his hands. They were cold, especially the burn-scarred palms. The telegram fluttered to the floor as she caught them to her chest.

His tone stayed flat. "We must go for Jeanette. Frances asked . . . that we take the child."

Abbie pressed in close to him. She couldn't bear the hard restraint she heard in his voice. "Of course. Oh, Monte, I'm so sorry."

He stroked her head but seemed miles away. He was blaming himself, though there was nothing he could have done. His sister, Frances, had been in his charge so long—through the war when they were young and afterward, when his father returned broken and maimed. After her grief this last year, the loss of her home and Kendal's death, Monte had tried to keep her with them, but she had refused.

Abbie tucked her head beneath his chin and reached around his back. She felt his tense muscles under her palms and knew he exerted great control over the emotion surging through him. Her own tears sprang loose and dampened his shirt. She hurt as much for his loss as for Frances's passing.

His voice was thick. "Will you pack? I have things to attend to before we can go, and I want to catch the morning train."

"Yes, of course." She drew away, but he pulled her close again and pressed his lips to her forehead. She raised her face and he kissed her, cupped her cheek briefly, then released her.

As she went up the stairs, she thought of little Jeanette. How was she faring with her mama gone? She had her mammy and her grandmother, Kendal's mother, but it was a mama the child needed.

Abbie's heart ached, remembering the little girl bundled in her arms as she took her down the hillside on the toboggan. She heard Jeanette's laugh, felt again the tiny mittened hands in hers. She longed to be there already, to wrap the child in her arms and hold her close.

Oh, Frances. She'd been so thin, worn by fear and anger and grief. Yet she'd seemed strong, more able to cope than before Kendal's death. Had it been a ruse? Had she mimicked strength to make her escape? Had she known Monte would never let her go unless he believed she would cope?

Abbie took out the carpetbags and satchels and pulled them open. Charleston. She was going to Monte's home. She needed only black, but it must be the very best. She had the black silk from Kendal's funeral, and the chintz, and the linen day dress.

She laid out Monte's frock coats, waistcoats, trousers, and

shirts. He looked so somber in black, but she supposed they all must. She debated between his chesterfield velvet collared over-coat and the inverness with the deep cape. What was she think-ing? What did it matter what they wore, when Frances . . .

Frances. All the unkind things she'd thought of Monte's sister haunted her now. Frances had been so proper, so condemning. And yet inside she'd had the same longings, fears, hopes . . . *Dear Lord, Frances rests with you now. I pray she's united with Kendal and their struggles are over.*

Zena tapped the door and came in, her assistance automatic, her dark hands swift and efficient. She packed the Saratoga trunk, and Abbie worked beside her. She couldn't be idle when her heart was so full it might burst. She felt a stabbing ache for Monte.

Frances was all he'd had left of his birth family. She thought of Mama and Pa and Sadie and Grant. She had so many to love, and he had lost all. She closed the carpetbag. "Will you finish here, Zena? I'm going to tell Mama we're leaving."

"Yessum. I's sorry 'bout Mizz Stevens."

Abbie pressed her hand. She wasn't surprised Zena knew al-ready. James and Pearl and Zena knew all their business and han-dled it as though it were their own. "See that Pearl has something hot for Monte as soon as he returns."

"Yessum."

For the second time that day, Abbie rode to Pa's ranch. She caught sight of Mama in the yard hanging linen on the line. It would freeze before it dried if the sun didn't show itself. She tied Zephyr to the hitching post and glanced at the buggy outside the barn. It was newer than Pa's and too fancy for—

"Hello, Abbie."

The voice came from the house, and Abbie closed her eyes and counted to ten . . . slowly. Didn't she have enough to deal with just now?

"Abbie, did you see our new buggy?"

Not even the chance that Grant was there, too, made facing Marcy Wilson . . . Martin any easier. Abbie turned. Marcy stood in the back doorway, one hand to her hip, the other on her newly bulging belly.

The fact that Marcy was carrying her brother's child did nothing to soften Abbie's feelings for her sister-in-law, and it only heightened her present loss. Frances at her worst was a rose to the stinging nettle, Marcy.

"Grant sent all the way to Denver for it to get the color I wanted."

Abbie glanced obligingly at the buggy again. The claret-colored side panels were attractive, and she could only imagine what Grant had paid for Marcy's selection. "It's a very nice buggy, Marcy. If you'll excuse me . . ."

"Ma's out back."

Abbie cringed. She couldn't help it, hearing her own mama referred to as Marcy's. "I know. I saw her."

"I can't take the cold. Doc says my condition makes my skin sensitive."

Abbie nodded dully. She didn't want to think of Marcy's condition or see the gloating look she wore when speaking of it. Her own failure to conceive Monte's child was starting to gnaw at her, and she could handle only one ache at a time. She turned her back on Marcy.

The moment she heard the door close behind Marcy's tender skin, she lifted her skirts and ran for the clothesline. Mama was at the far end with wooden clothespins in her mouth and a fresh, cleaned pillow slip in her hands. "Mama!" Abbie stopped just short of throwing her arms around her neck.

"Gracious, Abbie." Mama dropped the slip and took her hands. "What is it?"

"Frances. Pneumonia took her. Mama, Monte's in a bad way."

"Oh, dear."

"I know he feels responsible."

"He mustn't."

"But you know how it is."

"Yes, I know." Mama gave her shoulders a hug. "I'm sorry, Abbie. What can we do?"

26

Abbie shook her head. "We're leaving in the morning. Frances asked that we take Jeanette. I don't understand it, the way she feared for the child to be raised here. But I am glad. Just thinking of that little motherless girl . . ." She stepped back. "I wish I had her right now."

Mama smiled. "Soon enough. It will be hard on her. Losing her pa and now her mama so soon."

"I don't understand it sometimes."

"It's not our part to understand, Abbie. Only to accept."

"I know that." But knowing didn't make it happen. She knew that from experience, from her own pain when Monte married Sharlyn, when Buck Hollister killed Blake, when Sharlyn died of scarlet fever.

Yet what else could one do? Life and death were in God's hands, and refusing to accept that was next to stupidity. Some things were too sublime for mortals.

"Ma! Oh, Ma-a." Marcy stepped delicately across the yard with her hooded cape held close to her cheeks.

And then again, some things were only too mortal. "Mama, I have to run. Please give Pa my love."

Thankfully Mama refrained from comment at her disdain for Grant's wife. Abbie squeezed her and cut across the garden away from Marcy's path. Right now facing Marcy again was more than she could stomach.

◆◆◆◆◆◆◆

In the dim that preceded the dawn, Monte crossed the yard to where Cole Jasper stood awaiting his instructions. Ordinarily he had no qualms leaving the ranch in Cole's charge, but this time wasn't ordinary. After the losses Captain Jake Gifford had caused them, compounded by the loss of Abbie's stock certificates and the expense of this trip, the ranch was in a precarious position. One wrong move, one more setback . . .

He looked into Cole's hard, manly face. He'd learned well enough this last year to trust Cole. His loyalty and stubborn cussedness had saved Monte's life when Captain Gifford had him beaten and left to die. But until now, Monte hadn't revealed how desperate their circumstances were. This last he'd withheld through his own pride.

Cole tossed the butt of his cigarette and ground it with the heel of his boot as Monte stopped before him. His green eyes held their usual mix of respect and insolence. Monte could be thankful for that now.

If Cole Jasper had followed his orders to let him handle things alone, the coyotes would have feasted on his flesh. But Cole had let him take it as far as he could, then personally settled with Captain Gifford. Remarkably, it didn't rankle to consider Cole an equal.

Monte drew himself up. "We'll be on our way shortly. Before we go, there are some things you should know." Briefly but frankly he explained the situation. He saw Cole's surprise at both his honesty and the information. "So you see why it's critical you run things as tightly as possible. I hate to turn away hands, but . . ."

"Dunbar's hirin' on, and Ephart last I heard. If I cut loose a few, they won't be hurtin'."

Monte frowned, but Cole's response showed he understood the situation. "I trust your abilities, Cole. Make whatever decisions you deem necessary. I don't intend to prolong this trip, but there will be matters to attend to."

"I'll keep things in line here. I'm sorry about yer sister."

The words were sincere, though gruffly spoken. Monte forced away the painful rush and nodded. As long as he focused on the business at hand, he could hold the ache at bay. But the long hours on the train would be agony.

He turned as James brought their bags to the porch and the stable boy, Will, helped him load the trunk into the wagon. Abbie came to the door and stepped out. In black she seemed more slender still, her waist tiny in the corset to which she reluctantly submitted.

Her brown curls escaped the black ribboned bonnet and cascaded down her back. Hardly a matronly style, though her incredible blue eyes were somber enough. In spite of his heartache he felt his breath catch. Would he ever not feel that at just the sight of her? He hoped not.

He turned back to Cole and caught a similar reaction. The old jealousy flared, but he subdued it. How could he fault Cole for being as helpless in Abbie's presence as he was himself? "We'll be on our way, then."

As Abbie approached, Cole took off his hat and ran a hand through his unruly blond curls. "Have a safe trip. My condolences, Abbie."

"Thank you, Cole."

Monte lifted her into the wagon and climbed up. He felt the burn scars on his palms as he took up the reins. His hands were stiff but no longer so tender. He was thankful for even the limited use of them.

He had already instructed James and Pearl and bid them farewell. Now he nodded to Cole, who tipped his hat in salute. Abbie pressed close to his side as they drove. Will rode in the bed to keep hold of the trunk and bags and return the wagon. With nothing else to consider, the grief crowded in.

Abbie put a hand to his arm, as though sensing his pain. She would, she who was cleaved to him. He gave her a weak smile, and she returned it with tears sparkling in her eyes. He squeezed her in his arm. "If you cry, Abbie, you'll be my undoing."

"I won't, then." She raised her chin and blinked the tears away.

Too soon they reached town and separated. Monte and Will unloaded the luggage, and the porter saw it onto the train. Monte took Abbie's arm and helped her into a first-class carriage. No matter how precarious their circumstances, he would not have Abbie's first trip by train any less than the best.

For himself, it mattered little. Everything he felt was subdued. Nourishment had no flavor, life no zest. Even holding Abbie last night had not ignited his flame. He felt washed again in the waves of failure. How had he thought Frances could stand alone? How had he not seen she would perish in her sorrow? Why had he not insisted she stay? Why, why, why?

Monte's thoughts blended with the clatter of the wheels as the miles passed by. He became aware of Abbie's gaze and shook himself free of the cloud. "I'm sorry we haven't better circumstances for our adventuring."

She reached for his hands and kissed them.

"Abbie . . ." He smiled. "Mind yourself. Try to recall the proprieties expected of a gentleman and his lady."

"I was thinking more of my husband."

His heart quickened a moment, then stilled. "It would behoove you to recall the lessons my . . . sister . . . so painstakingly presented you."

Abbie sat back and sighed. "I do recall them, Monte, but like a foreign language. Frances was right in her assessment of me. I'm afraid I'll fail you in Charleston. As hard as I try, I'm bound to say or do something that will show everyone just how ill-bred I am."

Monte quirked an eyebrow. "Ill-bred? Never. As Kendal said, you're the new breed of lady. Be yourself, Abbie. Only leave me my decorum." He managed to warm his smile before turning again to the window.

He should entertain her, engage her in conversation to wile away the hours. But those few words had drained him. *Abbie understands*, he thought grimly. She understood too well.

They changed trains in Denver and continued on. Abbie urged him to eat and he made a good show of it in the dining car, though what he ate he couldn't recall. He thought of Frances's thin shoulders. She had wasted away from fear and grief for Kendal. She hadn't the fortitude to withstand a sickness. If he had kept her with them, built her strength . . .

A voice inside said she would not have thrived. She longed for the streets and shore of Charleston. She longed for her home, her people. She could not make the break as he had. She was bound to the South. If only Kendal had seen that!

If only he, himself, had seen it. He would have sent them both away, back to the place Frances belonged. The West was too rough, too unmade for her. Hadn't she said as much again and again? He should have known. He should have known. He leaned his head back and closed his eyes.

Abbie dozed across from him. He could hear her soft breath. Her presence was a comfort, though also, in a way, a torment. How could he hope to merit her love when he so frequently failed in his duty?

That she loved him he knew without doubt, and the miracle of that still shook him. But Frances had loved him, also. Too much, maybe. And depended on him. Why had she thought at the last to forsake his care? Why had she gone? Why had he let her go?

Sleep would not come, but lethargy settled in his bones. How could he make this right? Where was honor in the face of death? He thought of Jeanette. Yes, he could do right by his sister's child. Is that why Frances had asked it of him? Did she know his honor would require some service, some atoning?

Monte opened his eyes and watched Abbie sleep. He had thought by now to have her with child. He knew the lack burdened her. Having Jeanette would be good for Abbie. She mothered so naturally.

But he ached to see his own seed growing inside her, to raise up his prodigy to own the land, to carry on his work and his name. He sighed and sank back into a fitful rest. Jeanette would be a start, and he silently thanked Frances for asking.

Three

Abbie stared out the polished wood-framed window of the train at the live oak trees with the queer dangling masses of grayish green that hung and waved in ghostly tatters. When she'd wakened that morning, the landscape had seemed foreign, wholly new. Now it seemed eerie, unreal.

"We're in the Lowcountry, nearing Charleston."

She turned to Monte, surprised. He'd spoken so little, she was amazed he'd noticed her curiosity.

"That's Spanish moss draping the trees."

"I've never seen anything like it."

"There is nothing like it. There's no place like the Lowcountry."

Abbie pointed out the window. "What grows there?"

"Rice or indigo."

She looked at the distant, swampy fields and shook her head slowly. "I can't picture you here."

"I'm not actually from here, not from the Lowcountry, at least. Our plantation was inland. Chandler's is a half day's ride and ours some five miles beyond that. Frances moved to Charleston when she married Kendal. He was in commerce there, while we merely used the port to ship our crops."

"What did you raise, Monte?"

"Cotton and tobacco. Cotton we sold to England, tobacco had a native market."

"Tobacco. But you don't smoke or chew or snuff it."

"I never developed a taste. That was a sore point with my father."

"I'm glad you don't. Pa thinks it's unhealthy for the lungs, and spitting is—"

"Don't say that down here, Abbie. Tobacco's the lifeblood of many a planter." His voice had taken on a stronger slur as they neared their destination, but not the strange twang she heard some speaking.

"Why do they sound that way, Monte?"

"That's the Geechee speech. They come from the true lowlands along the Geechee River."

"What are those trees in the marsh there?"

"Cypress."

"Is the land always so wet?"

"The low fields drain and fill with the tides. Charleston is a peninsula, flanked by two tidal rivers and surrounded by islands."

Abbie felt him withdraw again. He seemed lost in his memories. She'd never seen him among his own people, in his own country. What was he feeling coming back? How would it be for her to approach the Rocky Mountains after making her home elsewhere for four years?

He seemed ... more refined, more cultured; his speech more accented, his tone softer, smoother. In his black frock coat, black quilted waistcoat, and white pleated shirt, he was magnificent. And he held himself with an elegance and calm she'd never manage asleep.

It touched her deep inside, how different their worlds were. This was Monte's place. It seeped into his bones, into his blood. With every breath he took on this journey, he became more the South Carolina gentleman and less the Colorado rancher.

The train pulled into a station so large it seemed a small city. Abbie stepped out into the cavernous depths filled with people and soldiers. Though the uniforms were like those the western cavalry wore, these men carried themselves differently. There was an awkward watchfulness in some, insolence in others, but nowhere the easy carriage of the men who patrolled the territory back home.

She glanced at Monte. If he noticed the Union soldiers, he made no sign. His face was set in that unreadable mask that concealed his thoughts and rebuffed intrusion. He led her through the station and out to the street.

The porter followed with their bags, and Monte instructed him to load them onto the hack waiting at the curb. He didn't lift a hand, but stood by while the driver helped the man load the trunk. Then he helped her into the seat.

Monte gave him the address. "We'll go straight to Kendal's mother. She's expecting us, and the train was remarkably near schedule."

Though December, the evening air was almost warm and bore a heavy tang. It felt damp when she drew it into her lungs with each quickening breath. "Where are we, Monte?"

"This is King Street. The heart of commerce in Charleston."

Abbie stared out at the stores they passed: dry goods, hardware, tobacconists, haberdashers, wines, medicines, and on the corner a store selling just books. She could scarcely take it in. They left King Street for a residential area, but it was no less wondrous.

She'd never seen so many tall, elegant houses, colorfully painted and graced with lacy wrought iron balconies. They were closely packed and lined with iron fences and walled gardens, many with palm and magnolia trees, climbing vines, and flower beds, some still blooming.

She watched a lamplighter start his rounds in the dimming dusk. A dog barked and she heard it answered distantly. Abbie felt overwhelmed by the age and languor of the place, so different from the raw birth pangs of Rocky Bluffs. She knew what the Union said of Charleston, the hot seat of rebellion, and she sensed its stubborn, rebellious spirit.

For the first time she wondered if another place could be as awe-inspiring as the Colorado Territory. A pure white bird with sharp tapered wings soared overhead, and another, gray and short tailed, settled to the street as they passed. Abbie looked back over her shoulder at them.

"Sea gulls." Monte's expression softened. "You look all of fourteen gaping like that."

Abbie ignored his jibe. "Sea gulls, Monte! Where's the sea?"

He pointed. "The harbor's through there, but you can't see it from here. We'll walk the promenade tomorrow." He squeezed her hand, then once more reverted to silence.

People strolled the walks in the balmy evening, and Abbie took it all in: the sight, the sound, the smell. This was Monte's land. If not the city itself, still the people, the air, the ground. How she wished it were not Frances's death that brought them here. How she wished ... but her wishing could be nothing to Monte's.

She tucked her hand into his, and he held it without speaking. It was enough that they were together. His loss would never pass, but the intensity of the ache would fade with time. She knew that. Thoughts of her childhood companion, Blake, no longer stabbed her as they had. And the regrets for her part in his death had dimmed as Monte's would—with time.

But for now, the pain was fresh and raw. Her remorse could hardly match his, but she ached for Frances leaving this world so soon after returning to these streets she'd missed so badly. She sighed.

The carriage stopped, and Abbie stared up at the pillared house. The portico alone soared far above her, and above it a white and rusting lacework balcony. Though the house was incredibly elegant, its rose-colored paint was chipping and pock holes marked its walls. Signs of war? Still?

Monte helped her down and led her up the steps. As they went inside, she pictured Kendal here. It echoed his flamboyant elegance. Here were people who lived by appearances, though she noticed the age and wear of the furniture and wall coverings.

She remembered Frances's remark, *If Kendal were not a gentleman, he would be a rogue.* In this dim, stuffy place, she'd be tempted herself to rebel. She followed Monte meekly into the vaulted drawing room where they were announced.

Not a shaft of daylight found its way through the heavy bro-
cades at the windows. Gas lamps along the walls provided weak
light as she walked across the carpet, flourished with reds and
golds, though the gold fringed edges were frayed. A gilt-framed
portrait of a long, narrow-nosed man filled the wall above the
green marble fireplace. Only his bushy eyebrows made him interesting, though he obviously found himself so.

The sable-gowned woman on the emerald velvet settee beneath him might have been carved of marble, the way she sat so
straight and still. Her white hair beneath the black cap framed
her face, but her skin was amazingly smooth and translucent. Her
eyes bore into Abbie without a glance for Monte.

Though certain her dress and coiffure were satisfactory, Abbie
felt like a bad apple with a smooth, rosy skin. She'd been caught
staring, and who knew what else the woman had read of her
thoughts. She tried not to squirm, and her sympathy for Kendal
increased. Had he, too, never measured up?

Kendal's mother at last turned to Monte. "Montgomery Farrel, time has been good to you."

Monte bent and kissed her hand. "As to you, madam."

She scoffed. "I am no longer in the spring of my years, nor
even the autumn. But I'll accept your compliment as I have few
enough flung my way these days. So this is your wife."

"Mrs. Stevens, may I present to you Abigail Martin Farrel."

Abbie didn't correct the "Abigail" and curtsied. "I'm very
pleased to meet you."

"I see you chose her on looks."

To Abbie's surprise, Monte smiled. "That definitely played its
part, madam."

Mrs. Stevens snorted. "I like a man who tells the truth." Then
she sobered. "I'm an old woman. No one should live to see her
offspring in the grave."

Abbie felt a pang and saw its shadow pass over Monte's coun-
tenance.

"You're here for the child, and it's a good thing. I haven't the energy to see to her as she needs." Something flickered in her eyes, and Abbie wondered at it. Did Mrs. Stevens resent Frances's request? Or was it something else?

"But first, you've traveled a long way and been nourished poorly, no doubt. Your wife needs meat on her bones regardless."

Abbie wondered if she would remain "your wife" for the duration of their stay.

"You'll stay for supper."

"Thank you." Monte bowed.

"I'll have it laid directly. You'll want to freshen up from your trip." She raised her hand and a servant led them away.

Abbie couldn't help feeling dismissed. Mrs. Stevens had the grace of an angel, the imperiousness of a queen, and the warmth of a reptile. But that was unfair. She was grieving as were the rest of them, and her sharpness could be due to her pain.

Abbie washed and primped meticulously, but in the long, narrow dining room, she felt Mrs. Stevens' eyes like needles. She sat at the table, trying to remember the tedious rituals Frances had taught her. *The body should be held tolerably upright, though not stiff as a poker. Appear comfortable, natural, at ease, but never lounge. It is vulgar to take fish or soup twice . . . be careful to touch neither your knife nor your fork before finishing your soup. . . .*

She caught Monte's eye and saw a flicker of amusement. He would enjoy her discomfiture, the knave. All this was easy for him. His impeccable manners were so natural he lived and breathed them without thinking. He was genteel to his core. Abbie was a poor imitator.

Her temper flared, and she relaxed in her chair. "This chicken is delicious, Mrs. Stevens. I must have your recipe."

"Cook doesn't use a recipe."

Undaunted, Abbie laid her knife across her plate. "Mama cooks that way, too. She always thought it best to feel your way through. A touch of this, a pinch of that, the feel of the dough, the aroma in the steam. It's much better that way. Personally, I haven't a cookbook to my name, but then Pearl won't let me near the kitchen anyway."

The corners of Mrs. Stevens' mouth twitched, though she merely applied herself to her meal. Abbie guessed she was being compared to Frances, and failing miserably. Well, fiddlesticks. But she caught a glimmer in Monte's eyes and her heart sank. Was he ashamed of her?

The delicate chicken caught in her throat, and she choked, stifled it, then tried to wash it down with the pale wine in the fragile stemmed glass. Abbie didn't care for the taste of wine, and Monte seemed content without it—especially after Kendal's decline with spirits. Today, though, Abbie hadn't dared refuse when the servant poured it in her goblet.

She refrained from further comment but thought of meals at Mama and Pa's table. She and Grant and Sadie had been boisterous, encouraged by Pa to engage with him in discussions and even on occasion to argue their points. And argue they had, though good-temperedly as a rule.

Mama had expected decent manners, no talking with their mouths full, no grabbing, no elbows on the table. But beyond that they'd enjoyed their meals tremendously, though nothing this fancy touched their plates. Still, she'd take biscuits and beans with camaraderie over this stiffness any day.

She sent Monte a defiant glance but found him lost in his thoughts. He'd spoken so little these last two days. She felt them drifting apart now when they most needed each other's strength. Grief isolated. Maybe Mrs. Stevens felt the same.

Abbie dabbed her mouth. "It was a joy to know your son, Mrs. Stevens. His high spirits were always a pleasure. And he could certainly tell a tale and appreciate a good one himself."

Mrs. Stevens went very pale, and for a horrible moment Abbie thought she'd be sent from the room. When the elderly woman looked up, her eyes were bright with tears. "And what tales did he enjoy, pray tell?" Her hand trembled, but a spot of color came to each cheek. "I would love to hear what gave him pleasure when he was away from me at the end."

Abbie drew a shaky breath and recalled the afternoon he'd found her in the library and wheedled from her the tale of her escape from Buck Hollister and his gang of outlaws. He'd been enthralled, amused, and bemused. She folded the fine linen in her lap and laid her hands atop it.

"As you know, law and order in the territories is not what you have here, Mrs. Stevens. There are men more ruthless than decency can describe. We had in the Colorado Territory one such man named Buck Hollister."

She felt Monte stir, but she was in it now. "He was a man of such nefarious character..." Abbie wove her tale, all the while watching the expressions play fleetingly over the woman's face. She purposely played up her fear in the grasp of the men who murdered Blake and her helplessness in Gray Wolf's camp. She finished with her realization that God had His hand in all things, even those beyond their understanding.

Mrs. Stevens stared at her long and pointedly, then turned to Monte. "I feel your wife has more than beauty to recommend her. But I pity you keeping her in hand."

He smiled. "Kendal recognized in Abbie the spirit that is winning the West. I'm afraid Frances was made of softer stuff."

"We are ill-equipped for life's woes. Strength comes through pain, but that pain either hardens or breaks."

Monte looked pensive, then nodded. "And I lacked the wisdom to see which way it would go."

Mrs. Stevens pursed her lips together. "Frances was at peace in her passing. If she regretted her choices, she never said." She turned and fixed Abbie in her gaze. "Tell me the truth about Kendal. Was the trouble that ended his life of his own making?"

Abbie felt her chest constrict. Telling the truth would dishonor the woman's son. Yet his mother was obviously not content with whatever Frances had told her. She recalled Kendal's drunkenness, his deceit, and his advances.

She felt the blood flame to her cheeks, but the words clogged her throat. "He ... was misguided in his choice of companions and misled by his desire to regain his losses."

Mrs. Stevens smiled dimly. "You've learned too well the subtlety that is not natural to you, my dear. Was he in love with you, then?"

Abbie flushed deeper. "No. He loved his wife, though for a time he lost sight of it." She glanced at Monte. She had never actually described all of Kendal's behavior toward her. The day on the snowy hill when he pressed his advances and she slapped him soundly, the kiss on the road when he made the irrevocable choice to continue his wrongdoing. "At the last, he paid for his mistakes with the highest honor."

"Frances said he died saving you." Her tone was bitter but not condemning.

Abbie could give her nothing but plain honesty. "Yes. He took the bullet meant for me."

Mrs. Stevens stared at her hands, then turned to Monte. "Forgive my overshadowing your loss. I know how dear Frances was to you, and she was a daughter to me, though I . . . sensed the disquiet between her and my son." She cleared the emotion from her throat before continuing.

"Their child, I fear, has tendencies toward the worst in both of them. You'll not find the task an easy one, though Mammy handles her tantrums to some degree. Yet, I think your wife will see the task through. You've not conceived children of your own?"

Monte sent a protective glance Abbie's way but answered simply, "Not yet."

"Perhaps it's better that way. At least for a time." She stood slowly, gaining her balance with her hands tightly on the table as her servant hurried to move the chair.

"I think it best you stay with me these next days. Jeanette will become accustomed to you on familiar ground, and your departure will be less trying. Jonah will show you to your rooms. Good night." Holding her cane, she walked away.

Abbie felt like a mouse played with by the cat—discarded, limp, and shaken, but amazingly intact. She glanced at Monte. His dark, handsome features were brooding, but he raised his eyes to her.

"Well, then, that's settled." He stood and tucked her hand in his arm, and they followed Jonah to their rooms. Abbie couldn't help wondering if his name weren't truly prophetic.

She walked into the well-appointed room chosen for her and stood in the center feeling small and altogether homesick. Another servant returned with Jonah carrying her trunk. When they left as silently as they came, she opened the carpetbag and took out her nightgown. She could hear Monte in the adjoining room. She suddenly felt tired.

She removed her clothes and hung them carefully in the maple wardrobe. Its cedar lining sent a pungent aroma into the room when she opened and closed the doors. She put on her white batiste lace-edged nightgown and let down her hair.

She shook it out and ran her fingers through the tangles. They loosed and fell thickly down her back. She turned when Monte tapped the door between their rooms and entered. His face was strained as he crossed to her and took her hands in his.

"I'm sorry, Monte. I didn't know how else to answer."

"You did fine." He stroked the hair back from her cheek, then kissed her softly. "And I was hardly ignorant of Kendal's . . . attraction. Don't think any more of it." He kissed her again, and there was warmth in it.

Abbie clung to him, feeling their love lessen the pain of loss, at least for the moment. His hands were strong on her back, and she pressed her palms to his chest and returned his kiss. His need was in his eyes and in his lips and in his hands.

He spoke hoarsely. "Whether we conceive a child is in God's hands. But it'll not be for lack of effort this night if we don't."

In spite of the august surroundings, he wakened her desire, and she surrendered to his love.

Four

The tall, elegant walls fairly shook with the shrill cries. Monte was stunned by Jeanette's vehemence as she hurled herself at Mammy's skirts, pounding with her fists. She was Frances all over again. Mammy stood stoically and let the child wear herself out, then took her in hand and led her from the room.

Mrs. Stevens sighed. "Well, you've seen it firsthand now. Are you still of a mind to have the child?"

He turned from the window. "We're of a mind to honor Frances's request, and even were that not so, we would hardly shirk at a little show of temper." He laid his hand on Abbie's shoulder where she sat across from Mrs. Stevens.

"And you?"

Monte knew Abbie's mind was more set than his. Hadn't she spent years ministering to the orphans at the mission? She answered softly, "Jeanette is my niece and I love her. We all have our failings, and those in one so young are hardly set in stone."

"Hmph. My experience says otherwise. Once they find their temper, they're not likely to lose it."

"Nevertheless, one can be trained to channel the behavior more acceptably."

"Perhaps. And your western territory may be wide enough to contain her. Well, then, I'll see that Mammy's and the child's things are prepared for travel, and you'll leave at week's end." Mrs. Stevens rose and left them, as was her wont after pronouncing their fate.

43

Abbie stood and gripped Monte's hand. "Monte, I must speak with you."

He quirked an eyebrow. "So speak."

"I have nothing personally against Mammy, and I'm sure she's done her best, but I want to take Jeanette alone."

"What?"

"I want to mother her myself, as Mama did me. I don't want other arms rocking her to sleep, other hands dressing her and plaiting her hair."

"Abbie . . ."

"Jeanette needs a mama, not a bevy of servants who give in to her every whim."

"You don't understand—"

"Yes, I do. I want a child, not a charge."

"If we have children of our own . . ."

"I'll still refuse a nanny or mammy or nurse or whatever you want to call it. I'll raise and nurture my own children, and I'll raise Jeanette as though she were my own." She clutched his hand to her chest. "Please, Monte."

Their intimacy last night had eased his sorrow and left him susceptible. He groaned. "Don't use your eyes like that. I can't stand against it."

She bent one knee up on the chair seat and leaned into him.

His blood kindled. "You're a minx and you know it." He cupped her chin in his hands. "And you use it as mercilessly as—" He caught movement beyond her dark curls and looked up. "Chandler."

Abbie spun, and Monte caught her from losing her balance against the chair.

"Mrs. Stevens' man let me in, but I've interrupted a tender moment, I see." Chandler came forward and bowed over Abbie's hand, then caught Monte's between both of his. "It's good to see you, Monte, though I'm so terribly sorry about Frances. Milton did everything he could, but . . . she hadn't the will. She was already declining before the illness."

Chandler's words burned into Monte's pain, confirming his

suspicions. She hadn't the will to live. She was declining already. How had he been such a fool? He forced a response. "Milton doctored her?"

Chandler nodded. "Doctor Graby had an outbreak of measles at the Myers' Plantation. But no one could have attended her more carefully than Milton. He never left her side. He knew how close you were and deeply grieves his failure."

Monte pictured Milton Rochester—next to Chandler, his closest friend. He knew Milton to be competent and conscientious, but for a moment the need to share the blame overwhelmed him. Milton was his own age. What could he know of urging to life one whose hope was shattered?

Monte turned away. He heard Abbie murmur to Chandler, but it took all his resolve to combat the emotions surging inside. Why had Graby left her to Milton? Why had Frances forsaken life? He felt Chandler's hand on his arm and contained his despair.

"Don't try to find blame, Monte, nor take it on yourself. It won't change anything. It can't bring her back."

Monte drew himself up. Chandler knew him too well, read his thoughts as though they were his own. He nodded stiffly.

Chandler released the grip on his arm. "How long will you be with Mrs. Stevens?"

"Through the week."

"Maimie and I would have you extend your trip and spend the following week with us. One week at least, a fortnight even better. Maimie is desperate to see Abbie, and I've not had a moment's peace."

Monte glanced at Abbie and read her hopeful gaze. He sighed. It was inevitable. Even the mournful circumstances of this trip would not preclude the required visits. Though his heart was not in it, Abbie and Maimie and Chandler, and countless others, must have the opportunity. "What of Jeanette?"

"She'll be with us." Abbie spoke without hesitation. "It'll be good to spend time with her here in the same city and climate but out of this house. It could lessen the impact of the trip and the changes."

"She's welcome, of course," Chandler added. "How old is she now?"

Monte turned. "Two, but very precocious."

"She's nearly three." Abbie smiled. "But she has, indeed, developed a vocabulary. And we worried so when she seemed slow to speak."

"Very well, Chandler. We'll accept your offer with pleasure." Monte bowed.

"Very good. And now I'll leave you, as I've business to attend to. Again, my deepest sympathy."

When Chandler had gone, Monte turned to Abbie. "I'm going to visit the grave. Will you come?" His throat was tight, but he needed to see these things through.

"Yes, Monte." Her eyes were somber as her tone.

"We'll have to walk. Only the *nouveau riche* have carriages."

"I can walk."

"We can take the horsecar from downtown."

He led her down the streets and to the graveyard, where too many lay beneath the earth, casualties of war, disease, misfortune. The peaceful dead, the violent dead, the hopeless dead. *Oh, Frances.*

His steps faltered as he stared across the rows of headstones at the Stevens family plot. The monument to Kendal's father loomed over the newly carved stone near the edge. The pristine stone was white as her skin, sharp as her tongue . . . and final.

He walked forward and gripped the iron railing, then opened the gate and went in. Abbie was not at his side, though when they had separated he didn't know. He stood over the bare earth and read the headstone.

In loving memory of Frances Marie Stevens.

His eyes blurred at the dates. So young. Twenty-four. He swallowed the tears clogging his throat and felt Abbie's hand on his back.

She said nothing but her touch was comforting. He reached around to press her to his side. "Was there some way to prevent this?"

"No," she said softly.

Lord, what could I have done?

Heaven was silent. As with Sharlyn, death had plucked a fragile bloom before the petals had faded and withered. As with Sharlyn, he was helpless to prevent it, but acceptance was slow in coming. He laid the hothouse gardenias and zinnias on the mound and straightened. When he turned, he saw Milton Rochester outside the railing.

"Mrs. Stevens said I'd find you here."

His friend's face was bleak, the small black eyes and compact features pressed tighter than usual. Monte's anger flared, then passed. He held out his hand and Milton gripped it.

"It's dreadful to lose a patient, but horror when it's one dear to you and yours." He shook his head. "I tried everything medicine had to offer."

"I'm sure you did your best for her." Monte's chest tightened with the words.

"I'm sorry, Monte." Milton's gaze held, then flickered to Abbie.

"Forgive me. Milton Rochester, may I present my wife, Abbie."

Milton bowed over her hand. "A rare pleasure. Chandler spoke of your beauty, but I thought he exaggerated. I see now that every word was true."

"I'm pleased to meet you, Doctor Rochester."

"Milton, please." He stepped back as Monte swung the gate open and followed Abbie out. "Have you plans for the day?"

"I'm taking Abbie along the promenade. She's never seen the ocean."

"Never seen it! Well, it's a sight on a day this fair."

Monte smiled. It would be a sight for Abbie regardless. He recalled their first outing when he'd described the ocean for her mind's eye and brought her to tears. Oh yes, it would be a sight for Abbie. He tucked her hand into his arm. "Will you join us, Milton?"

"If it's not imposing."

"Of course not. We've too many years between us to miss the

opportunity now." Monte glanced back once more at the grave. His step faltered.

"It was peaceful, Monte. I don't think she suffered."

Monte nodded, felt his throat tighten, then drew a long breath. "I'm thankful for that."

◆◆◆◆◆◆◆

Abbie leaned on the iron pipe rail that lined the promenade and stared with wonder at the sparkling expanse of water fed by the tidewaters that rushed into the bay from either side of the city. The ocean was more green than blue in the main body and deep, churning brown beneath the dock at her feet. The massive pilings, encrusted with salt and barnacles, stood solidly amid the surging, slapping waves.

The breeze flapped the rolled sails of the ships at port. Gulls circled and cried and perched on their skeletal masts and cross-beams as they rocked and swayed. Abbie breathed the sour, salty tang and gazed past the low tree-covered islands across the water to the blending line of water and sky.

She felt Monte's gaze and turned to find both his and Milton's eyes on her. She squeezed her hands at her chest. "It's incredible. Oh, Monte, I'd love to climb aboard ship and head out there where the water is all around, the gulls diving, and the wind full in the sails."

He smiled. "With the wind today, you'd learn soon enough if you had the stomach for it."

"What do you mean?"

"Have you heard of seasickness?"

She pushed back the hair whipping her eyes and looked out at the rising waves. "It would be worth it."

She saw the amusement flicker in Monte's eyes as he took her elbow, and they started on down the wide promenade. Milton pointed out the different boats and told them who owned them, who captained them, and all he knew of their previous successes or failures.

"You sound like a seaman yourself," Abbie said.

"A hobby only. My heart is in medicine. Always has been. Even with its limitations." Abbie saw him glance regretfully at Monte, and his narrow shoulders sagged. She felt the strain between the two men. It was unlike Monte to place blame erroneously, but he said nothing to ease Milton's distress.

"Will you lunch with us, Milton?" Monte asked.

"No, I'm afraid I can't spare any more time. I'm sharing Doctor Graby's rounds."

Monte nodded. "Then we'll take our leave."

Abbie walked briskly beside him as he led her down a narrow way to a small teahouse in sight of the wharf but far enough away to be free of the rough traffic of sailors. Monte seated her and took the chair across. He ordered coffee and sweet rolls, then returned his attention. "Well, Abbie, you've seen the ocean. How does it compare to your plains?"

"I can't compare them. They're too different. But it's wonderful, as wonderful as you described. Do you remember?"

"I was thinking of it as I watched you take your first look. One day I'll take you across the sea to all the places you've imagined."

She smiled and gripped his hand. "I'm glad we came first to your home, Monte. Will you take me to see your plantation?"

"It's no longer mine, Abbie."

She felt a swell of remorse. "I'm sorry. I didn't mean . . . I just thought . . ."

"It's all right. I'll show you the plantation, if you like, when we go to Chandler's."

"Is it very painful to come back?"

He sighed. "Painful? Yes and no. Things change, I know that. Would I trade what I have now for what was before? No. Yet . . . I could wish that the difficulty, the hardship, and even the suffering that I see around me were not so. Everywhere are the signs of destruction, poverty, struggle."

He sipped his coffee and shrugged. "But with it, or perhaps because of it, there is the bravery, the unconquerable spirit of the South, especially South Carolina. That, Abbie, will never be equaled nor destroyed. No matter how long the soldiers remain, how strict the curfews or the restrictions, they'll never break our spirit."

Abbie felt alienated by his use of "our." It reflected the closed expressions she saw all around her.

He laughed low. "I guarantee you, the life of every Yankee in Charleston is one of frustration."

"Why?"

"They can occupy the houses, walk the streets, even give the orders, but they'll never belong and they know it. They can't break into the circle, and the knowledge gnaws at them. They're like dogs at the gate, whimpering for one glance from the people inside. And they'll never get it. Never."

Abbie was astonished by his fervor, though his voice was low and his drawl pronounced. Her heart sank. She, too, was an outsider. Perhaps she was admitted through the gate by marriage, but she would never belong. She suddenly ached to be home on the rough, dry ranch, in the scrubby hills that clung to the feet of the towering mountains.

Monte read her distress and pressed her hand. "It's just the way it is, Abbie."

"The belle who doesn't fit the mold. I'm not even a belle. How could Mrs. Stevens tell from the first moment?"

Monte smiled, spread his hands. "Abbie . . ."

"I did everything Frances told me. I—"

He caught her hand between his. "You can't change who you are. And I wouldn't have you change. I could have had any southern lady I wanted. I chose you."

She knew that was true. Monte with his fine looks and finer ways. She sighed. "I guess that counts for something, but I feel . . . more like the dog at the gate."

He threw back his head and laughed. It was the first he had laughed since the terrible news, and she was not the least concerned that it was at her expense.

"You shouldn't paint those pictures if you don't want me to take them seriously."

He bowed over her hand. "I should know better indeed. For-give me."

For a moment she felt close to his heart, then his grief settled again, and he released her hand. "We should go."

"Yes. I want to spend time with Jeanette." Even if it meant being closed inside Mrs. Stevens' dreary walls. At least they would spend Christmas with Chandler and Maimie.

♦♦♦♦♦♦♦

Abbie found the child in the upstairs room that served as the nursery. She was dressed in white with peppermint red stripes and ruffles and ruffles of lace. It was difficult to tell where the lace left off and the child began. Mammy bustled around when she entered, picking up the discarded dolls from the floor.

"Thank you, Mammy, that will be all." Abbie waited for the woman to leave. It felt uncomfortable to speak to another person that way, but she'd seen that it was expected and didn't want to stand out more than she already did.

Jeanette eyed her from her perch at the child-sized table. "Do you want tea?" She held up the miniature handpainted teapot, confident in her abilities as a southern lady. Just shy of three, Jeanette probably already contained the elements of decorum she herself lacked, Abbie thought grimly.

Abbie smiled and took her place on the other small chair. "Yes, thank you."

"That's 'Manda's chair, but you may use it."

"Amanda?"

Jeanette pointed to the French porcelain doll in the corner of the window seat.

"Ah. It's kind of her to allow me."

"*I* say you may, not 'Manda. She can't say in my room. Only I can."

Abbie bit her tongue. Now was not the time to instruct. First she must have Jeanette's trust. "Jeanette . . ."

"I'm Jenny." Her face looked fierce a moment. "Mama calls me Jenny. Grandma calls me Jeanette, and I don't like Grandma."

"Jenny's a lovely name." And she understood the child's difficulty with her grandma, though it was disrespectful to say so.

"I have ap'rcot crumpets and tea."

"Very nice indeed. I'm privileged to be your guest." She took the cup of imaginary tea Jeanette handed her. "Do you remember when we took the toboggan down the big hill at Uncle Monte's ranch?"

"Papa spoiled it. He made us go home."

The child had a more remarkable memory than she expected. But if thoughts of Kendal upset her, she didn't show it. "Uncle Monte and I are going to take you back to the ranch with us. Would you like that?"

Jeanette handed her a tiny fluted plate. "Have a crumpet."

Abbie took the plate and mimicked eating. Jeanette's eyes stayed on her as she delicately dabbed her lips with the scrap of linen. "The best I ever had."

" 'Manda can't have any."

"Why not?"

"She sassed Grandma."

"Oh dear."

"It doesn't matter. Mammy will sneak her some. And then she'll cry and cry to get some more."

Abbie nodded slowly. "I see. That isn't very honest, is it?"

Jeanette looked at her pointedly, her little chin coming up in exact replication of Frances. Suddenly she knocked over her chair as she jumped up and ran to the window. She shook the doll and cast her to the seat, then rushed to the cupboard and threw all the doll's clothes on the floor. Then she threw herself with them and set up a wailing to rally the town.

The door flew open and Mammy descended like a great dark hen.

Abbie stood up. "I'll handle this, Mammy. You may go."

The woman sent her a dark look, shook her head, and puffed her lips, reminiscent of Pearl. Well, Abbie was used to such disapproval and more determined than ever that Jeanette not grow up as self-centered as Monte's sister. Three years of indulgence was enough.

When the door closed behind Mammy, Abbie took her place at the little table again. Though Jeanette's caterwauling set her teeth on edge, she made a great show of pouring herself another cup of invisible tea and helping herself to another excellent crumpet. She didn't speak as she ate and sipped but admired the view from the window.

After a full five minutes, Jeanette stopped screaming and watched her from the floor. Abbie turned her attention to the doll. "What a great many things you can see from that window, Amanda. It must be very interesting in your seat." It didn't matter that the doll lay head down with her pinafore over her face.

Jeanette raised up on one elbow to study the window. She stood and walked slowly over, then climbed up on the walnut shelf and kneeled against the panes. "They took Mama away in an ugly black carriage."

"Yes."

"She can't come back."

Abbie climbed into the seat with the child. "Yes, I know."

Jeanette turned on her and beat her fists against her legs. "I don't like you! I want you to go away! Go away! I want Mammy! Mammy . . ." She wailed again.

Abbie caught her little fists and pulled her into her lap. She curled the child against her chest and held her while she cried. There was grief in this outburst, and that she would not ignore. The hollering became sobs, and Abbie rocked as she stroked the dark, damp curls. So much hurt for one so little.

Dear Lord, comfort your little one. And give me wisdom. Abbie kept rocking as the child stilled. "Shall I tell you a story?"

Very slightly, Jeanette's head nodded against her.

"Once upon a time, there was a little girl named Red Riding Hood. She was called that because . . ."

Abbie kept her voice soft while she continued to recite the story and stroked Jeanette's soft head and small, curved back. "And the wolf gobbled up the granny in one swallow."

The child looked up with wide eyes.

"Then the wolf put on the granny's nightcap and climbed into the bed." She felt Jeanette press close against her. "Red Riding Hood knocked on the door . . ." As she spoke, Abbie smoothed the child's tangles and felt the dampness dry on her cheeks. " 'My, Granny, what big eyes you have.' 'The better to see you with,' the wolf said."

Jeanette took Abbie's fingers in her little fist.

" 'My, Granny, what big ears you have.' 'The better to hear you with,' the wolf said." Abbie covered the little hand with hers. " 'My, Granny what big teeth you have.' 'The better to eat you with!' And the wolf jumped from the bed and swallowed Red Riding Hood in one gulp."

Jeanette pulled away and stared up. Her little mouth made a perfect O.

"Now a woodsman passing by had heard Red Riding Hood's cries." Abbie caught the two little hands and held them firmly. "He came into the house, saw the wolf, and split him open. Out jumped Red Riding Hood and her granny safe and sound."

Jeanette smiled. It was radiant, and Abbie was struck again by her likeness to Frances, and for that matter, Monte. They all favored his mother's side.

"You see, Jenny, the wolf is death, and Jesus is the woodsman. He conquered death, and when we pass through it He brings us to new life." She turned at the tap on the door, and Monte entered.

He raised an eyebrow at the two of them curled in the window seat, and she knew the nature of his inquiry. Likely as not, he'd heard the commotion and come, albeit reluctantly, to her rescue. She smiled. "Jenny, go give Uncle Monte a hug."

Five

Abbie tucked her knees up under her skirts and settled onto the apple green spread at the end of Maimie's bed. The rose-and-green chintz curtains were pulled into puffs at either side of the tall, narrow windows to let in the December daylight, and the tasseled ties fascinated Jenny, who cupped and petted one with her small hands.

It was a cheerful room, so like Maimie, and Abbie drew up her knees contentedly. She'd spent most of the last three weeks there, as Maimie was in the final months of her pregnancy. After the stillbirth of her first child, the doctor was taking no chances and had ordered her to bed.

Abbie was just as glad after what she'd endured with Mrs. Stevens—an extended week of her very proper lady friends and callers coming to gape, and later gossip, about her. She more than suspected Mrs. Stevens drew great pleasure in watching her writhe, though she never gave any indication, maintaining her carved marble poise. Abbie was thankful Maimie's condition precluded callers. She'd had quite enough of that.

She glanced down as Jenny now dug her fingers into the button box. She had found the box filled with multicolored and faceted buttons at the bazaar and presented it this Christmas morning to the child, remembering the fun she had when Mama let her rummage in her buttons.

When Jenny raised her hands and scattered them across the floor, she bit back the reprimand. Their battle of wills was still tenuous, and she chose her conflicts carefully. When she turned back, she found Maimie's heart-shaped face and frank brown eyes steadily on her. Abbie shrugged slightly.

Maimie smiled. "You'll do fine."

Abbie sighed. "It's ... harder when there's been so little discipline."

"Yes, but you have the instincts. And so does Monte, only ... perhaps it's not fair, but ..." Maimie shook her head.

"I know. I think it's his grief that keeps him separate."

"Forgive me, Abbie, but I don't think it's grief alone."

"What, then?"

"Guilt. I saw it when Sharlyn died. He blames himself for Frances."

Abbie fingered the quilted spread. "She depended on him so. He took the responsibility seriously."

"Too seriously."

"Maybe. But what else could he do? Even with Kendal—I shouldn't speak ill of the dead and I know he did his best—but Monte saw his failure. How could he not continue his responsibility?"

Maimie laid a hand on her belly beneath the coverlet. "He did all he could for her. But there comes a time where he must release it, Abbie. Frances is gone, and I fear ..."

"What, Maimie?"

"I fear that as long as he holds himself responsible for her death, he'll not take Jeanette to his heart."

Abbie glanced down at the child as she scrambled under the bed for the errant buttons and climbed out victorious. Maimie had spoken her own fears. Though Monte was gentle with Jenny, he made no attempts of his own to kindle a relationship. Indeed, he spent most of his time away with Chandler on the plantation.

He was out with Chandler and two others right now for the traditional dove and quail hunt. But if it wasn't that, it would be something else. In Maimie's company, Abbie didn't fret, but she felt his distance.

Nor would he speak of his loss. When she mentioned Frances, he grew quiet and pensive. Unlike Abbie, delving into memories to ease the loss, he seemed determined to bury it, ignore it, and hide it in work.

That he enjoyed his work with Chandler, she couldn't deny. And it was good for him to have an outlet. He was tender and close with her at night when they were alone. He loved her with a need she'd not felt in him before. But during the day he was cool and distant, as though daring grief to touch him.

Abbie sighed. They'd extended their stay a third week already, and though she loved her time with Maimie, she wondered at his reluctance to go home. What if he wanted to stay for good? She had heard the tone in his voice when he showed her his land, the house he grew up in, the soil that bore the crops that had sustained his family for generations.

They'd spent less than an hour looking at his old plantation, but he seemed to age in that time. At twenty-seven, he bore too much on himself. She shook away the clouds. "I'm worried, also, but he has to find his own way out. It will take time. It always does."

Maimie rubbed her hand over her stomach, mothering already without thought. Abbie felt a pang. Would she never know that joy? And then she felt remorseful. God had given her Jenny. "Monte will grow close to Jenny once we're home and he's settled into his own."

"I hate to think of you going. If only it weren't so far."

"The train helps. I have to admit, as much as I hated it coming through, it has made travel easier."

Maimie laughed. "Monte wrote of your despair at the coming of the train. Chandler and I laughed so."

"Well, it seemed so ... civilized. So settled. I like the land wild."

"I know. That's what Kendal loved about you."

Abbie shook her head. "Poor Kendal. He was so lost."

"Not entirely."

"No. At the end, he found his way."

"And Frances?"

"When she left us, I believe she had put her trust in the Lord. She was in His hands."

"Then help Monte to see that. Life and death are not in our control. But if our souls are in order . . ."

Abbie felt Jenny's hand on her knee and turned. The child held up the string of buttons and Abbie smiled. "It's lovely, Jenny. Well done."

Jenny scrambled up beside her and hung it over her head. "For you."

"Thank you." She gave her a hug. "Now, then, it's time for your nap."

Instantly Jenny's lip protruded and her eyes took on stormy depths.

Abbie held her gaze firmly and the child relented. She took her by the hand and stood. "Come. I'll tuck you in."

◆◆◆◆◆◆◆

In the glow of the lamps that evening, Monte stood between Abbie and Chandler as the guests arrived. Though Maimie could not participate, Chandler had insisted on this soirée. The family had dined at three, and now the guests arrived for sweets and liqueur.

As he and Abbie had not been there for the funeral, this enabled people to offer their condolences as well as share the festivities. He was hardly in the mood, but Chandler was right. It was expected.

Beside him, Abbie was obviously dazzled by the finery and array, though she could hardly not notice the shabby condition of the garments and slippers. Even so, the gowns had been exquisite in their day. The gentlemen's swallowtail coats were impeccably clean and tailored if well worn, and those with jewels bore heirlooms, though many who had possessed such no longer did. Courtesy of Yankee and, more painfully, Confederate marauders.

The Yankees he could forgive. But much of Charleston's destruction, especially that of the planters' homes in the outlying area, had come at the hands of the southern forces. The white trash farmers bore a hatred for the ruling planter class deeper than anything the Yankees felt. They were quick to take advantage in the lawless days before military rule set in, and their vicious pillaging scarred more deeply than any other.

Of course, Abbie knew none of that. He glanced at his wife. She looked fresh as a mountain rose, even in black. Her eyes had that sapphire glint surrounded by lashes that drooped at the sides and quickened his pulse, but her color seemed pale and her step uncertain. That was not like her at all, and he chided himself for leaving her so much to Maimie.

Had he missed something with his lack of attendance? Did she mourn more deeply than he thought? But there had been no love lost between his wife and sister, though he could hardly blame Abbie for that. She had done her best.

He turned and greeted the Blackwells from Columbia. Edward Blackwell had overseen several of Monte's father's business ventures. "How do you do, Edward. Fine to see you, sir."

"And you, Monte."

"May I present . . ." Each time he presented Abbie, he felt more fortunate. He was a lucky man. More than lucky. God had blessed him beyond his deserving. And yet with that emotion came the companion fear. What if something happened to Abbie? What if he were unequal to keeping her safe, well, whole?

Perhaps his fears were unfounded, ridiculous even. Hadn't she proved herself strong and brave and well nigh invincible? But he could no more control the feeling churning inside than he could the events of this life. He could only mask them and put on the face of courage.

He accepted Edward's condolences and turned to the next couple. He would be glad to leave the line, but as Chandler's guest of honor his responsibility was clear. He felt Abbie sway beside him and turned in alarm. Never had he known her to grow faint, not even in the face of death and horror and despair.

She was as strong and hale as a yearling thoroughbred. But as he caught her arm, he read the confusion in her eyes. "If you'll excuse me," he murmured to Chandler and led Abbie away from the entry into the parlor. He helped her to sit. "Abbie, what is it?"

"I don't know. I feel . . . I must be catching something."

He felt a wave of fear and pushed it away as irrational. "I'll take you to bed."

"I don't want to miss Chandler's party in our honor. I feel stronger now. If only this fool corset weren't so tight. I swear when we go home, I'll never wear one again."

"Don't put those thoughts in my mind, Abbie. I won't be fit for polite society." He bent and kissed her. "Are you certain you're all right?"

"Yes, I feel fine. A little squeamish, but everything I've eaten lately has been so different. Something must not agree with me."

He laid the back of his hand on her forehead. "There's no fever."

"No. I'm sure it's nothing." She stood up and collapsed against him.

Monte caught her with alarm as she fainted in his arms. Gently he laid her on the settee, then rushed to the hall. Milton stood in a cluster of gentlemen, and Monte hesitated only a second before gripping his arm. "Pardon me." He bowed to Milton's companions. "But I must borrow Milton immediately."

Milton turned in surprise. "Monte?"

He tugged him from the room. "It's Abbie. She's fainted."

"Oh, well . . ."

"No, you don't understand. Abbie's never had a faint moment in her life." He rushed Milton to the library, fighting to control his concern.

She stirred when Milton dropped beside her and slapped her hand. Monte felt his chest constrict. Surely nothing serious was wrong, surely . . . Milton held the salts to her nose, and her eyes fluttered open.

Abbie startled. "Good heavens . . ."

"That's right. Take it easy, now. Monte, will you leave us a moment? And send a man for my bag. It's in the cloakroom."

Monte frowned at Milton's clipped orders. He didn't want to

leave Abbie, not . . . in Milton's hands. Wasn't that what he was thinking? Goodness, it wasn't Milton's fault. When would he accept that? He forced his legs to obey and went for the bag himself.

Milton took it and ordered him out again. Monte stood outside the door, staring at the knotted oak panels.

"Monte?" Chandler touched his arm. "I could only just break away. Is Abbie all right?"

"I don't know. Milton's with her." He said it more gruffly than he intended. "He ordered me out."

"And well he might. Come, have a brandy, a cup of syllabub."

"No, I'll wait."

"Monte, she's in good hands."

Chandler tugged his arm and Monte followed. Brandy would be good, but he declined as he did the frothy cream concoction. He wanted nothing dimming his reactions or thoughts when Milton returned. He ran his hand over his face and glanced at Chandler.

"Relax, man. Abbie's as hearty as they come."

"Then explain her fainting."

"I'll leave that to Milton." He nodded, and Monte turned.

"Is she ——"

"She's fine," Milton assured him.

"Then what was wrong with her?"

Milton smiled. "Nothing that won't be right in nine months. Or more precisely, eight, I'd guess."

Monte stared at his friend's smile. Was the man daft to be amused by his wife's illness? Was he as incompetent as he'd feared? What was this nine months, eight months. . . ?

Chandler clapped him on the back. "That *is* good news, man."

Monte turned. An extended convalescence good news?

Chandler laughed. "Abbie's with child, Monte. Your offspring."

Abbie with child. He felt staggered. How had the thought not occurred to him? Because he avoided that thought, studiously, lest he dwell on the disappointment. And because his thoughts had been preoccupied by death. *With child.* His child. He spun and strode to the parlor.

Abbie looked up when he entered, and her pale cheeks flushed.

He dropped to his knees before her and took her hands in his. "Abbie . . ."

"It's nothing I ate."

He pulled her hands to his chest and found himself without words.

She slipped her hands around his neck. "Oh, Monte . . ."

"My darling." He kissed her forehead, her eyes, her mouth. "What did Milton say? Is everything all right?"

"Yes, fine. It's normal to feel queasy and dizzy and tired. It'll pass soon enough."

"You'll have the best care. I'll find the finest doctor in Charleston. . . ."

"In Charleston? He'll have a dreadful long trip, then."

"What do you mean?"

She caught her fingers in the hair at the back of his neck. "You're surely not thinking of staying here."

"Only until the baby comes. I'll not risk—"

"No, Monte. This child will be born on the Lucky Star. He'll be a true Colorado baby."

"But, Abbie . . ." Monte groaned with the vision of Sharlyn wasted with fever, his tiny cloth-wrapped son lifeless in his hands.

Abbie gripped his head between her palms. "I'm not Sharlyn, Monte. I'm strong and healthy, and Mama's there and Doctor Barrow. Everything will be fine. But I have to do this in our own home, Monte, with the Colorado granite under my feet."

Monte shook his head. "I'll discuss it with Milton. If he feels it's safe . . ."

"Monte, I know what I want."

He smiled wryly. "You always have."

◆◆◆◆◆◆◆

Though Monte's breath was deep and slow beside her, Abbie couldn't rest. She felt miserable, more miserable than she would let him know. It took all she had to keep her supper down, and her head swam every time she moved. She was bone tired, but her mind raced.

She was carrying his child. At last she held his baby inside her. "Sweet Lord," she murmured again and again. "How good you are to me." Her emotions swung between ecstasy and concern. Jenny must not suffer by this. She must see that the child's needs were kept as important as her own. She must not allow Monte to continue his overindulgence of her to the neglect of Jenny. She must encourage his relationship with the child. She must . . .

The night wore on. Her body cried for sleep, and when Monte stirred and pulled her close, she let his warmth lull her. She carried his child. *Oh, thank you, Lord.*

Six

Abbie handed Jenny into Monte's arms and followed him from the train, stepping carefully over the tobacco slime on the floors surrounding the spittoons at either end of the cars. Behind her, the porter carried their bags to the luggage car where he collected her trunk and the two that held Jenny's things. Abbie climbed out and breathed in the keen mountain air. Her lungs exulted in its freshness, though the March sky had the tone of light that belongs to lingering winter.

Her breath misted, and Monte turned. "Are you cold? I wired James to send the carriage."

"I'm fine, but let me get Jenny's bonnet." She straightened the bonnet and tucked the soft curls into the child's collar. After Charleston's muggy warmth, the chill would be especially sharp to the small girl, though tomorrow might be as fair and warm as one could wish on a spring day.

Abbie could see that Jenny's eyes were still puffed from fussing all day and much of the night. Maybe she'd been wrong to leave Mammy behind. Maybe she truly wasn't up to raising the child without those sturdy hands taking the brunt of Jenny's temper.

But that had been her compromise. She would stay with Chandler and Maimie through January, February, and most of March—until Milton declared her hale—if Monte would agree to leave Mammy behind. Perhaps it hadn't been fair to trade on his protectiveness. She felt a pang of conscience, but only for a moment.

They had been there for the birth of Chandler's son, Nathan.

Maimie had labored two days and reached the point of exhaustion. Abbie recalled the long hours at her side, bathing her brow, but the joy of her healthy son had renewed her, and Abbie felt more determined than ever that her child be born on the ranch.

She glanced at her husband. With gentle words she'd broken through his fears, and now they were home. Did he feel any of the surging joy that rose in her? She caught sight of James, his dark face and grizzled head, his shoulders hunched as he brought the carriage up. Will jumped down from the seat beside him. He'd grown out of his pants again, and his brown hair hung in his eyes, but his grin was broad.

She smiled back as he took the carpetbags and tossed them into the carriage. He would be a big man when he grew into his legs. Unlike many in his position, stable boy from the time he was small, Will could read and write—thanks to their school sessions outside the stable with their backs to the wall. He gave her a hand into the carriage while Monte tucked Jenny under the warm lap robe.

Abbie's heart swelled as they drove. The land around was brown and dry, with pale green yuccas spotting the prairie between the patches of snow. Snow streaked the sides of the mountain slopes beneath the dark blue pines. She glanced back over her shoulder at Pikes Peak, crowned in white and huddled beneath ponderous gray clouds.

She turned back and caught sight of the ranch. The cottonwoods around the house and along the creek behind made a skeletal streak across the rough brown land clumped with twiggy scrub oak and olive green juniper spears. The Lucky Star. Unconsciously she put her hand to her belly. *We're home, baby.*

She caught Monte's eyes on her and smiled. His returning smile was so full of warmth and joy she could hardly keep from throwing her arms around his neck. But Will was altogether too impressionable, even if James would have ignored it.

She was surprised by how tired she felt climbing the stairs to the porch. Though the queasy stomach had all but passed and removing the corset had stopped the dizziness, she couldn't avoid the weariness that made her far less active than she wanted to be. She hoped it would pass, but if it didn't it was a small price to pay for the miracle that would come. The miracle that was returning joy to Monte's eyes.

✦✦✦✦✦✦✦

Sirocco was testy as Monte rode him across the open range among the herd. He'd likely not been exercised as much as he needed in their absence. But now that he was back, the stallion would see some use. He reined in beside Cole.

Astride his large palomino, Cole took one last draw on the cigarette, then rubbed it out on his boot heel and tossed the stub. "So you're back."

Monte gazed out across the backs of the herd to Breck Thompson and John Mason bringing in a pair of strays. The cattle breath steamed the air as the animals grazed and stood chewing their cud. "Everything looks good."

"Got a couple hundred cows with calf. They'll be droppin' anytime."

"How many men have we?"

"Those two plus Matt, Curtis, and Skeeter. And Charlie, of course. I didn't think you'd want to cut loose a good cook with roundup close." Cole rested his hand on the pommel. "When the time comes, we'll need to take on some, but for now..." He shrugged. "We got what we need."

Monte nodded. "I hope running it lean will give us the edge. Beef prices are up. If they stay that way until autumn, we'll ship the four-year-olds out with the full weight steers. I've some other ideas to discuss with you, but I want to study on them first."

Cole nodded. "Padriac Beard sent a man after beef for the fort. I told him next week we'd deliver."

Monte frowned. Lieutenant Beard had been more than willing to truck with the scoundrel Gifford. He'd accepted stolen Lucky Star cattle re-branded with the double diamond, but Beard wasn't fooled. He knew well what he was doing, aligning with a fellow Yankee against the southern rebel.

Cole must have read his expression. "Their money's as good as any. The men are hard up for meat and willing to pay extra for Lucky Star stock. I let 'em know the hardships caused by Cap'n Gifford drove the price up." He pulled a crooked grin. "The man all but groveled."

Monte eyed Cole, his slow smile meeting his foreman's. Cole required no thanks or congratulations, but as their eyes met they shared the triumph. One small step back on track. "Good" was all he said.

Monte rode back to the house, left Sirocco to Will, and found Abbie in the parlor with Jenny, as Abbie insisted they call her. He flinched at the sight of the child so like Frances. Looking at her brought him back to days when Frances and he had trifled away the time riding their father's land. He recalled swinging her on the long oak swing in the hot, lazy days before the war.

Abbie glanced up from the book she read to Jenny. "All in order?"

"Cole's managed admirably. I want a word with Joshua. Would you like to see your folks?"

Her face brightened. "Yes. I'll just bundle us up. Want to go for a ride, Jenny?"

"May 'Manda come?"

"Of course. We couldn't leave Amanda."

"And Chalky and Spark?"

"No. We'll let the kittens stay here."

Monte frowned at the two scraggly kittens in the box beside the settee. "Where did they come from?"

"Will found them in the barn out of season. It's a new mother, and she seems to have all but abandoned them. He thought Jenny would enjoy caring for them."

"The barn seems an appropriate place."

"I want them in my room." Jenny stood, her face ready for battle.

"Well, we don't have animals in the house, Jeanette." He saw Abbie wince and corrected himself. "Jenny. The cats belong in the barn."

She screwed up her face, but he turned to Abbie. "I'll fetch the buggy. Wrap warmly." He escaped as Jenny warmed her lungs on Abbie's ears.

◆◆◆◆◆◆◆

Abbie kept Jenny snuggled between herself and Monte. The clouds had devoured the mountains to the roots, and they entered the fog at the foothills of Pa's homestead. Her heart sank when she eyed the claret buggy also parked in the yard, then soared as Pa and Grant came from the barn—next to Monte, her two favorite men, even if Grant had dismal taste in women.

Grant lifted her down, and she reached back for Jenny. "Jenny, you remember Uncle Grant." She spoke cheerfully, though in truth the child had possibly seen him once or twice and likely never spoken at all. But she hoped to keep Jenny from feeling overwhelmed by all the new places and people.

Jenny pressed her face to Abbie's neck and eyed Grant warily. Abbie caught sight of seven-year-old Tucker coming out of the barn swinging a stick. She waved and he hurried over.

"Jenny, this is Tucker."

Tucker dug the end of the stick into the ground and eyed Jenny. "Wanna see the chickens?"

To Abbie's surprise, Jenny detached and scurried after him.

"I'll keep an eye on her," Pa said. "Mama's inside. Go in out of the cold."

She pushed open the door and went through the front room to the kitchen. Mama looked up from the stove, her face rosy and moist from the steam. "Abbie."

Abbie rushed in and caught Mama's hands between hers. "Oh, Mama, I have news."

Mama's eyes teared. "You're expecting."

"Mama! How did you know?" Abbie pressed the rough, worn hands between hers.

"I see it in your face. You've never looked lovelier." She turned. "Wouldn't you say, Marcy?"

Abbie silently groaned as Mama turned her to face Grant's

wife. She hadn't seen her at the table, so eager was she to greet Mama. Marcy's smile was thick as sorghum.

"Certainly, Ma. Of course, she's still awfully thin. Have you been ill, Abbie? Perhaps the travel . . ."

"I'm perfectly fine." Abbie tied on an apron.

Mama turned back to the pot. "Have you told Pa?"

Abbie glanced out the window. "No. But by all the back-slapping outside, I'd guess Monte has."

Mama smiled. "I *am* happy. Monte's been so patient."

"I'd stand and congratulate you, but my back aches so." Marcy waved a hand. "The doctor says I have delicate bones."

"Well, don't strain yourself." Abbie took the pot of boiled potatoes from the stove to the board. "Shall I peel?"

"Thank you, Abbie."

While Marcy carried on about her house and the new addition for the baby, Abbie rubbed the skins from the potatoes. She tried to think charitably and bit back the rude remarks that came too readily to her tongue. She prayed that the penance of Marcy's presence would count for something.

"We've had to move the bed to the ground floor since I can't use the stairs. Grant carries me if I really need to get up there."

Abbie felt a recurrence of morning sickness.

"He's so attentive. I hope you find Monte half as considerate when things get difficult for you, Abbie."

"I don't expect any difficulty." Abbie dropped the potatoes into the bowl, atop the chunk of butter. She shot Marcy a glance in time to catch the sour expression that hastily faded when Mama turned.

Marcy shrugged. "Of course, you can't say. Especially with it taking so long to get with child. Why, there could be any number of problems. Doctor Barrow might even order bed rest for you."

"Nonsense. I'm as healthy as ever." Abbie gently stirred the potatoes to coat the butter, then pulled a branch of parsley from the bunch tied to the ceiling beam and crumbled it over them. And one thing was certain; she'd never confess a single pain to Marcy.

The men crowded in, Pa with Jenny on his shoulder. He swung her to the floor, and she ran to grab Abbie's skirts. Abbie stroked her head. Let the child get acquainted, and she'd likely forget her shyness. Look how well Tucker was doing. If a little transplanted orphan could thrive on good, loving care, surely Jenny could, as well.

They gathered at the table and Pa offered thanks. Abbie felt a surging joy at being once again with those she loved most in the whole world. She'd even try to like Marcy. There must be something to like if Grant doted on her as she said. She'd just missed it for so many years now, she wasn't sure where to look.

And speaking of looks, the ones Marcy gave Monte were enough to turn her stomach. If she was playing some game with Grant's emotions, trying to make him jealous, she'd better be careful. And if she was seriously mooning over Monte still . . . Abbie forced a smile when Marcy passed the rolls.

After supper she pulled her coat tight and carried the scraps to the compost heap. The moon made a dull glow in the cloud canopy. Monte was heading to the barn to harness the horse as she started back. Inside, she passed Mama drying the last of the pots and went in search of Jenny.

Tucker had been sent to wash and get ready for bed, so she couldn't be with him. Marcy sat alone in the front room, and Abbie guessed Grant was likewise hitching up his buggy. She stooped so Marcy wouldn't have to strain her delicate neck, in case the doctor had warned her of that, too. "Have you seen Jenny?"

"She went out with Monte. I tried to keep her, but she's so flighty."

Abbie bristled. "She's hardly flighty. She's very young and she's suffered much." In the dim light, she saw the glint in Marcy's eyes.

"Well, time will tell. At least now—if you carry through—you won't have only your borrowed child."

If Abbie had been just a little younger and hadn't her family to think of, she'd have slapped Marcy soundly.

"Good-bye, Mama," she called as she buttoned up her coat and walked out. Monte was just leading Toby from the barn.

"I'd have come in for you. Have you been out here long?"

"I only just stepped out. I was escaping something venomous."

"Patience, Abbie." He lifted her in beside Jenny, already tucked into the lap robes.

The child was drowsy and laid her head in Abbie's lap. Abbie stroked her curls as Monte drove. She fought her anger at Marcy's words. *Borrowed child.* Marcy knew that would cut deep. She didn't dare say "foundling," but her intent was the same. And then Monte all but making excuses for her. Abbie seethed.

Monte nudged her with his elbow. "Come, Abbie. Let it go, whatever it was."

"I don't understand you . . . or Grant."

"What don't you understand?"

"How can you be taken in by her? Did you see how she looked at you? I've never seen anyone flirt so brazenly. Makes me wish Grant would take his hand to her."

"That's hardly likely in her condition, and I didn't—"

"Of course, you didn't. You're used to women adoring you. But you enjoyed every moment."

He grinned crookedly. "I believe you're jealous of Miss Marcy."

"Jealous! Of all the ridiculous notions." She pushed his soothing hand from her knee. "The day I'm jealous of that she-snake . . ."

"Well, she's certainly jealous of you."

Abbie put up her chin and turned away. Didn't he know there was such a thing as simple spite?

He spoke softly. "You beat her out in her pursuit of me. Soundly, I might add. And, no, I wasn't blind to her attentions. Grant adores you and no doubt defends you against her railings. And now she has not even her coming child to set her above."

Abbie stared at him.

He tipped his head. "It puts me in mind of Rachel and Leah. I always felt a little sorry for Leah."

"Rachel and Leah loved the same man."

Monte was quiet.

Was he suggesting. . . ? Surely Marcy wasn't still in love with Monte. Hadn't she all but thrown herself at Grant's feet? And the way she went on. "Grant does this . . . Grant does that." Abbie shook her head. And as for Marcy's opinion . . . she'd never received anything but scorn and ridicule from Marcy.

Monte was wrong. Her motivations were spite and meanness, but there was no convincing Monte. His innate gallantry would never see it. She drew a long breath. The air smelled of snow. That was good. The land was dry.

✦✦✦✦✦✦✦

The snow didn't come in the night, and the clouds dimmed the morning, still masking the mountains completely as Abbie crossed the yard to the stable. She slipped inside, found Zephyr in her stall, and spread the saddle blanket across her back. As she reached for the saddle on the rack, a voice surprised her.

"I'll get that."

She jumped and spun. "Cole! Don't you know better than to sneak up on someone?"

"My apologies." He pulled off his hat and held it to his chest, but there was a glint in his green eyes and a wry twist to his smile. "But I wasn't sneakin' up. I was already here when you snuck in." His rascal smile broadened.

Abbie frowned as he replaced his hat and swung the saddle to the mare's back. He brushed close, and she smelled tobacco and sage and horses. He always smelled of the outside.

He reached under and fitted the cinch strap, pulling it tight. Then he gently kneed Zephyr's belly to release the trapped air and tightened the strap again. "So how'd you fare in fine, uppity Charleston?"

"All right." She bristled at his dubious glance. "Why shouldn't I?"

"Don't get yer hackles up. I just figured a place like that might not be to yer liking."

"A place like that? You've been to Charleston?"

"Not Charleston, but others like it."

She set her chin and challenged him. "What others? I thought you came up from Texas."

"I did. That don't mean I never spent a day outside it."

She reached up and stroked Zephyr's muzzle. "Charleston was lovely, in spite of the war damage."

"I wasn't meanin' the buildings and streets." Again his eyes mocked as he pressed the bit between Zephyr's teeth.

"What were you meaning?" She didn't want to hear it, but couldn't let it go.

He slid the bridle over the mare's ears. "The folks. The ladies and gents."

"And why wouldn't I fare well with the people of Charleston?"

The corner of his mouth twitched. "Forget I said anything, Abbie. Where're you off to?"

"Do I answer to you?" She snapped without thinking and saw his mouth tighten. She had treated him as high-handedly as Charlestonians treated their servants. Well, he deserved it. He . . .

Cole stepped back and handed her the reins without reproof.

Her conscience stung. "I'm sorry, Cole. It's just . . . I wish it weren't so obvious."

"What?"

"My social deficiency."

He grinned crookedly.

She drew herself up, all pangs of conscience forgotten. "You needn't laugh at me."

"I ain't laughin'. And it ain't you who's deficient. It's the rest of them stiff old cats."

Abbie bit back the smile at his apt description of Mrs. Stevens' friends. She smarted still from the guarded, all-knowing glances they'd sent one another, glances that said Monte had married beneath him, poor boy. She led Zephyr to the stable door and scanned the yard.

"What's goin' on, Abbie? What are you sneakin' off from?"

"I'm not sneaking."

"Heck you ain't."

She turned on him. "Well, if you must know, I'm going for a ride."

"I figured that much."

"That's all there is to it."

"Then why're you jumpin' and peekin' around like you're guilty?"

"I'm not guilty. Doctor Rochester said it was perfectly fine to ride for a few months yet, but Monte..." She stopped. She shouldn't complain to Cole about Monte, and the look on Cole's face would have silenced her anyway.

He pulled a paper from his pocket and a pouch of tobacco. "So you're expectin'."

"Yes," she said softly. It didn't matter that a proper gentleman would not have mentioned his guess. In a way, Cole was entitled to know.

He sprinkled the tobacco onto the paper, rolled it, and licked the edge. "Mr. Farrel's right, Abbie. This is wild country, and it's fixin' to snow."

"I know that as well as you."

He struck a match on the wall and held it a moment, then blew it out without lighting the cigarette. "Sorry."

His thoughtfulness touched her. "That's all right, Cole. I'm past the sensitive stomach."

"Ain't right to smoke in front of a lady, 'specially the boss's wife." He gave her a hand to mount. "Take 'er easy out there."

Abbie swung up. "Thank you, Cole." She smiled down at him and felt doubly guilty knowing he wouldn't go to Monte. But she had to get out, feel the wind in her face, feel Zephyr's spirit as she carried her over the land. A buggy ride to town or to Mama's just wasn't the same. Anyway, she'd confess it if Monte asked.

She urged Zephyr to an easy lope, confident the mare's smooth stride would not jar the baby within. She understood Monte's concern, but Zephyr was far less skittish than she'd been. They understood each other now. Zephyr anticipated her commands, and she sensed the mare's moods.

She'd sensed Cole's, too. Did her news distress him? She remembered how she'd felt when Sharlyn told her she was carrying Monte's child, proof of their marital devotion. The ache tightened her chest. Cole had behaved better than she had.

Maybe he'd put his feelings for her behind him. Maybe he no longer cared as he once had. She hoped that was so. Though he swore he'd never be so inclined again, she suspected Cole could love a woman well. If only he hadn't chosen her.

Abbie sighed and slowed Zephyr's pace. The cold penetrated her woolen coat and she breathed its keen bite. For all his teasing and scolding, Cole was still a good man. If she hadn't given her heart to Monte from the first, she might have cared for him more deeply than she did.

But God had made her for Monte. She would never love another. Abbie brought the horse around. At least she and Cole remained friends . . . even though he provoked her like no one else. He seemed to think that, after Monte, he was in charge of her. The truly annoying thing was that Monte thought so, too.

She supposed that was only right. Cole had proved himself worthy of that trust. Hadn't he risked his life to save her from the rustler, Jip Crocker? Still, he didn't have to be so exasperating. She wished he didn't understand her so well. Sometimes he saw more clearly even than Monte.

And she didn't understand him at all. What did she know about him, about his life before he signed on with Monte? What did Monte know? Likely little more than she did. Monte judged a man by the character he showed, not by his past or pedigree. In that, he was unlike his Charleston associates.

She frowned. How had Cole known she'd failed in Charleston? Not that it took much to reckon it. And why did she care? She'd always disdained the refinement she now coveted. Did she really covet it?

Would it matter to her if not for Monte? If he were a man like Pa, well educated and intelligent but simple and respected for his good sense and good humor instead of his position and standing.

If that were the case, she wouldn't care if she could properly simper over tea.

But Monte was a gentleman. Everything about him bespoke his genteel roots, more so now after seeing him in the company of others like him. It was no wonder Cole suspected her inadequacy. It must have been glaring to all.

Not all. Maimie and Chandler took her as she was. She warmed at the thought. And Monte did, too. He loved her with all her flaws. She put a hand to her belly. *Oh, baby, you'll be the best of both of us.*

That thought convicted her of her disobedience to Monte's wishes. How could he expect her not to ride? But he did, and that was what mattered. She turned Zephyr around.

The first flakes fell in large white clumps when she neared the yard. It would be a wet snow—the spring snows always were—and from the look of the clouds, a heavy one. She turned Zephyr over to Will at the stable and hurried to the house. Already snow clung to her hair, and her cheeks were red from the gusting wind.

Startled, Monte looked up from his desk when she rushed into the study.

"I'm sorry, Monte. I disobeyed and took Zephyr out. As you can see, no harm came to me or the baby, but I realize it was wrong to disregard your request and I've come to confess." She stooped down beside him and rested her hands on his thigh.

"Good heavens, Abbie. I'm not Father Dominic." But his eyes flickered with amusement. He took her hands in his. "You're cold."

"It's snowing."

He frowned. "Then you're lucky you made it back before it started in earnest. Abbie . . ."

"Please don't scold. I had to go. I've been too long from the land. I had to see it spread out around me, taste the wind and smell the sage. I . . . what are you laughing at?"

"Nothing, my wild mountain wife." He pressed his lips to her fingers. "But I will have your promise it won't happen again."

"If the urge comes on me so much I can't bear it, I'll find you first and beg."

He groaned.

"Besides, the snow will keep us inside a day or so at least."

"A day or so? Abbie, you've more than yourself to think of now. This baby..."

"...will be as strong and healthy as the Colorado land itself."

His eyes burned. "That is my fervent prayer. And that's why I've asked you not to ride or go far afoot."

Abbie softened. "I know, Monte. I understand your concern."

"Good. I trust it will keep you honest."

Seven

Monte stared out at the swirling mass of white. The first day of snow had been bad enough, but this day he'd watched at the window for it to relent until the daylight vanished and the night deepened. Only the lamplight through the glass illumined the flakes, which were falling more densely than he'd ever seen.

The cold, too, was unusual for March. The bitter wind felt as though it came straight from the polar ice caps and drove the snow in gusts. He thought of the cattle out on the open range. The horses and those cows with calf had been gathered into the fenced pasture, but all were without shelter.

With their long legs and powerful build, the Longhorns were better suited to handling such weather than other breeds, but even they would be hard pressed in this storm. This infernal, unpredictable western weather. He turned from the window when Abbie touched his elbow.

Her eyes were alight as she gazed on the scene. "Isn't it lovely? It's like a Russian fairy tale."

He swallowed his concerns and smiled. "Yes. You're up late. I thought you retired long ago."

"I did." She lifted the silk lapels of her wrap as proof. "But you never came up."

He glanced at his desk. "I've had business to catch up on."

"You work too hard."

He chuckled. "Hardly."

"Come up now." She reached her arms to his neck, and her eyes held the blue depths he could drown in.

His pulse quickened, and he took her in his arms. He had barely tasted her lips when a pounding at the front door drove them apart. "What now?" He hurried from the room and met James in the hall. "I'll get it, James."

"Yessuh."

Monte pulled the door open to Cole, who stood hat in hand. Snow clung to his coat and jeans and mustache.

"What is it, Cole?"

"Snow's driftin' up four feet already, Mr. Farrel. The calves in the west pasture are gonna be in trouble."

"What are you suggesting?"

"We gotta get them out to a cleared space."

What cleared space? Monte looked at the blizzarding snow in the halo of light. "Is it possible?"

"Won't be easy, but they'll drown if we don't."

"Drown?"

"Breathe the snow into their lungs. Some are likely buried already. And if they can't move they'll freeze."

Dear God. "Very well, let me get my coat. Have you roused the others?"

"I'm on my way." Cole glanced at Abbie.

She responded immediately. "What can I do?"

Monte opened his mouth to send her up to bed, but Cole spoke for him. "Get somethin' hot goin' for the men to drink. The wind's nasty, and we'll need to be fortified." He turned and hustled down the steps.

Monte closed the door. Cole was wise. Abbie would have never agreed to rest quietly while they were out. It was good to assign her a task that kept her in the house.

"Strong coffee, Abbie. As much as you can make." He pulled on his long coat and fastened the buttons, then found his gloves and hat and started for the door.

"Monte." She took a muffler from the hook and wrapped it around his neck. "Please be careful."

"It's the cattle at risk, Abbie. Don't worry." He kissed her forehead and went out. The snow flew in his eyes and nostrils as he

crossed the yard to the stable. He could see none of the outbuildings and only several feet ahead of him, but he knew the way
blind. He stepped inside and found Will, bundled up himself,
with Sirocco and another already saddled.

"Can I help, sir?"

Monte eyed him. He stood almost at height with him, had a
huskier build, and his young voice had cracked with coming manhood. Monte guessed for this night they could use all the hands
they could get. "We'll need extra horses. Ride up with us and you
can rope a remuda, as many horses to the man as you can manage."

"Yes, sir." Will grinned broadly.

Oh, to be young and worry free. Monte took Sirocco's reins and
led him out. He mounted as Cole and the others came from the
bunkhouse with their own steeds. In minutes they were coated
with snow, and hats did little to keep the wind from blowing it
into their eyes and mouths.

Cole rode up next to him. "Better stay together until we get
the pasture in sight. Then we'll have the fence to guide us."

Maybe, Monte thought. The way the snow was drifting, the
fences could be buried. The horses fought, chest deep in some
places, toward the pasture that held the new calves. Surely the
cows would provide some protection against the wind and snow
for their young.

He heard Cole hollering, but the wind snatched away the
words. Monte kept his head down and urged Sirocco on. The stallion was trembling with exertion, puffing at the snow in its face.
Beside him he heard Breck swear and understood the sentiment.
He tried to see the others, but in the dark and storm they were
lost to view.

Cole's powerful palomino burst through, and he reigned in
before him. "We're off course, Mr. Farrel. Turn north." He pressed
past to give word to the others.

How in heaven's name Cole could tell anything about their
position was beyond him, but Monte pulled Sirocco to the right
and started on.

"Is that the fence line, Mr. Farrel?" John Mason asked beside him.

Monte followed his outstretched arm and squinted through the storm. "Can't tell, John. Just keep on." Next to Will, John Mason was the youngest of them out there, but he'd grown up some since signing on with Gifford and learning from hard experience the value of loyalty. And where was Will, anyway?

Monte wrenched around to look for the boy. This was hard enough on the rest of them with more years and strength. "Have you seen Will?"

"No, sir." John held an arm to his eyes against the cutting blast of wind.

Monte wheeled and followed the trench back that Sirocco had just cut. He passed Curtis and Breck and found Cole coming back. "Did you see Will?"

Cole nodded. "He's with Charlie."

So even the chuck wagon cook had come to help. It cheered him, the loyalty of his men. He swung Sirocco again and followed the path already cut by Cole's horse, Scotch. It seemed they'd been out there for hours, but all sense of time was wiped away by the storm. It was worse than Cole had indicated. No moon penetrated the cloud cover except to give a dull illumination to the whirling flakes stinging their eyes.

Cole pulled up and jumped from Scotch's back into the snow that rose to his chest as he shouldered into the drift and dug through with his arms. "Found the fence, Mr. Farrel."

Monte stared along the crested ridge only slightly higher than the mounding snow beyond it. Where were the animals?

"No time to find the gate." Cole took wire cutters from his saddlebag and snipped the wire, then dug down for the next and the last. "We'll cut through here." He mounted Scotch and brought him through the gap.

Monte followed and heard Breck calling the others through. Sirocco staggered against the chest-high snow, and Monte scoured the dark land for sign of the other horses. He strained his eyes toward a darker mass ahead and heard a frantic whinny.

He hollered to Cole and leaped down, thrashing with his arms from side to side and pushing his weight to clear a way to the horses huddled there.

He stumbled and fell to his knees against something solid, then groped with his gloves until he uncovered the swatch of frozen, matted fur. He sat back on his heels and felt Cole stoop beside him. Cole dug into the larger mound to his left and found a dusky hide. Cow and calf had perished together.

Monte stared through the swirling madness. He could make out a few horned heads above the surface of the snow, and his throat tightened. "Have we a chance?"

"For some of 'em, maybe. If we work quick." Cole stood. "Get the men to walk abreast and trample the snow to the gap in the fence. I'll see what I can locate."

"Get to the horses, Cole."

"I reckon they'll manage a mite better than the cattle at this point. I don't think we'll salvage any calves."

Monte shook his head and turned back. He passed Cole's orders and fought beside the men to cut the swath through the snow. Sirocco was spent and made no move when he left him standing behind. Shoulder to shoulder with Breck, Monte dug through the drifts with his body, feet, and hands, but even as they pressed and trampled, snow piled again behind them.

Still they made steady progress to the fence, then dropped, exhausted and oblivious to their soaked and freezing condition. The wind had long since numbed his face, and Monte was thankful for the muffler Abbie had wrapped about his neck. His chest heaved with exertion, and he rolled to his side against the wall of snow they'd created.

He raised his head as two figures loomed up outside the fence line. Two riders on horseback, one with a lantern that barely penetrated the storm, the other slim and . . . He leaped to his feet as Abbie slid down from Zephyr's back. His angry frustration warmed him. "Abbie!"

"I brought coffee" was all she said.

Monte glanced at her companion on the other horse. James

held the lantern, looking abashed. He was not to blame. The servant had no chance against Abbie's wheedling.

Monte grabbed her shoulders and turned her. She was bundled into her coat and, he noticed with annoyance, his trousers. Her head was tied in a scarf but covered thickly with clumps of snow. The hair at her forehead was matted with ice and her lashes likewise.

"What are you doing here? You could have been lost in the blizzard!"

"I followed your tracks." She reached for the large canteens that hung over blankets on the mare's sides.

His exasperation left him speechless.

"Here." She produced a tin cup from the saddlebag and poured. "Drink this."

He took the coffee and sipped, letting the steam thaw his nose and cheeks. She poured cups for the others, and he couldn't help notice their relief and adoration. He released a slow breath. Why was he surprised? Abbie home, warm and safe, while others toiled in danger was not a picture he could conjure with even his best imagination.

Monte watched her hand a steaming cup to Cole, who had just ridden over and dismounted. He didn't look the least surprised. Had Cole anticipated her extending his orders? Probably.

Monte drained the cup. The heat and bite of the coffee brought life to his system, as it would the others. He joined Cole and his wife. "Well?"

"There's a few still fightin'. We can get through, but it'll take all of us."

Monte turned. "Abbie, you and James get back to the house. Thank you for the coffee, but please, don't come back again. We'll have more when we're through here."

"I can help bring the animals. Zephyr's fresh still—"

"No." He bristled when Abbie looked to Cole.

"Git back to the house, Abbie. You heard yer husband." Cole nodded his head toward the house, but his tone was less convincing than it might have been. Monte wondered if Cole would have agreed had the order not already been given.

Abbie raised her chin. "You said yourself it would take all of you. Well, James and I are two more."

Monte took her arm and marched her toward the fence. "Now is not the time. Every minute counts, and we have a job to do."

"I can help, Monte."

"If I have to escort you personally, that's one less man to bring in the stock." He sent James a scathing glance. "Take her in hand." He turned on his heel and heard James's plea behind him.

"Come on, now, Mizz Abbie. You got no cause to be out here."

Monte refused to look back and give her hope. Cole had sent Will on to rope fresh horses, not that any would be fresh in this, but at least they hadn't worked as hard yet. With the other men, Monte stripped the saddle from his tired mount, resaddled, and went after the band of cattle huddled at the south fence. His stomach sank when he saw that they stood on the bodies of others less fortunate.

Cole barked orders, and like his men, Monte followed them. He had no experience to match Cole's and knew well enough to do as he was told. The wind took his hat, and he scrambled through the drifts after it. He was nearing exhaustion and guessed the others were, as well, but they continued to dig out the survivors and prod them toward the trench.

Some of the cattle seemed dazed, others dropped and could not be roused, but some gained new strength and pressed through the trench and beyond, following the tracks the men had made from the yard to the pasture. Monte dug with his hand to free one long-horned cow and found a calf huddled beneath in a pocket of air created by the mother's legs.

He eased the calf loose and both made their way along the trench. He leaned against the snow wall and fought the trembling of his limbs. How much longer could they sustain the exertion? He turned and saw Will collapse.

Monte made his way through to the boy and pulled him up from the drifts. "Get on a horse and go back to the house."

"I'm sorry, Mr. Farrel. I can manage still."

"No, you can't. Nor can the rest of us. We've done what we can here. Now go." He turned and helped Matt free a steer entangled in the stiff, frozen legs of three others, then ordered him likewise back to the house. Matt was too weary to argue. He nodded and fished his hat from the snow.

Monte turned into the buffeting wind and almost sat back in the drift, so shaky were his legs. He pushed forward to Cole. "I'm sending the men home. We've done what we can."

"I reckon so." Cole slapped the flank of the horse he'd extricated. He rubbed his face with his arm. "Dawn's comin' on."

Monte peered up at the swirling darkness. Cole's sense was keener than his to detect that, but he was weary enough to believe they'd worked through the night. "You coming?"

"I'll make one more sweep."

"Don't linger."

"Nope."

Monte released the mount he was riding into Breck's care, resaddled Sirocco, and rode him back. The track was well trampled by the animals following in line, and he found they'd gathered in the yard between the house and outbuildings where the structures had kept the snow from accumulating as deeply. It looked odd to see them huddled about the walls of the great house, but he shook his head and rode past. He tended Sirocco, then went inside.

The warmth hit him so powerfully he almost collapsed, but forced himself to the kitchen where Abbie flitted like a ministering angel between Matt and John and Will, already there. Pearl ladled cups of hot soup into bowls for them, and they ate it at the rough table on stools.

Monte took his gratefully and let it warm his hands before lifting the spoon to his lips. The life returning to his fire-scarred palms was painful, but the hearty beef and vegetable stock renewed him. He sent Pearl his thanks with a look.

Abbie put a plate of hot biscuits on the table. "Help yourselves, gentlemen. There's more coming."

Seeing her working side by side with Pearl brought a smile to his lips. No one but Abbie could have invaded Pearl's domain and remained intact. She'd had an upward road of it, but Pearl had at last taken her to heart. He watched the men flush when she ministered to their weary souls with hot food and a smile. Dressed now in a blue cotton skirt and white shirtwaist, she was a welcome sight.

Curtis and Breck staggered in with Cole behind them.

"Drop your wet things on the floor there, then come and get warm." Abbie poured fresh cups of coffee as Pearl ladled more soup. The wind whistled at the window, but the glass steamed from the warmth in the room. Even James and Zena crowded into the doorway.

His household. His people. Monte ached for the stock he'd lost this night. There were certain to be more when they searched the open range. But gathered here was his family, all but Jenny, who no doubt slept blissfully upstairs with Abbie's stories driving her dreams. He looked at his wife and she met his gaze. In the dawning light he felt a surge of love for her. *Thank you, Lord, for this woman and all those gathered here.*

Eight

Abbie stood in the entry when Monte came inside, stamping the slush and mud from his knee-high boots. The sunlight through the open door was bright, but his expression bleak. Her heart sank. "Is it as bad as all that?"

"Worse. We've lost eight hundred head that we know of. Others have wandered so far, driven by the storm, that it will take weeks to search them out, if we ever find them at all." He sagged against the wall.

Abbie went to him and took his hands. "What will we do? How can we bury so many?" She'd driven past the west pasture on the way to Mama's and seen the carcasses half covered in snow.

"We can't bury them. The ground is frozen. Once things dry, they'll be burned."

She heard the desolation in his voice and had no words that would not be empty solace.

He shook his head. "We've lost steers that were marketable at full size. And Longhorns are such slow growers; four years for the calf to mature, eight to ten to reach full weight. How can I put in that kind of time again?" He shook his head. "I was counting on this year's beef herd to pull us out."

She tightened her grip on his hands. The sunshine through the window behind him seemed mockingly bright. "Surely there will be some to market. And with that you can buy—"

"I can buy nothing," he snapped, then bowed his head. "Forgive me." He brushed her fingers with his lips and pulled away. "I'll be in my study. Would you send Pearl with coffee?"

Abbie watched his back until the door closed behind him. He hadn't even removed his muddy boots. Zena hurried over with a cloth to wipe his tracks from the wood floor. Abbie went to the kitchen and gave Pearl his request. She would have brought it herself, but his dismissal was clear. She wandered upstairs and found Jenny dressing Amanda, or rather undressing her. The doll's things lay strewn across the floor.

Jenny looked up. "May we sled now?"

It was on her lips to refuse outright. She certainly shouldn't risk a toboggan ride herself. What happened the last time was evidence of that. Maybe Will . . . The distraction would keep worry at bay. Abbie held out her hand. "Come. We'll see what we can do." Downstairs, she bundled the child, took her by the hand, and headed for the stable.

Will met them, toboggan in hand. "I saw you comin'. I guess this is what you're after?"

Abbie smiled. "It's impertinent to assume you know a lady's mind, Will."

"Ain't I right?"

"*Aren't* you right?"

"Aren't I, then?"

"Yes, you are. Jenny would love a slide or two."

"You too?" He grinned.

"Yes, I would. But I won't since . . ."

He blushed. "I forgot about the baby."

"How did you know?"

He kicked his boot in the snow. "Heard the men talkin'. Come on, then."

He carried the toboggan he'd made from barrel slats to the hill behind the stable, and she followed. Had Cole told the men, or had Monte? It wasn't unlikely Monte had alerted them to be especially watchful of her. She felt the joy of his care like a great downy quilt about her heart.

Abbie looked down the slope and remembered the disastrous ride with Kendal. Had he intentionally swerved the sled off into the trees and around the turn of the hill, tumbling her off in order to make his advances? She frowned. How was it two men from the South could be so different? Monte with his devotion to honor, and Kendal . . .

Will settled Jenny onto the front, then gave the sled a shove and jumped on behind. Jenny's laughter was musical. The sun dazzled Abbie's eyes as she watched them go. Overhead a chickadee warbled, and looking up, Abbie felt spring touch her heart. Even though the snow lay deep on the north slopes, elsewhere the sun was quickly turning it to rushing torrents down gullies that lay bone dry most of the year.

Thoughts of their losses depressed her spirit, but wasn't the spring proof that God would bring them through? Surely if they lived simply, cut back on their expenses . . . she wouldn't need anything new. Monte had given her gowns enough to last for years.

And they could dine just as well on plain fare as on the sumptuous meals Pearl turned out. What other expenses were there? Payroll for the men, and wages for James and Pearl and Zena. That was the worst of it, she guessed. Household expenses, coal for the stoves and braziers, oil for the lamps, repairs and upkeep, feed for the horses.

Unless they still owed money on Kendal's fraud. Monte was determined to cover that and retrieve her stock certificates . . . at the escalated price Mr. Driscoll was asking. She wasn't supposed to know that, but she'd come across the discarded response to Monte's inquiry. From the condition of the paper, she could imagine Monte's rage when he received it.

Then there were the previous debts he had vouched for in Kendal's collapse and those he took on to support Frances until her death. She had no idea what that amounted to, but the burden obviously hung heavy on him. *Oh, Monte, must your honor extend to everyone else's shortcomings?*

Will tugged the sled up the hill with one hand and Jenny with the other. Their cheeks were red, their eyes bright. From her perch at the top, Abbie tried to look as cheerful as they.

◆◆◆◆◆◆◆

Monte tethered Sirocco and crossed the walk to the bank. Everything in him cried out against what he was about to do. But what choice had he?

The blizzard had destroyed him. They could eke along, as were his fellow ranchers Dunbar and Ephart, but Monte knew from experience that catastrophe brought collapse. He'd seen enough plantations go down because they'd hung too long by a thread.

Though he knew the risk of taking a loan, it was better to run strong and get back on top. Even if it meant groveling to Mr. Driscoll. He still stung from his last encounter when he tried to reacquire Abbie's holdings. But he would swallow his pride to save his land, especially now with a child coming to inherit it all and Jenny to think of, as well.

He rang the bell on the counter, though he was certain Driscoll had seen him coming. Elam Blanchard, the clerk, hustled out from Driscoll's office. "Yes, Mr. Farrel?"

"I'd like to see Mr. Driscoll."

"One moment, please." He scurried back in.

Monte looked around at the small paned windows, the fine wood trim, the brass cagework. A small spider wove a web across the corner of the ceiling where the sunrays caught in the delicate threads. A cloud passed over and the web disappeared.

Minutes passed. Driscoll was toying with him. He refused to turn when the door opened behind him. Two could play at that game.

"Mr. Farrel?"

He turned.

"Mr. Driscoll will see you now." The clerk opened the half gate and let him pass through to the inner sanctum of Driscoll's office.

Mr. Driscoll stood up behind the desk, smug in his brocade waistcoat and ankle-length gaiters. His fox-colored side whiskers bunched when he smiled. "Good afternoon, Mr. Farrel. Cigar?" He held open the brass tin.

"No, thank you." Monte waited while Driscoll lit up. He hoped it was Chandler's leaf. "I sent notice of my request. I've come to see if you've had time to consider it."

"Well, now, Mr. Farrel, I have had a chance to look over your situation. An unfortunate business, your losses these last few years."

Not unfortunate for you. "I would prefer we limit our dealing to the present."

Driscoll leaned back in the tight leather spring chair. "In banking decisions, Mr. Farrel, past history is an integral part of the puzzle. And whereas I can't fault your business sense, nor your diligence, there is some question as to your judgment."

Monte bristled. "The Lucky Star is prime land, my stock the finest in the area. The financial losses last year were due to circumstances that no longer exist. They had nothing to do with the good standing of the ranch."

"Nonetheless, you've shown a propensity to overextend, albeit for humanitarian reasons. It's still not good business. Covering other men's debts to your own detriment may earn you treasure in heaven, but this bank deals in earthly gold." He laughed at his own joke, then cleared his throat. "And then the blizzard. Well, you're not the only one to have suffered losses. Surely all the ranchers could claim just a need as yours, yet . . ."

Monte drew a long breath. "Are you refusing my loan?"

"Refusing? No. I just want you to understand why I'll need collateral."

Monte felt the muscles tighten in his jaw. He'd expected this but it rankled nonetheless. "I mentioned certain stock certificates."

"Unfortunately, the stock certificates you mentioned don't interest me."

Monte gripped the arm of the chair. "They're perfectly good mining stocks."

"Mining is precarious, especially now with so many playing out and the uncertainty of the government's coin policy."

"The mines I've invested in are solid." Though trying to sell his shares now with the current lag would mean more losses.

Driscoll shrugged. "No, I'm afraid the only collateral I can accept is the deed to the Lucky Star."

Monte fought to control the surging fury. He forced himself to calm. "The Lucky Star is worth far and above the amount I requested."

"So it is. And when you've paid back the loan, you'll have your deed."

"This is usury."

"If you think you can do better elsewhere . . ." Driscoll spread his hands.

Monte felt his pulse throb in his temple. By the time he established relations with a Denver bank and brought his suit to them, with no guarantee they'd be any more flexible than Driscoll, he'd have defaulted on his payroll and starved his family.

He thought of Abbie and the child within her. He thought of Cole and the men who had fought with him through the drifts to rescue the animals they'd saved. He thought of the land, his father's dream, and groaned silently. Then he looked at Driscoll, smug behind the desk.

He stood up. "Thank you, Mr. Driscoll, but I cannot accept those terms." He turned.

"Think about it, Mr. Farrel," Driscoll called. "You'll be back."

Nine

"Jenny?" Abbie looked under the white ruffled bed and in the wardrobe. She'd already searched the other rooms but with no success. Pearl hadn't seen the child, nor had Zena. Abbie had left Jenny to nap after the birthday party she'd thrown her. April twenty-third, and Jenny was three going on thirteen.

Abbie cringed when she thought how imperiously Jenny had treated Clara Franklin's little Dell and Melissa's daughter, Suzanna. Then, true to form, she'd thrown a rousing tantrum over one of her gifts, and Clara and Melissa had left, thanking God Jenny wasn't their responsibility. Abbie went from the last guest room into the library. "Jenny?"

Nothing. She glanced into the drawing room and the parlor, then searched the cloakroom, growing crosser by the minute. She checked under the coats hanging nearly to the floor, then put one on and went outside. Standing on the porch, she shielded her eyes and gazed out over the yard.

The barn where the kittens were was the likeliest place. She crossed the yard and pulled open the broad wooden door. The April chinook blew hard and whistled through the cracks. The barn was warm, though the sun was now sinking in the west. She breathed the smell of hay. "Jenny, are you in here?"

No answer. Abbie's concern and irritation grew. Where could she be? She went out from the barn to the bunkhouse. Breck and Matt Weston had dismounted and penned their horses in the east corral. Breck greeted her with a tip of his hat on his way back around the side. "Can I help you, Mrs. Farrel?"

"Have you seen Jenny? I can't seem to locate her."

"We just came in from the range, ma'am."

"Where's Cole?"

"I don't know. Matt and I were runnin' down strays."

Abbie peeked into the bunkhouse but it was empty. She turned with a sigh. She wished Monte was back from the Dunbar ranch. But he'd said it would likely be dark before he returned. She headed for the stable. That was not a safe place for a small, curious girl. Surely Will would return her to the house . . . if he was in there. Lately he'd spent more and more time out with the men.

The wind caught the door when she pulled it open, but she held tight and stepped inside. She stopped short at the sight of Jenny perched high on Cole's palomino, Scotch, with his big sheepskin coat about her. Cole had his back to her, but Jenny looked over, smiled, and gripped the pommel. Cole turned.

He looked stubbornly defensive, and Abbie thought better of teasing him. She joined them at the stall. "Jenny, I've looked all over for you."

Cole slid the bridle from Scotch's teeth. "I found her in the yard."

"Don't you think she's a little small for Scotch?"

"Nope."

"No?"

"Not if I'm leadin' him. Don't want her growin' up prissy like her ma, do you?" He reached up and swung Jenny from Scotch's back to the stall railing. "Sit there, now, while I take his saddle off." He loosened the cinch, sliding the belt through the double metal rings.

Abbie reached out. "Come down from there, Jenny."

"No. Cole said I can watch."

"That's Mr. Jasper to you, young lady," Abbie instructed.

"Cole's fine by me." He unbuckled the belly strap and turned on her. "Abbie, I'll bring the young'un up soon as I'm done here with Scotch."

"I think she should come now."

He crossed his arms and leaned his shoulder on the stall. "How come?" His green eyes went over her. They were the color of the sea in the Charleston harbor, and they held a touch of the ocean's stormy peril.

"She needs to know she can't just wander off on her own."

He turned back to the saddle. "Well, she ain't wandering, she's helpin' me."

Abbie stared. Of all people, Cole was the last one to whom she'd expect Jenny to attach. And who'd have suspected Cole would have a soft spot for little girls in his obstreperous heart? She could see she was defeated, and the shine in Jenny's eyes was too rare to squelch. She could scold her later, when Cole wasn't there to gainsay every word.

"Bring her straight in. The night's coming on."

"Yes, ma'am."

She hated it when Cole used that roguish tone. She spun, swirling her skirts behind and stalking out of the stable. Her eyes must have held fire, because Monte looked concerned when she nearly collided with him outside the door.

He had Sirocco by the reins, but reached an arm to her. "Abbie?"

"Cole has Jenny. Will you see that he brings her in as soon as he finishes?" She flounced past. There, let Cole explain himself to Monte.

◆◆◆◆◆◆◆

Monte rolled his eyes to the library ceiling. Jeanette's screams coming through the floor made him want to scream himself. What demons possessed the child? He could hear Abbie's voice raised over the din, but steady and firm, not angry. How did she maintain her calm? What Jenny needed was a thrashing.

And he ought to administer it, but he didn't dare. It was Frances all over again. He drew a long, shaky breath. He had indulged his sister in everything, letting her pouting and tantrums sway his better judgment. And he had done everything in his power to protect her from the consequences of her actions.

He had raised her to become the weak, self-indulgent woman she'd been. Never mind that he'd loved her, that it was his father's place to raise her, not his, that the war had created extraordinary circumstances. Frances was his charge, and he'd failed her. How could he now take responsibility for her child?

He'd imagined some cathartic experience. The chance to undo his wrong by loving Jenny. But it was impossible. She was impossible. Only Abbie seemed able to break through, yet he knew it took its toll on her. He read the weariness in her eyes after a battle. It wasn't fair to leave it to her, but then, she'd refused to bring Mammy.

He sighed. Maybe Abbie was right. Maybe Selena's child-rearing was superior. Hadn't she produced Abbie?

Then let Abbie handle it. The pounding on the ceiling signaled the tantrum had moved to the floor-kicking stage. Monte took up his hat and went out.

◆◆◆◆◆◆◆

Abbie pulled open the sash to let the morning light into Jenny's room. The child rubbed her sleepy eyes and sat up in the bed. She looked exhausted, and Abbie knew the fits of temper that preceded her sleep nearly every night were wearing on her. But as much as she hoped for Jenny's love and trust, she must establish authority or Jenny would never break the pattern that had ruined Frances.

"Good morning, Jenny." Abbie bent and kissed her cheek. She expected no act of affection in return. Jenny's clinging to her skirts and burying her face against her neck were nothing more than self-protective gestures. At best, Jenny suffered her company as long as she was entertaining enough.

Jenny slipped out of bed and stood in her bare feet. "I want Zena to dress me."

"She will, dear, as soon as you've had your bath."

Jenny bunched her fists at her sides. "I don't want a bath. I want to help Cole with Scotch."

"Yes, well, Cole is working now. He's with the herd."

"I want to see the cows. Cole said he'd show me. He promised."

Abbie squatted down before the child. "And maybe he will. But right now, you need your bath." She took her hand but Jenny yanked it away.

"I won't. I want to see the cows." Jenny crossed her arms and stuck out her lip stubbornly. She looked for all the world like an Arabian knights's genie from a bottle, but Abbie knew she'd be granting no wishes.

Abbie sat back on her heels. "Do you know what happens to little girls who won't wash?"

Jenny's stance wavered.

"They develop a scent. They smell. And out here when people smell they attract wild animals, coyotes and wildcats and bears." She watched Jenny's eyes widen.

"And wolfs?"

"Perhaps. And another thing, Jenny. God likes us to be clean."

Jenny put her hand in Abbie's. Abbie smiled. She knew well which part of her message had affected the change. But hopefully some bit of the second part had sunk in, as well. She had a pang of conscience thinking how many times Mama must have clung to that hope with her. She led Jenny down to the back room and drew her bath.

Zena put her head in the door. "You wants me to bathe her, Mizz Abbie?"

"No thanks. I can manage."

The child was so beautifully formed it thrilled Abbie to see her as God had made her, without all the ruffles and layers. She sponged the warm water down Jenny's back and sudsed the fine dark hair, then rinsed her clean and dried her. "There now." She wrapped her in a towel and carried her upstairs, then allowed Zena to dress her and fix her hair.

Abbie longed to do it herself, but Zena deserved more than housework to fill her days, and she could see she delighted in the task. When Jenny came out dressed in the blue woolen habit and boots, Abbie laughed.

Zena wrung her hands. "She say she ridin' with Mistuh Jazzper."

Abbie took Jenny's hand. "Thank you, Zena." She went downstairs, pulled on her own coat, and led Jenny to the stable. "Saddle Zephyr for me, please, Will." Monte couldn't fault her this ride.

She and Jenny waited in the sunshine until Will brought out the stormy gray mare. Yes, it meant riding against Monte's wishes, but she could hardly take the buggy to the herd on the open range. With only a slight pang of conscience, Abbie mounted, and Will handed Jenny up. She settled the child into the saddle before her and urged Zephyr with her knees. She would teach Cole not to make promises he didn't mean to keep.

The herd came into sight, scattered over the greening range in clumps. She caught sight of Cole riding the edge, swinging his hat to bring in a stray. Even without Scotch and at that distance she would know it was he. Only Cole rode a horse as though he'd been born on it. She urged Zephyr down the gentle slope.

She'd never taken the mare in among the cattle, but no doubt Cole would spot her long before she neared them. Sure enough, he spurred Scotch and met her at the base of the slope. He tipped his hat, revealing the unruly blond hair, but didn't remove it. He was working and didn't take kindly to interruptions.

Abbie smiled smugly. It would make her point that much stronger. "Good morning, Cole. Jenny said you promised to show her the herd."

Cole looked from her face to Jenny's and back. His scowl pulled into a crooked grin. "That's right."

Abbie stared, unbelieving, as Cole pulled Jenny from Zephyr's back and tucked her in before him. Jenny's eyes danced, and Abbie felt her mouth fall open on words that vanished before they came.

"Did ya have other business, Abbie?"

"No, I . . ." She hadn't intended to leave the child.

Cole tipped his hat again and headed off.

Her anger flared. He'd read her purpose and thwarted her intentionally. What on earth would he do with a little girl in his saddle? She pressed her knees to go after him, but he spurred

Scotch and took off with Jenny firmly in his arm. She could hear Jenny's laughter all the way.

She turned Zephyr crossly and started back. If he thought she'd wait and watch his shenanigans, he had another thing coming. He could just bring Jenny back to the house himself. She took Zephyr out on the range as far as she dared before her exasperation eased. The last thing Jenny needed was Cole encouraging her.

Her stomach made a serious complaint, and she looked up at the sun high in the sky. She felt crankier than ever by the time she got back, washed, and met Monte in the dining room for lunch. She'd been so caught up in Jenny's scheme she'd forgotten to have breakfast. With a start, she realized Jenny hadn't eaten, either.

She exulted in wicked delight at the thought of Cole with a hungry, whining child. She hadn't long to savor it, though. She'd hardly taken her place when James admitted Cole with Jenny in hand.

"She washed at the pump."

Abbie caught Monte's surprise when Cole lifted Jenny to the chair, then turned to go.

"She must be starved," Abbie threw at him.

He glanced back over his shoulder. "Nah. She had jerky from my pack."

Abbie seethed. Of course. Cole Jasper was never caught short, never without a solution . . . or a retort.

Monte quirked an eyebrow. "What was that all about?"

Abbie glanced at Jenny taking it all in. "Maybe it would be best to discuss it later." Thankfully Monte didn't push it. He obviously had his own thoughts to contend with. She bit into the salt-cured ham they'd brought back with them from Charleston. Somehow it lost its flavor when she thought of Cole feeding the child on jerky from his pack.

She should have known he would figure out something. Cole Jasper never had a moment's indecision, nor was there any difficulty he couldn't master. For some reason that both annoyed and comforted her.

After lunch, Abbie read to Jenny and tucked her in for her nap. Jenny made no argument. Her morning with Cole must have worn her out, for she was asleep within moments. Abbie sat beside her, watching her chest rise and fall. She was worn out herself. She lay down beside the child and stroked her chubby fingers. For all her tyrannical tendencies, Jenny had her sweet moments—and not just when she was sleeping. If only she could reach inside where Jenny's affections lay.

At this moment it overwhelmed her to consider the task of training Jenny, especially with so much to undo: Frances's disinterest, Mammy's overindulgence, Kendal's desertion. No wonder the child fought every step of the way. But Abbie would not give up. She would persevere until she convinced the child she was not only there to stay, but that she loved her.

Ten

Abbie stood on the boardwalk outside the newspaper office in the sparkling May sunshine that illuminated the new leaves and settled like warm honey on her face and hands. Together with Pa she watched the unusual procession stop in the street; two wagons with canvas covers, three boys with sticks to herd the motley sheep that followed the wagons, and an assortment of blue-eyed, red-headed men, women, and children on foot. A like-wise fiery-headed man leaped down, and Abbie saw his Roman collar. "He's a priest, Pa."

She was jostled by Eleanor Bailey and her sister Ruth pushing forward among the gathering crowd. "It's the Irish." Eleanor nudged her sister.

"Stinkin' Irish," someone murmured, but Abbie didn't catch who.

Pa stepped down from the walk and met the priest in the street, hand extended. "Welcome, Father. I'm Joshua Martin, but my mother was an O'Neil, and my wife's name was McKenna."

"Both goodly names." The priest pumped his hand. His eyes crinkled at the sides when he smiled. "I'm Father O'Brien, and this is my flock from County Meath. We've traveled all the way from New York City."

"That's a good long stretch."

Abbie couldn't hold back any longer. She hurried down to meet him.

"This is my daughter Abbie."

"And as fair a daughter as a man could wish. If lookin' can

tell, you'll have a grandchild soon to dandle on your knee."

"That's right." Pa beamed. "That'll make four."

"A lucky man, indeed."

Abbie glanced over the huddled forms in the wagons. "How have you come all the way from New York City, Father?"

"We've come as you see us, with all our earthly treasure. Irish are not appreciated in New York. But I've heard this is God's country in the West. We've come to homestead. We're farmers all."

Abbie couldn't help but notice the worried faces on most of the women. They looked haggard and weary, as well they might, but there was a cheeriness, too, a seeming irrepressible good humor.

Pa patted the neck of the lead ox. "Where are you headed?"

"Where the Lord leads us. Is there a church to worship in?" Father O'Brien scanned the street to the white frame church near the end.

Pa shook his head. "That one's Reverend Shields'. He's the Methodist minister."

"But there's the mission, Pa."

Father O'Brien turned. "The mission, lass?"

"Father Dominic and the Franciscan brothers built a mission east of town to minister to the Indians. Until last year it served as an orphanage, as well, but Father Dominic passed on and the brothers were called back east. It's been empty, but it's not in disrepair. At least it wasn't last time I rode out." She glanced up and saw the wondering, hopeful glance of a young woman with pale blue eyes and curling red hair.

"Well, then. That sounds a good place to start. Can you direct me?"

"I'll do one better. I'll ride out with you." Pa hooked his thumbs in his suspenders. "There's lots of empty country around the mission. I'd guess you could file to homestead out there."

"We'll have a look, then. Sounds as though the dear Lord's diggin' a furrow."

Wes McConnel joined them from the smithy in his leather apron, and when Pa introduced him, Father O'Brien clamped his hand with gusto. "A pleasure it is to find countrymen farin' well. This is a goodly land, I think, for all its barren looks."

"It's a good land, Father." Abbie smiled. "The best."

"I'd not be knowin' that yet, lass. It's a bonny green place we've left, and our hearts are heavy with the leavin'. But we'll see, now, won't we?"

She nodded. "Yes, you'll see. Pa, may I ride out with you?"

"We'll take your buggy. You folks need supplies or anything before we start?"

"We'll water the horses, but we've naught left to purchase supplies. The good people back home took a collection, and it's gotten us this far. Now we'll live by our wits."

"If there's anything you need . . ."

"We're not askin' charity, friend. But if you've a mind to barter, I'd not say no to a pint, nor would the lads."

Abbie hid her smile behind her hand.

Wes McConnel laughed, his lined and sooty face as delighted as a boy's. "Then come on. We'll slake our thirst at the saloon." No wonder he'd bred a son like Blake.

"Have you no decent Irish pub, then?"

" 'Fraid not. But the beer's just as good."

"It's the company I'm missin'."

"Well, you've two Irishmen in Joshua and me. We'll make merry enough for you."

Abbie watched the three of them and five younger men head off, but Pa would keep his head and usher them out again in short order. Else he'd answer to Mama for it. She turned to the women. They seemed not at all chagrined that the men had left them marooned in the street, and they leaned on the wagons laughing and chatting.

She stepped close. "I'm sorry to interrupt, but hadn't you better clear the street?"

The woman she'd noticed first turned to her. "And where would we go, then?"

"Well," Abbie waved her arm, "just down to the end there."

"Will you walk with us, Abbie Martin?"

"Yes, I will. But I don't know your name yet."

"Nora. Nora Flynn." She climbed up onto the lead wagon the Father had driven and nickered to the horse. A dark-haired woman who looked nearly Mama's age drove the second wagon, and Abbie walked among the sheep and children to the end of town.

Nora jumped down beside her. "That's Mary Donnelly in the other wagon, and my sister Glenna, there. She's married to Alan O'Rourke."

The tall, red-haired Glenna smiled and shifted the rosy baby on her hip. "And when's your baby due?"

Abbie rested her hand on her belly. "September."

Nora took the arm of a demure woman with broad teeth and auburn hair. "This is Peggy McSweeney. She has the big dark husband, Connor, and she bears babies the like that'll grow as big as their da." The women laughed. "I'll not introduce the little ones. You'd never keep 'em straight thrown together like this. But that's my youngest sister, Maggie, in the braids. She's fourteen this day."

"Happy birthday." Abbie sent a smile to the bony girl with red braids. She pushed a curious sheep away from her skirts and laughed. What a wonderful, fun group this was. She guessed Nora was unmarried, since she hadn't mentioned a husband of her own. But she seemed of an age with her, and Abbie felt a quickening of friendship.

"Peggy's mother, Moira, is in the wagon restin' from fever, so we'll not disturb her."

Pa and Wes and Father O'Brien came out of the saloon three blocks down, followed by the other Irishmen. Abbie identified Connor McSweeney at once. His dark head was fully above all the others, and he had shoulders like an ox.

"That's my brother, Doyle, behind Father O'Brien, Nolan and Kyle Donnelly, and Alan O'Rourke beside them. Glenna made the catch lots of girls were hopin' for. Isn't Alan handsome?"

Abbie looked at the ruddy man she indicated. His thick auburn hair and easy smile were attractive indeed.

"I was more than half in love with him myself, but he never

had eyes for any but Glenna since we were small."

Abbie thought of Blake, of the closeness they'd shared growing up and his devotion to her. Her heart ached to think how he'd have enjoyed meeting these folk from County Meath.

"What did I say?"

Abbie turned, surprised.

"I must have touched somethin' unknowing."

Had Nora read her so clearly? "You reminded me of a dear friend I lost."

"It's sorry I am to bring that sadness to your eyes. You have a sparkle otherwise. I saw it the first moment."

Abbie sighed. "It's been two years since Blake was killed. But sometimes I feel it fresh. He would have liked you all immensely. He was Wes McConnel's son."

"And he was fine, I'm sure."

"Yes. He was fine."

"So where's your husband, Abbie Martin?"

"It's Abbie Farrel."

"Och, of course. How silly of me."

"He's with the cowboys and ranchers at roundup." She read Nora's lack of comprehension. "Every spring, the ranchers band together to gather the cattle from the open range, separate out the herds, and brand the new calves. They do it again in the fall for any late calves and to put together a beef herd to ship to market."

"Yes." Abbie thought of how hard Monte worked these days.

"I'd like to meet him."

Her heart swelled. And she'd like nothing more than to introduce her fine husband. "Once you've settled in and he's back, I'll have you over."

Abbie climbed into the buggy Pa drove with Father O'Brien. The small children were bundled into the wagons, and they all started out along the track to the mission. The sheep and herders would follow more slowly, but the rutted track was easy to see, with the winter grass low and matted and the new green grass springing through.

The second day of May was as pretty a spring day as Abbie could hope for. A meadowlark sang from somewhere nearby, and overhead white puffs of clouds hung from the sapphire sky. The breeze was neither warm nor cool, just the touch of air on her cheeks.

Snow clung still to the crevices of the mountains, but the earth was soft and the breeze smelled fresh. It was hard to think that the blizzard had come just over a month before. How was Monte faring? Was he finding the lost cattle that had wandered so far in the storm? Cole would know what to do. There was no one who knew cattle better; of that she was convinced.

As they neared the adobe buildings encircled by trees, she pointed. "There, Father O'Brien, is the chapel and garden. Beyond that, the house that also served as school for the orphans."

"Ah yes. And where are the orphans now?"

"With families in the area. Wes McConnel has Jeremy, and Mama and Pa are raising little Tucker. I believe they're all well situated, but I can't say I don't miss going to the mission and finding all their cheerful faces. I schooled there with Blake McConnel when we were young, then taught the children with Father Dominic. It'll be good to have children there again, though I don't suppose any will actually live at the mission house."

"All in good time, lass. The good Lord will show us what's to be done and if the land will yield."

"I'm sure it's different than where you've been, but things can be raised here."

Pa reined in, and Father O'Brien climbed down from the buggy. He bent and dug his fingers into the hard, dry earth. "It puts me in mind of Adam's fall from the garden. Like the moist but stony soil of Erin, this land will be worked with the sweat of our brows."

Abbie couldn't argue. It was land that gave grudgingly to those who would tame it, more suited to grazing than farming. The sheep would thrive. Pa's small flock was evidence of that. But whether the ground would bear what they planted depended on the rain and what irrigation they could dig from the creek that flowed in the gully.

Father O'Brien walked to the door of the chapel and stepped inside. She knew what he would see: cool dark walls, wooden benches, the carved crucifix of the Savior that always reminded her of the first priest martyred by the Indians he'd come to serve. They'd lashed him to a tree and burned him after extensive torture.

But Father O'Brien knew nothing of that. He'd see only the Lord Jesus in His final sacrifice. And he'd sense the devotion, the commitment, the peaceful purpose of those who had served inside those walls before him. She saw it in his face when he came out.

"Glory be. The Lord has planted us."

As Pa drove her back to the ranch, Abbie turned to him. "What did Father O'Brien barter for the beer?"

"Stories."

"Stories?" Abbie asked, confused.

"The man can spin a yarn as long as the territory."

Eleven

The next day, Abbie put the two chickens into the crate and waved her thanks to Mama. She set the crate onto the buggy seat beside the rose bush wrapped in burlap. Nora would be pleased. She nickered to Toby and started for the mission.

The ride was long and bumpy and, as much as she hated to admit it, uncomfortable in her condition. It had surprised her how openly the Irish women had discussed her pregnancy without the least embarrassment. Even Father O'Brien. They seemed to have an uninhibited enjoyment of life, even after trekking across the country with next to nothing to their names.

She reined Toby in outside the long, low mission house, and Nora came to the door. Her hair was loose over her shoulders like a coiled red mane, her skin fair with a scatter of freckles over the bridge of her nose. Her wide-set eyes and bone structure were like Mama's, though Mama's coloring was anything but Irish, thanks to a single gypsy ancestor who'd passed on the brown eyes and hair.

"Good mornin' to ye, Abbie Farrel."

Abbie smiled at the way she pronounced "morning." It was a strange but pleasant accent, somehow warm and real, and she realized Mama's own speech had hints of it still. Strange how she'd never really considered Mama's Irish background until these visitors arrived. Their very Irishness seemed to bring it out in the rest of them.

"Good morning, Nora. Come see what I have for a house-warming."

Nora came out with a red-haired cherub at her heels. "This un's Danny, Glenna's second."

Abbie climbed down and ruffled Danny's thatch of hair. Then she reached for the crate of chickens and held the pair out to Nora. "A chicken and a rooster, to start your own flock."

"Och, imagine. Can you spare them, then?"

"They're from Mama. She has only Pa and little Tucker and herself to feed. She's been sending extra eggs to the hotel for two years now. Even after Pearl took three layers and a cock."

"Pearl?"

"Our cook."

"Your cook, Abbie? Have you servants, then?"

Abbie cringed. She hadn't meant to show Nora up. "They came out with Monte, my husband, from the South. After the war, they had nowhere else to go except to try to make their own way. The poverty and destruction were horrible."

She shuddered at the memory of the utter filth and hopelessness she'd seen the Charleston Negroes living in. "Even though they were freed, they stayed with Monte."

Nora's eyes widened. "Your husband's a slave owner?"

Abbie drew herself up. "Of course not. Slavery is abolished, and even were that not so, Monte treats them as part of the family."

"I'm sorry, Abbie. It's surprised I am, not judgin' you. And I'm thankful for the chickens. They're a bonny pair."

Abbie turned. "I've something else for you." She took down the rosebush. "You'll have to plant it near the creek, but it blooms red and smells sweet."

"You're too kind." Nora set down the crate and gingerly took the plant.

"Just welcoming you." Abbie swung her arm. "Now that we're neighbors. Monte's ranch, the Lucky Star, is just down that way some miles, beyond the low bluff. It's the same creek that flows past our house."

"Then I'll think of that when I'm at the water and wonder if you're drawin' it same as us." Nora smiled.

"We've a well that pumps it up from underground, but I spend a lot of time at the creek. There's a spot I'll show you that's lovely. Monte took me there on my first visit. It's very special to me."

"It would be a joy to see it and to meet your Monte. I see ye love him mightily. Come an' have a cup of tea."

Abbie followed her in, past the pallets and blankets laid out on the floor of the long room and into the large kitchen where Brother Thomas had once rolled the mounds of bread dough and steamed the vegetables he and the children raised in the garden out back. She looked through the window at the handful of tots playing out by the garden wall. It was good to see children there again.

She took the cup Nora handed her. "Where's everyone else?"

"Out lookin' at the land. They'll be choosin' their plots an' breakin' ground."

"What about you?"

"I'll live here at the big house and do for Father O'Brien, since I've no husband."

Abbie heard something in her tone but couldn't identify the emotion. Surely Nora wasn't ashamed to be unmarried. She was lovely and hale and would no doubt be swarmed with offers.

"I'm keepin' the little ones while the others are out."

"I'm sure it's wonderful to have such close ties; your sister and brother and their families all here together."

"Aye."

Again her tone was reserved.

Abbie sipped her tea. It was strong and hot in the crockery cup. On the stove a huge pot of potatoes simmered, but she saw nothing else cooking or in readiness.

"I wonder, Abbie, would your husband have a milkin' cow we could work for?"

Abbie pictured the rangy Longhorns. The eastern Shorthorns Monte had tried to crossbreed had died of Texas fever, carried, Cole said, by a tick that the Longhorns were immune to. The Longhorns were hardly tamed to milk. But Pearl had a pair of milk cows, and Monte had gotten Belle to replace Buttercup, who had died in the fire.

She looked into Nora's pale, hopeful eyes. "I'm certain he can get you one. He knows the market."

"We've no funds, though."

"We'll figure something out." A thought jumped to mind. "My pa runs the newspaper. Maybe Father O'Brien would sell him stories to print. He's always looking for something new."

Nora assessed her quietly. "I don't think folks would care to hear our stories, Abbie. Not unless it's in their blood like you and your da and Wes McConnel."

"I don't think that's so. People aren't divided here so much as other places. Out here we need each other, and our differences are . . . overlooked." *At least to some degree*, Abbie thought to herself.

"If that's so, then it's like nowhere else I've been." A shadow passed over her eyes, and this time Abbie recognized it. Bitterness, grief, and anger. But it passed as quickly as it came.

Abbie heard a horse outside and turned. "Are you expecting someone?"

"Who would I be expectin'?"

Abbie stood with Nora and walked to the door. She pulled it open.

Davy McConnel swung down from his horse and sauntered over with the same nonchalant stroll she remembered in Blake. He pulled off his hat and tossed back the brown hair that hung in his eyes. "Howdy."

"Nora, this is Wes McConnel's son, Davy. Davy, Nora Flynn."

Davy smiled. "Pa thought you might have some work fixin' up the place. I came to offer my help."

Nora crossed her arms and leaned her hip on the door frame. "And what help can ye be?"

"Anything you need." He looked up. "Check yer roof, breakin' ground . . . anything."

"I suppose you've come hungry, too."

Nora's manner surprised Abbie. Why was she so prickly and defensive?

"Nope. Ma stuffed me before I set out. She said the last thing you all needed was another mouth to feed."

"She's right at that." Nora straightened. "The others'll be troopin' in soon. You can ask Father O'Brien what he's needin'. For m'self, I have no use for you."

Abbie met Davy's eyes as Nora turned from the door and disappeared into the house.

"Well, that was a fine welcome." Davy scratched his head and replaced his hat. "Guess I'll have a look around and see for myself what's to be done."

"She must be tired and overwrought. They've come so far and not had an easy time of it, I gather."

Davy shrugged. "Might be the McConnel men just aren't lucky with ladies." He sauntered around the side of the house.

Abbie's cheeks burned. Had he meant that to cut her as it did? *Blake*. Here, where they'd spent so many childhood hours, she always felt him near. But Davy was right. She'd been bad luck for Blake. He'd loved her as she couldn't love him. He wasn't content being like a brother to her. And that's why he left.

She sagged against the jamb. Davy had his own heartache from it all. It was his two brothers, Mack and Blake, who were killed by the outlaws. And he knew well enough Blake had gone as much for her as to find gold in the mountains. Was she bad luck for Monte, too?

She went inside. Nora sat in the kitchen with Danny on her knee and a fresh cup, smiling brightly as though nothing were amiss. Abbie stopped in the doorway, but she motioned her to sit.

"I suppose I'd better get home."

"Finish your cup before you go."

Abbie sat. "There's a chance the men'll come back today."

"From their roundup?"

"Yes. It's been longer than usual already. The blizzard scattered the cattle, and I suppose the men are riding farther afield to find them."

"Did they break through the walls, then?"

Break through the walls? Abbie tried to picture what Nora

meant. "Most of the range isn't fenced. It's just open country. Monte's one of the only ranchers so far to fence some of his pasture land, but he uses that mostly for the horses."

"Then how do you know whose cows are whose?"

"By the brand and the earmark. Monte's cattle have a star brand and a single notch on the left ear. This year they started roundup at the Farringer range down to the south, so they'll end on Monte's. We're the farthest north in the district."

"And the cattle all run together?"

"They mostly stay near their home ranges, but those encompass miles of open land. And the blizzard scattered and confused those that survived."

"You've mentioned this blizzard. Surely it's been months since winter."

"Out here snow can come all the way into June, and the next day'll be as warm and shining as summer. But the blizzard we had last March was devastating. We lost nearly a thousand cattle, including all but one of the new calves, and thirteen horses."

Nora's eyes widened. "That's a staggerin' blow for sure, but have you so many to lose?"

"I don't know what we have left." Abbie stared into her cup. "Monte's concerned."

"It's a rich man ye've married, Abbie."

Abbie nodded slowly. "We have much to be thankful for." She heard Davy hammering at the back of the house. Nora tensed but said nothing, and Abbie finished her tea and stood. "I'll come again if I may."

"Of course you may. You're welcome anytime."

Then why wasn't Davy? Abbie climbed into the buggy and turned Toby for home. Next time she'd bring Jenny with her. It would do the child good to have others her age to play with. The encounter on her birthday had shown Abbie the need. If Jenny was to behave, she must learn she was not the only child who mattered.

◆◆◆◆◆◆◆

Monte turned from his stance at the study window and smiled when Abbie rushed over. He folded her hand in his. "And why was my wife not here to welcome me home?" He said it playfully but meant it nonetheless.

"I brought a pair of chickens from Mama to the new folks at the mission."

He raised an eyebrow and she explained at length, with every detail down to the sheep. Her face fairly shone with the excitement of it all.

"And Nora wondered if you might find them a milk cow, only they've no money to purchase it."

His heart squeezed and he released her hand. "Nor have we, Abbie. We've scarcely seven hundred head surviving, and . . . our funds are depleted." He felt stripped and barren.

She stared into his face. "Seven hundred?"

"There are carcasses all the way to Walsenburg." He couldn't tell if she truly understood what that meant. Many of those surviving were not of marketable weight, and it would be years before he built up the herd to what it was—if they held on long enough to accomplish it.

"Oh, Monte!"

He turned back to the window. "I'm not sure what to do, Abbie. For the first time in my life, I'm not sure where to turn."

"Turn to the Lord, Monte. He's never failed us before."

He smiled dimly, then stared once again out the window. He knew God was in control. God had given him Abbie, brought him victory over Captain Gifford, sustained him through loss and sorrow. He had surrendered his will to the Almighty, serving Him as honorably as he could. But he was not a man to wait only on the Lord and do nothing himself.

Yet he was caught now between indecision and inability. What he would do, which was build up the herd with fresh stock, he could not for lack of funds. What he would never do, turn over the deed to Driscoll and the bank, would give them the funds he needed.

But at what risk? His child's inheritance? His land? The land

117

was the difference between bond and free. Land had separated the planter from the poor white farmer in the South. Land ... and honor. The swamp farmers and poor whites had turned against the landowners, grasping what they'd never earned, destroying what they coveted.

He would not forget their betrayal easily, nor would he surrender to their kind, in the person of Driscoll, his ranch, his home, his freedom. He could refuse to pay Kendal's debts. He could disavow responsibility. But even so, they had already drained his reserves. Driscoll was right. It had not been good business to step in where Kendal failed. It had been honor.

And by honor he would continue. He could live no other way. He glanced down at his wife, silent beside him. "Don't be troubled, Abbie. We'll find a way through, God willing."

"I know we will, Monte."

Twelve

"Oh, for heaven's sake, Marcy." Abbie put her hands to her hips. "It won't hurt you to gather lettuce from your tiny little garden. You're not doing yourself or your baby any good acting so helpless." It was only at Mama's insistence that Abbie was there in Marcy's kitchen instead of out enjoying the fine May afternoon.

She would have preferred to be at Nora's, where the laughter always matched the hard work, where stories flew as fast as their fingers over the tasks at hand. She longed to drop by Clara's and hear her chatter. She yearned to be home with Monte and Jenny. Anywhere but here with Marcy's whining.

No doubt Mama would frown at her exasperation, but truly Marcy took it too far. She reached out and tugged her to her feet. "A little exercise certainly won't hurt."

"But I can't go out in the sun. Doctor Barrow—"

Abbie slapped a straw hat over Marcy's shining blond curls. "You won't even know it's there." She propelled her toward the door. "And it's not fair to expect Grant to do all his work and yours, as well. The least he can expect is supper when he comes home."

Marcy sent her a scathing look and waddled over the small patch of garden to the rows of early lettuce that glowed in the golden sun rays. "I certainly hope you don't expect any sympathy when you get this big and awkward. Because I'll remember—" She drew in her breath sharply and pressed her hands to her cheeks.

"What is it now?" Abbie's annoyance with Marcy's theatricals

119

made her voice sharp. Marcy doubled over and gripped the fence, and Abbie felt a jolt of fear. "Marcy?"

"Something broke. It's gushing down my legs and—" She broke off with a cry.

Good Lord, the baby. Abbie put an arm around Marcy's shoulders. "Can you walk?"

Marcy straightened, then cried out again and clutched Abbie's arm until the circulation stopped. "I don't think so! I—"

"You can't have the baby out here in the garden."

"Have the baby?" Marcy looked at her with stark terror.

What did she think was happening? Had she no sense at all? "Here, lean on me."

"No! This wouldn't have happened if you hadn't forced me out here." She bent double again and wailed.

Abbie looked quickly at the next house over. No help there; it was Howard Murphy's place, and he'd be at the saloon with the other single men who roomed with him. If only Grant were here. But he was coming in on the evening train, and the Lord only knew when it would actually arrive.

He should have known better than to accept that legal case in Denver, even if it was a favor to the judge. But, then, the judge was Marcy's father. Abbie girded herself for battle. "We're going inside. There's nothing else for it." She took Marcy by the shoulders and propelled her gently but firmly toward the house.

"You're hateful, Abbie Farrel. You did this on purpose." Her hat slipped sideways, and she yanked it from her head and tossed it to the ground. "You've always—Ohhh!"

"Stand here until it passes." In spite of her steady tone, Abbie was concerned. The pains were far too close, and there was a good deal of blood in the wetness on the ground where Marcy had stood. "Okay, now. Slowly." She took Marcy's weight against her. *Please Lord, don't let her faint.*

She got her to the back stoop before the next pain made her scream. If she could just get her inside. Thank God the bed had been moved down. In truth there was no way Marcy could have gone upstairs in this condition.

Marcy cried out. "How could you? You think you're so smart. I told you . . ." She gasped.

"Just a little farther now. You're almost there." Abbie pushed the door open and eased her inside. She glanced at the trail of blood on the stoop, but said nothing. No sense making Marcy any more scared than she already was. She got her to the side of the bed and sat her down. "Can you strip off your things?"

"Of course I can."

"Then do so while I get Doctor Barrow."

She was glad Marcy didn't argue. She rushed from the house and down the rutted lane. Thank goodness Grant and Marcy lived near town, but it was still a good mile to the main street. She ran, though her own increasing bulk made it difficult. She passed McConnel's smithy and Pa's newspaper office. A handful of men parted before the saloon to let her pass.

"Everything all right, Mrs. Farrel?"

She scarcely looked to identify the speaker, but knew Ethan Thomas's voice. "It's fine." She said it as much for herself as for him. "But I need the doctor."

He caught her arm. "You stand here, ma'am. I'll run for the doc."

Abbie stopped, held her side, and leaned against the wall. "Tell him Mrs. Martin's having her baby." She drew long breaths, more winded than she had any right to be.

"Here ya are, Abbie." Wes McConnel brought her a glass of cider from the bar. As she drank it, she watched for the doctor and Ethan to come out. *Oh, please be there.* Down beyond the hotel, she looked at the station, but it would be some time before the train arrived.

Come on, she begged inwardly. It seemed interminable, but at last the doctor stepped out with Ethan behind him. They climbed into Doctor Barrow's buggy and drove up. Ethan jumped down and Wes gave Abbie a hand in.

Doctor Barrow took up the reins. "She's at home?"

"Yes."

He slapped the reins lightly. "Well, these things take time. Likely there's no hurry."

"It doesn't seem normal. The pains are very close, and she's bleeding more than I'd expect."

He frowned, then increased the horse's pace. When they reached the house, Abbie directed the doctor to Marcy, then went to the kitchen. She started the water heating on the stove and searched the cupboard for clean cloths. The water warmed reluctantly. Everything seemed to take longer than usual, each moment hanging on the last.

Come on, come on. When the water boiled, she joined the doctor and Marcy in the dining room that now held the bed. Marcy was drenched with sweat. Her gown clung to her, and her face was taut. She bared her teeth as she thrashed.

Abbie felt a stab of fear. What if she had pushed Marcy too far? What would Grant say if anything happened to her? *Please, Lord.* She watched Doctor Barrow remove his cuff links and roll his sleeves.

He scrubbed his arms in the basin and wiped them dry. "Get to her head and soothe her while I see where we are." Doctor Barrow spoke without turning, then delved beneath the blankets.

Marcy screamed, and Abbie wet the cloth from the pitcher and smoothed it over her brow. Marcy opened her eyes and panted, "Grant?"

"He's not here yet."

Doctor Barrow sat back, and Abbie looked with panic at his bloody hand. Mamie's delivery had not been like this. Fear clutched her heart.

The doctor stood and plunged his hand into the basin. "I was afraid of this. The baby's breech."

Abbie's thoughts raced. Breech. That meant turned wrong, not positioned to be birthed as it should. At least that wasn't her fault. She couldn't be blamed for the baby's position.

What was she thinking? How could she think of herself when Marcy's life and her baby's were at risk? What would Doctor Barrow do?

He checked Marcy's pulse and felt her abdomen. "It might yet turn on its own." He applied pressure and Marcy wailed. Abbie soothed her brow, willing her strength. Her pains were too close, too sharp, her fear too intense. Abbie could almost smell it.

Doctor Barrow watched and waited while Marcy labored in pain and fear, but seemingly to no avail. The clock ticked and the hands moved. With frightening regularity the pains came on Marcy, but they seemed to do nothing. Abbie soothed, but Marcy's screams increased. If only she wouldn't fight it. On and on it went.

None of the pain and effort seemed to accomplish anything. When fresh blood gushed, Doctor Barrow stood abruptly. "The placenta may have ruptured. I'll have to take the child now." He twisted a cloth. "Give her this to bite down on."

Abbie's heart sank, but she took the cloth and eased it between Marcy's teeth. Marcy's eyelids drew back from the whites of her eyes. She tried to fight, then gripped the bedding until her knuckles turned white. She screamed through the gag. Abbie held her shoulders down against more strength than she thought Marcy possessed.

"There, now," she soothed. "He's turning the baby so it can come out. You'll be fine. You'll be just fine." *Oh, God, she will be fine, won't she?*

How could it take so long to turn the baby? She kept her eyes on Marcy's face and refrained from pleading with the doctor to hurry. Her job was to keep Marcy calm, and Marcy's frantic gaze was riveted on hers, as though she could draw strength from Abbie's firm demeanor.

"There, now." She held Marcy's eyes with more compassion than she'd ever felt for her. She shared her woman's agony and ached for her.

Marcy screamed again and gripped Abbie's arms to the bone.

"That's right. Hold on to me. It's almost over." What did she know? For all she knew it could be days still, just like Maimie. No. Marcy would be dead by then. This birth was too violent to be sustained. *Oh, sweet Lord . . . help her. Bring the baby soon.*

"Mrs. Farrel." It was more a bark than a beckon. "The baby's tangled in the cord. Come hold the head while I loose it."

Hold the head? Abbie's heart raced as she reached down to secure the tiny bluish head protruding from Marcy's body. *Oh, Lord in heaven.* She closed her eyes when he reached inside. Marcy seemed beyond caring. Abbie moved one hand, then the other as the doctor worked the cord free from the baby's neck. Marcy wailed, and with a sudden rush the baby girl came free into Abbie's hands.

Doctor Barrow turned the infant and smacked her backside. The baby cried.

Oh, thank you, Jesus. Abbie's own breath came in gasps as she held the baby while Doctor Barrow tied off and cut the cord. The infant was small and gangly, but she cried with all the power she had.

"Wash and wrap her," Doctor Barrow ordered. "I'm not through here."

Abbie took the baby just as Marcy thrashed again. From Doctor Barrow's expression, she was not out of danger yet. Abbie bathed the crying baby in tepid water, then diapered and dressed her in the gown she found in the dresser upstairs. Her crying stopped when she bundled her tightly into the blanket she'd left warming near the stove.

She carried her back to Marcy. Doctor Barrow was washing the blood from his arms at the elbow. Marcy lay still and quiet, and Abbie's chest constricted.

"She's sleeping."

Her breath released audibly.

"I hate for you to see that with your own turn coming soon, but I'm awfully glad you were with her. We'd have lost them both. Even now..." He cleared his throat. "She's lost a good deal of blood, though the worst of the hemorrhaging has passed."

Grant burst through the door and stood panting. He'd obviously gotten the word and run all the way from the station.

"Congratulations, young man. You have a daughter."

Abbie remembered she was holding the baby and brought her

to him. Grant stood dumbfounded, then slowly reached out and took his child into his arms.

Abbie smiled at the awe in her brother's eyes. "Have you a name for her?"

His throat worked. "Emily. Emily Elizabeth."

She squeezed his hand and left the room. Marcy and the baby were in his care now, and the doctor would no doubt fill Grant in. She was as fatigued as she could remember being. Her arms and shoulders ached, and she was famished. They never had made Grant's supper.

She rubbed the back of her neck and went outside. It was dark and Monte would be worried. She wished she hadn't unhitched Toby but reattached him wearily, then climbed into the buggy and started home. She had barely made it from the stable to the lane when Monte rode up on Sirocco. His face was stern, and she recognized his concern.

Sirocco stamped and snorted as he reined in and dismounted. "Abbie."

"Marcy had her baby. A daughter."

His expression lightened. "That's marvelous." He looked toward the house, then tied the stallion behind the buggy and climbed in beside her. She gratefully handed him the reins and leaned against his shoulder. She was asleep before the lights of town faded from view.

Monte felt Abbie's weight against him as he drove. Her breathing was deep and her body limp, signs of exhaustion. Would she never realize her limits? Did she not understand the terror he felt when she failed to arrive on time or pushed herself beyond her strength?

Did she not know how much he wanted this child, how deeply he feared burying another son or daughter? Would Abbie never settle into the wifely mold? He sighed. He had not married her because she fit any mold. Precisely the opposite. A smile pulled the corners of his mouth.

His youthful rejection of the rigid strictures of his southern upbringing had landed him a woman as unlike his first wife as the Colorado Territory from South Carolina. While part of him struggled to tame her, the rest exulted in her strength and audacity. She would bear him a child the like of whom he'd never seen.

◆◆◆◆◆◆◆

Abbie slept clean past noon the next day. She was appalled to see how high the sun was when she opened her eyes, but Monte sat on the end of the bed and laughed.

"I hope this teaches you." He handed her a cup of tea.

"Goodness, Monte. Why didn't you rouse me?"

"I wanted you to realize that you have limits."

"As if I didn't know that." Abbie sat up and sipped the tea. He stuffed a pillow behind her.

"I'm not an invalid, Monte. I don't need you to pamper and attend me as Grant does Marcy."

"Is that what this is all about?" Monte's tone was suddenly stern.

"What?"

"Are you trying to prove to Miss Marcy that you're stronger than she?"

Abbie bristled. "I resent that. I've no need to prove anything to Marcy."

He clasped her free hand. "Then do me a favor and refrain from heroics just long enough to bring our child into the world."

"What are you talking about? What heroics?"

"I spoke with Doctor Barrow this morning."

As though that told her all. "And?"

"He said without your help he could not have turned or untangled the infant. He also said you ran the mile to town and stayed on your feet through all the grizzly hours without once quailing at the sight of blood. I let him know you weren't given to faints."

"Thank you, Monte. It's all a bunch of nonsense to think any of that was beyond a woman's natural inclination. Of course I had to hurry, and I'm not so large yet that I can't run."

"Even if it means sleeping fifteen hours straight." His amusement was tempered with concern.

"Well, I haven't an answer for that." Abbie closed her eyes and savored the tea.

"I have. You overtaxed yourself."

She sighed, snuggling back into the pillows at her back and resting the cup and saucer against her chest. "Thankfully, Marcy's baby is delivered. You've no idea what an ordeal she endured. She was utterly spent by the end."

"It's a miracle they both survived. Doctor Barrow said a breech birth doesn't always turn out that way. Your quick action made it possible."

"There, now. You can't scold me further."

"I'm not scolding." His voice was gentle.

"What, then?"

"Appealing. With all my heart. Don't strain yourself."

"If it makes you feel better, I'll spend the day in bed. Jenny can join me and we'll have stories and tea and . . . what?" She caught the contradiction in his expression.

"Cole took her out this morning to see the new foals. With his help, one of the mares birthed twins last night. I needn't tell you how unusual that is."

"Oh, Monte! And they're healthy and strong?"

"And pretty. She'll enjoy it."

"Did Cole take her on Scotch?"

Monte nodded. "And she looked for all the world like Cleopatra astride an elephant and in complete charge of everything."

Abbie could well picture it. And Cole encouraged her naughtiness. "Is she back?"

"She wasn't when I came up, but I'm sure she's safe with Cole."

Abbie set the cup down on the bed stand, tossed back the covers, and swung her legs to the floor.

"What happened to your promise?"

"I can't stay in bed wondering where she is. Anyway, I'm perfectly well rested, and I want to see the foals. Colts or fillies?"

"Fillies, and I should have known better."

Abbie caught his face between her hands and kissed him. "*You* may escort me."

He helped her stand and pulled her close, resting a hand on her stomach between them. "Will nothing induce you to stay?"

"Not as long as Jenny's twisting Cole around her finger and spoiling whatever headway I've made these last months."

"Really, Abbie."

"Really."

He released her. "I'll await you downstairs. But I insist you eat before we go."

"You needn't insist. I'm starved."

♦♦♦♦♦♦♦

The foals were pretty indeed, cinnamon brown with white blazes, and they tumbled skittishly about the mare when the buggy drew up to the fence. But Cole and Jenny were not at the pasture. Abbie turned. "What do you say now, Mr. Farrel?"

"I'm sure they're somewhere close." He turned the buggy and drove back to the yard.

Abbie rested her hand in his and climbed down, but she didn't go toward the stairs. He shook his head when she headed off, but he didn't stop her. Nor did he join the search. He went up the stairs and inside as she rounded the corner, passed the stable, and headed for the bunkhouse. Jenny's laughter carried on the breeze.

Abbie rounded the south wall of the bunkhouse and saw them. Cole, squatting, elbows on thighs, untangling the small loop of rope from his neck and shoulder. He handed it to Jenny who stood before him in skirt and petticoats. Laughing, she tossed it onto his head again.

Abbie leaned into the shadow of the wall and watched. Jenny's back was to her, but she could imagine the light in her eyes to match the laughter. Cole made a to-do about her snagging him, then gave her another try. This time the rope caught him in the face, but he picked it up from where it fell and adjusted it in her hand. "There. Now, try again."

Instead, she dropped the rope and stretched her arms around his neck. Abbie could see Cole's expression as he hesitantly closed his arms around her and patted her small back. Feeling ashamed to witness the tender moment without their knowing, she moved back from the corner. A twig snapped under her foot, and Cole looked up.

Abbie stepped away from the wall. "Hello, Cole, Jenny."

Cole stood and gathered up the rope. "No need to eavesdrop, Abbie. If you want the child, just come an' take 'er."

"I didn't mean to eavesdrop. It's just . . . she was enjoying herself so. I love to hear her laugh."

Jenny clapped her hands together. "Cole taught me to rope."

"A fine skill for a lady." Abbie caught Cole's frown and stooped down to brush the dust from Jenny's skirt. "Auntie Abbie has a few such skills of her own."

Cole snorted. "Such as?"

"Oh . . . spearing fish, tracking animals, climbing trees."

He eyed her. "I don't reckon you practice them much."

Abbie stood. "No. Not lately."

"I always believed a girl had as much right to knowin' things as a boy."

"Then would you say a boy ought to learn to sew and cook and clean?"

Cole rubbed his jaw, and Abbie saw the sunlight catch in the blond stubble beside his mustache. "I reckon if a body has a mind to learn somethin', he ought to learn it regardless."

"And if he hasn't a mind to?"

Cole hooked his thumbs into his belt. "Some things ought to be learned anyway. But oftentimes before you realize that, the opportunity's gone." He bent and chucked Jenny under the chin. "Run along, now. I got work to do."

Jenny caught his rough hand and kissed his knuckle, then skipped over and took the hand Abbie extended. Abbie had never seen her so free with her affection. As they walked back to the house, she watched the sunlight play in Jenny's curls. "Jenny, what is it about Cole that you like so much?"

"I like how he smells."

Abbie bit her lip against the surprised smile and looked across the yard. What did Cole smell of? Tobacco and horses and the wind off the range; strong, manly scents. No wonder Jenny snuggled close. Did she even remember her pa? Did Cole somehow conjure feelings of comfort and familiarity?

She pictured the child in his rough embrace, only it hadn't been rough. It was amazingly gentle. That's what had made her step away. She'd glimpsed a side of Cole he didn't often show.

Jenny suddenly tugged her hand free and pointed. "Look. A bunny." She scurried after the cottontail that disappeared under the porch, but the rabbit disappeared out the far side with Jenny none the wiser.

Abbie stooped and lifted her to her feet. "The bunny's gone, Jenny. Come inside and wash now."

Thirteen

Abbie stayed dutifully close to home the next two weeks, but on the Sunday following, she took Jenny and drove out to the mission chapel. Monte declined, saying his day of rest would be better spent in peaceful solitude. It was no doubt in reaction to the earsplitting tantrum Jenny had thrown the night before.

Though lessening in frequency, the incidents had increased in volume and duration. Abbie prayed for wisdom, but it seemed long-suffering was the answer she received. Jenny was no further along the road of self-control than a wild thing. As she stood in the yard with Ma and Pa, the McConnels, and Pat Riley from the lumber yard, Abbie watched her dealing imperiously with the Irish children, Meghan and Danny and Katie Lynn.

They had rushed out together to play in the yard in the sunshine after Mass. Now Jenny was prancing like a princess and demanding their adoration. Meghan seemed willing enough and Danny, as well, but Katie Lynn gave her a push. Before Abbie could reach them, Jenny had two fistfuls of Katie's red hair and Katie had slapped her across the face.

Both girls were yammering to wake the dead. Abbie hooked an arm around each and demanded they retreat. Jenny refused to let loose Katie's hair, and Abbie pried her fingers off, then clamped a hand around the small wrists and dragged her back. Glenna took hold of Katie.

"Your Jenny has a temper to match Katie's own. Sometimes it's best to let them fight it out and see what comes of such."

"I'm very sorry."

" 'Twas Katie that pushed. It's not often someone stands up to her."

Abbie glanced up to see Nora watching, then took Jenny firmly in hand, and joined her friend in the shade.

"You've your hands full, Abbie Farrel."

"She's had a lot to contend with in her short years. Too much loss."

"Aye. Loss is a debilitatin' thing for a wee lass. Or not so wee." Abbie glanced up, but Nora turned her gaze to Father O'Brien. "A grand homily he spoke this mornin', eh?"

"Yes. I've always related too well to the prodigal son. It seems that his fault was not so much truly wickedness as impulsiveness."

Nora smiled. "Are you impulsive, Abbie?"

"Only to a fault."

Nora laughed. "Aye, and you remind me of someone." The laughter died in her eyes and faded from her lips. She took a stick and shooed the chicken from the chapel doorway. "I'll be about Father's meal, now. 'Twas good seein' you."

"And you, Nora. Will you come to tea tomorrow?"

"Can my own feet take me there?"

"I'll send James to fetch you."

"I wouldn't feel right. I'll borrow Mary's wagon."

"Just follow the track and take the right fork."

"I'll do that. Good day, Abbie."

Abbie watched her retreat inside. What secrets did Nora Flynn harbor behind her smile? She glanced up and saw Davy McConnel watching, as well. He stood in the yard beside his mother, Mary, and sister, Mariah. But his attention was on the door through which Nora had passed.

She knew from Wes that Davy had come out every day and worked on repairs to the mission chapel and house. But it seemed by his expression he'd still not received a welcome. Why did Nora disdain him? He was a fine man, strong and hearty if not outright handsome. He had Blake's contagious smile, though she doubted Nora had yet encouraged it.

Abbie shook her head and stooped down to Jenny. "How would you like to go see baby Emily?" Abbie had promised Mama before Mass to check in on Marcy.

"May I show her my critters?"

"What critters?"

Jenny ran to the little bag she had left lying on the step, snatched it up, and ran back. "The critters Cole made me." She shook the bag.

Abbie heard the wood pieces clatter together and smiled. "Certainly. I'd like to see them, too."

Thinking of visiting Marcy brought none of her usual animosity. Maybe experiencing the trauma together had melted the boundaries of her dislike. At any rate, seeing the baby would provide a distraction for Jenny.

Pa hoisted Jenny into the buggy, then gave Abbie a hand. "Tell Grant I have a matter to discuss with him."

"All right." Abbie took up the reins.

Jenny was quiet as they drove. She fingered the bag at her side and took in everything around her: the squirrel that skittered up the ponderosa and chattered from the branch, the magpie calling from its tip. But she seemed to shrink into herself as they neared town.

"What's the matter, Jenny?"

She spoke without raising her head. "I don't like Aunt Marcy."

Abbie could hardly correct her honesty when it so closely paralleled her own feelings. "Why not?"

"She doesn't like me."

"That's not true, Jenny."

"Do we have to stay long?"

"No. We'll see the baby and ask if there's anything Aunt Marcy needs." Abbie reined the horse to a stop before the green frame house. She noticed Jenny tucked the bag of animals into the corner of the seat.

"Don't you want to bring them in?"

Jenny shook her head.

"May I see them?"

Jenny pulled the bag out, loosed the drawstring, and dumped the carved wooden creatures into her lap. Abbie recognized Cole's workmanship, another facet of his personality that seemed incongruous. It was amazing how he captured the nature of each animal with the fine strokes of his knife. She examined a Longhorn steer, an antelope, and a running horse, then a chicken and a bear and a rabbit.

"When did he give you these?"

Jenny shrugged. "I don't 'member."

Abbie slipped them back into the bag. "Why don't you bring in the bag. You don't have to take the animals out."

Jenny pulled the string and clamped the bag in her little fist. They knocked and Marcy's mother opened the door to them. Abbie was not at all surprised or put off by the haughty look she gave them. She was used to it. Like Marcy and her husband, the judge, Darla Wilson saw most of the world from the end of her nose.

"Good morning, Mrs. Wilson. We've come to pay Marcy a call."

"Come in, Mrs. Farrel. I'll see if she's up to callers."

Abbie waited in the front room as Marcy's mama ascended the stairs. Grant must have moved their bed back to the bedroom. A few minutes later Darla Wilson returned. "You may come up."

Abbie was surprised. Surely Marcy wasn't still bedridden. She bit her tongue and headed up, Jenny in hand. Marcy was indeed ensconced in pillows and covers on the large bed. She held the baby in her arms, but her face reflected none of the radiance Abbie would have expected.

As soon as Darla Wilson left the room, Marcy put up her chin. "Have you come to gloat, then?"

Abbie stopped short. "Gloat?"

"I know what you're thinking, Abbie Farrel. How I disappointed Grant producing a baby girl. And how dreadful a time I had. Of course, that was thanks to you, bringing on the labor before I was ready."

Abbie felt her ire burn. All her natural animosity returned, but for Jenny's sake she masked it. "I don't know what you're talking about. Grant's thrilled with Emily, besotted. He's not foolish enough to expect a son. He's as happy as can be. And as for the rest . . ." She swallowed her pride. "I'm very sorry if what I did brought on your labor. Truly I am, but it has worked out for the best."

"Oh yes." Marcy tossed her blond ringlets. "You got to be the center of attention . . . again! I'm so sick of Grant and Doctor Barrow telling me you saved my life." She screwed up her face. "'Abbie ran all the way. How lucky it was that Abbie was there. Abbie didn't flinch even with all that blood.'" Marcy's lip protruded. "It was my blood, my suffering, but no one can talk of anything but you."

Abbie forced herself forward to the end of the bed with Jenny clinging to her skirts. "You were incredible, Marcy. I've never known anyone to suffer like that so bravely."

Marcy's color left her cheeks. "Are you mocking me?"

Abbie shook her head. "Not one bit. You brought that baby with the worst of circumstances, and did it . . . heroically."

Marcy sank back into the pillows. She seemed at a loss, and for a moment Abbie saw something flicker in her eyes. Then she turned up her nose. "Of course Grant wouldn't say so."

"He didn't see it. He doesn't know. No man could understand, not even Doctor Barrow." Abbie stroked the post of the footboard. "They do their part, but have no inkling what it's like for us."

Again Marcy seemed at a loss, and Abbie felt chagrined that she had never made the effort before to reach out as she was now. Was it possible Marcy was vulnerable? Marcy with all her haughty airs?

"May we see the baby?"

Marcy looked down as though only realizing the infant was there in her arms. She held her out and Abbie took her. She sat at the edge of the bed and held the baby for Jenny to see. Three weeks of feedings had filled in her cheeks. Emily had Marcy's blue eyes, at least so far. Her dark hair had fallen out and a pale fuzz covered her skull in the loose-fitting bonnet.

"She's beautiful. How could you think for one minute Grant is disappointed?"

Marcy looked toward the window. She was quiet so long Abbie thought she'd ignore her question. Then she sighed. "I know how Pa felt about me. Especially when Ma never produced a boy."

For the first time, Abbie glimpsed inside Marcy. She'd never even wondered what made her so mean, so faultfinding. "I promise you Grant is as happy for this baby girl as he'd be for a son. You have nothing to be ashamed of."

For the fleetest moment, Marcy's eyes held gratitude, then they hardened again. "I never said I was ashamed."

Abbie glanced at Jenny laying out the little animals along the edge of the bed. Of course Emily was too small to notice, but Marcy glanced over.

"What's all that?"

"Animals Cole carved for Jenny."

"Cole Jasper, your foreman?" The haughty tone was back in her voice.

"Yes. He has quite a talent."

"What has he to do with your niece?"

Abbie smiled down at Jenny. "They're fond of each other."

"I certainly hope you won't foster that," Marcy sneered.

"I've no need to. They've developed it on their own," Abbie answered honestly.

Emily mewed, and Abbie handed her back to Marcy.

"Well, if you've any hope of making a lady of the child, rough men like Cole Jasper—"

"Marcy." Abbie eyed her squarely. "I'll not have you say a word against him. He's a fine man. He's saved Monte's life and mine at his own risk."

"That's all fine and good, as long as he knows his place."

Abbie's temper flared.

"Don't be so innocent, Abbie. He's only using the child to get to you. You know how he feels about you. Everyone knows he proposed marriage."

Abbie sprang to her feet, scattering the little animals. She saw the look of triumph in Marcy's eyes and realized she'd been baited. How had she thought to change a pattern that had been cast between them from childhood. Jenny scrambled to gather the wooden animals into the bag, and Abbie contained her fury.

"You have a lovely daughter, Marcy. I hope your recovery is swift." She took Jenny by the hand and walked out. *And I hope your whining and nastiness don't drive Grant stark raving mad.*

Fourteen

The noon sun bathed the wood floor of the entry, and Abbie smelled the linseed oil Zena had rubbed into the tight, fitted planks. She took a long, slow breath. She had slept poorly, thinking of Marcy's words. How was it she could have such heartfelt sympathy for Marcy one moment and such scathing contempt the next?

Each time she tried to break through she was rebuffed. She and Marcy were oil and water. They'd never mix. Marcy had always possessed a sharp tongue and aimed it her way. Abbie didn't hold her solely to blame, though. She'd fired plenty of shots at Marcy, as well, and she knew they'd hit bull's eye. How could anyone undo that kind of bad blood?

Maybe it was foolish to think they could find common ground. Especially when Marcy held such a poor opinion of the people Abbie cared for. Cole, in particular. Marcy's attitude toward him was nothing short of contemptuous, though why it should be, she couldn't say. Just plain snobbery, she supposed.

She heard wheels in the yard and hurried to the door. It was early for tea, but maybe Nora had expected the trip to be longer. Her heart jumped at the thought of seeing her friend, someone who shared a laugh and a chat without malice.

She opened the door in surprise to Reverend Shields, then smiled. "Good day, Reverend."

He removed his hat and nodded. "Mrs. Farrel. Is your husband home?"

"Yes. I believe he's in the study. May I take your hat?"

"Thank you. I hope I'm not intruding."

"Not at all. I'm having a friend for tea. Won't you join us, as well?"

"I'd like that very much, if it's not too much trouble."

"It's no trouble at all." Abbie tapped and opened the door to the study. "Monte, Reverend Shields is here to see you."

Monte looked up from his desk. "Come in, Winthrop."

Abbie left them, closing the door softly behind her. She went to the kitchen and found Pearl. "Reverend Shields will also join us for tea, Pearl."

"I already seen him, Mizz Abbie. I's warmin' a pie."

Abbie smiled. "He loves your pie."

"Don' you say that. Don' you gimme the big head." But her cheek dimpled with the suppressed smile.

Abbie wandered upstairs. Waiting for Nora now, the time seemed to hang. She glanced in the nursery at Jenny. The child was dressed in sky blue satin with ribbons to match tied into her dark ringlet curls. She looked exquisite, too pretty to touch. She looked like Frances, and Abbie felt a pang.

Zena looked up from the ring of marbles between them. "Is you needin' Mizz Jenny now?"

Jenny frowned, and Abbie felt as though she'd been caught longing for something she shouldn't have. But that was ridiculous. Jenny was hers to love. Why couldn't it be as easy as it seemed to be for Cole Jasper? She shook her head. "No. I'll call when tea is served."

She walked back down. She was eager but at the same time anxious about this visit. What if Nora was overwhelmed or offended by the discrepancy in their circumstances? Maybe she shouldn't have asked her so soon. Maybe they hadn't yet become close enough. But how could she continue to receive Nora's hospitality without returning the invitation?

She looked out the window, but except for Will watering the minister's horse, the yard was empty. What did Reverend Shields want with Monte? No doubt he was collecting for some cause or other.

The fire she'd lit in him when they placed the orphans had kindled to a blaze, and there was always some need. He came to her when a matter required personal attention, and to Monte when it was financial. She sighed. This time he might leave disappointed.

She heard a horse and wagon and looked out to see Nora. The wagon stopped at the end of the drive, and Abbie knew her friend was getting the full effect of the majestic pink-and-white house, the grounds, and the outbuildings with the mountain peaks behind. She half expected the wagon to turn around, but after a few moments, Nora came on.

Abbie sighed her relief. She hurried down to greet her. It would not do for Nora to be shown in by James who, bless his heart, maintained the formal manners and attitude he'd learned in the South. She opened the door and went down the stairs as Will handed Nora down from the wagon.

Abbie reached out her hands and grasped Nora's. "Welcome. I'm so glad to have you. I see you found your way."

"No trouble at all." Nora's eyes went up the house. "But I don't know as I'd've come if I'd known it was this grand."

"It's a fine house Monte built, but it's a home like your own."

"Not exactly like." Nora grinned.

"Will you come in?"

"I'd like to see that special spot you told me of first, if you don't mind. Maybe it'll build me courage."

Abbie slipped her arm through Nora's. "I'd love to show you."

They walked along the creek under the cottonwoods to the circular pool where Monte had first taken her. The chokecherries had finished blooming, and green berries clustered on the branches. The Queen Anne's lace stood white beneath. Wild lupine and fairy trumpets colored the grass, and the creek gurgled over the rocky bottom.

She watched Nora view the wild beauty. What did she think of when her eyes settled on the clear, cold water?

"It's a lovely spot, Abbie. I can see why it's special to you."

"And Monte. It is his favorite place on the whole ranch. But then, I doubt he'll ever truly love the wide, empty prairie as I do."

"I admit I've no love lost on this barren land meself."

Abbie smiled. "That doesn't surprise me. One day I'll take you to Pa's homestead where I was raised. We'll go up into the hills and you'll see the beauty of the mountains up close."

"The mountains are fearsome tall."

"We'll just climb the feet."

Nora shook her head and gave a little laugh. "These are not the bonny green hills of Erin, of that you can be sure."

Abbie started back toward the house. Monte and Reverend Shields would be eager for tea. As they came around to the front, Nora eyed the buggy in the yard. "Have you other company?"

"That's Reverend Shields' buggy. He came to see Monte about some matter or other."

"And your husband received him?"

"Of course he . . ." Abbie paused at the look in Nora's eyes. "Reverend Shields is our friend. He's the Methodist minister. Monte was raised Methodist."

Nora's eyes widened, then hardened. "You married a Protestant . . . and a landlord."

"My husband knows and honors the same God."

Nora's glance went over the house. "Forgive me, Abbie, but I'll not go inside. I won't set foot in a manor house, not even for you. Ye're welcome at the mission anytime."

She turned on her heel, climbed into the wagon, and slapped the reins without another word. Abbie stood, stunned. How could Nora judge Monte and Winthrop Shields without even setting eyes on them? How could she refuse to come into her home? Abbie sank to the lowest stair. She felt worse than she had from any insult Marcy had ever thrown her way. The door opened behind her, and Monte stepped out.

"Abbie, I requested Pearl lay the tea. Are you . . ."

She looked up to him.

"What is it?"

"Nora won't come into the house of a Protestant landlord."

He looked out at the wagon disappearing down the track. "I'm . . . sorry."

Abbie stood up and turned. "There's no need to apologize." She climbed the stairs to him. "Whatever Nora Flynn might think, I know God draws no distinctions. He sees the heart and knows its surrender." She glanced back over her shoulder. "Or the lack."

She took Monte's hand. "Come, let's not keep Reverend Shields waiting." She was sorry for whatever bitterness was stirred in Nora's cup, but she would not allow division in her heart. If Nora could not accept her husband, she was not accepting her.

◆◆◆◆◆◆◆

When Sunday came again she found Nora friendly, but by the looks of all the women, she knew word had passed that she was the wife of a Protestant "landlord." Though why that word seemed to connote such contempt, Abbie hadn't a clue. She allowed Jenny to play in the yard and chatted with Nora and Glenna about baby Delia's new tooth.

Glenna hurried away to retrieve Danny from the dirt when he'd tumbled, and Davy McConnel approached. He removed his hat. "Mornin', Abbie. Miss Flynn, I wondered if you'd care to walk a bit."

She scarcely smiled, but nodded. "The name's Nora, and I'll take a stroll, Davy McConnel."

Abbie caught the look of triumph that passed over Davy's features. Maybe compared to Monte, Davy McConnel didn't seem such a burden to Nora after all. Or maybe she was not eager to be alone with her any more than she had to. Abbie's heart sank. She had counted Nora a friend. Not since Sharlyn died had she had any but Clara to truly call friend.

She gathered Jenny up and took her home.

◆◆◆◆◆◆◆

Cole sat astride Scotch in the mild June heat. He'd been riding the fence of the pasture where they'd contained what remained of the herd. He looked for damage and repaired what he found: loose wire and broken or leaning posts demolished by the weight of the snow or washed out from the melting runoff. But just now he couldn't keep his mind on the stretch of fence beside him.

He looked again at Abbie walking the prairie. She seemed to be deep in thought. Her hair blew back from her face in the warm wind, and she covered the ground as naturally as any lithe prong-horn. Lithe she was, except for the bulge where the baby grew inside her. That's what had her on foot instead of riding her spirited mare. Mr. Farrel was taking no chances.

Cole could hardly blame him, though he knew Abbie chafed. She was not the compliant doll his first wife had been, nor anywhere near as fragile. She reminded him of a Comanche squaw he'd come upon in Texas, giving birth out on the plain with nothing but the wind to help her. He'd ridden away with a sense of having witnessed something that shamed him in its simple endurance.

Abbie had that same courage, that brave stubborn quality that made her a survivor and kept her close to his thoughts no matter how hard he tried. Montgomery Farrel was a lucky man. Cole dismounted and strode to a post where the wire hung loose. He took a nail from the bag at his hip, pulled the wire into place, and hammered it in.

Abbie stopped at the noise and looked up. He returned her wave with a brief salute. Front on, he couldn't help but look at her belly. It wasn't the loss of her figure that bothered him, nor even—he hoped—that it was another man's child. It was the thought that she might change, become like the married hens who cackled around the house and became plump and complacent.

He didn't want Abbie to lose her spark. That was what set her apart. That—and her wit, and her smile, and her eyes—and countless other details he didn't want to think on. He stood when she approached, then took off his hat. He rubbed the sweat from his brow with the back of his sleeve. "Nice day fer a walk."

"It's a beautiful day, though I'd rather ride."

"You've gone a fair piece."

She shrugged but didn't complain about Mr. Farrel's protectiveness. She had grown up some there, keeping to herself things she might have told him before, things that made it hard to keep his head straight.

She touched the post. "Damage from the blizzard?"

He looked along the fence. "That and the dry. Makes the wood crack and the nails slip out. Just a matter of puttin' 'em back in."

She nodded. "Need a hand?"

He grinned. "You're desperate, ain't ya?"

"I am not desperate." She put her hands to her hips. "Just because someone offers help—"

"I know what stir crazy feels like. Here, hold that wire and keep yer fingers free of the post."

She held the wire while he hammered. He couldn't help noticing how the tips of her fingers tapered down to her fine pale nails. But her hands were strong, not the limp, useless hands of some ladies. He remembered the feel of them in his and frowned. "I can get the rest."

"I don't mind." She walked to the next post and pulled up the wire.

With the least effort, he could get used to working beside her. "Look, Abbie, I work better alone."

She dropped the wire. "Suit yourself." She started down the slope.

"Abbie..."

She paused.

"Don't go far."

She tossed her head and increased her stride. She'd probably head for Kansas just to spite him. He banged the nail into the wood with such force the post split. He swore under his breath.

Fifteen

Cole eyed the new men he'd signed on to drive the herd. Ben Smythe looked like he'd barely passed peach fuzz, and Jeff sat on a horse like an eastern sissy. But with the railroad through, men with any real experience driving cattle were hard to come by. They'd moved on up to Montana or stayed in Texas. With Mr. Farrel tight on payroll, this was the best he could do.

He glanced at Breck and Matt Weston. At least he'd have two decent cowboys, and John Mason would serve as wrangler. He already had the remuda ready, eight horses for each man. He'd need to know each horse by sight and keep track that none strayed along the way.

Charlie sat in the chuckwagon, and he was an old hand at it. Cole left it to him to pack the bedrolls, supplies, water, wood, and tools. Skeeter would see to things on the ranch while they were gone. Skeeter was steady enough to leave in charge. Breck would have been his preference, but he needed him for the drive.

Cole drew himself up in the saddle. Fact was, a real cattle drive sounded mighty good just about now. They'd catch the branch of the Santa Fe Trail coming from Bent's Fort and follow it out to Dodge City, Kansas. He could almost hear the clamor of that city already. Yes, indeed.

Since the railroad had come through, they'd driven the cattle to the stockyards east of town and freighted them to the markets. It had been too long since he'd actually taken a herd across country to the cow towns in Kansas or beyond. That Mr. Farrel hadn't the funds for freighting the herd was downright advantageous, not that he'd tell Farrel so.

But now that Charlie had pulled up the wagon, he and the men were ready to hit the trail. He looked over the herd, spread over the land east of the yard. Six hundred and ninety of their own and twice that again gathered from Dunbar, Ephart, and Hodge, with some two hundred head between Farringer and Bates.

He turned when Mr. Farrel came out of the house dressed in chaps, a denim shirt, vest, and a red kerchief. Cole frowned down young Ben's surprised hoot. Mr. Farrel might look the southern gentleman, but he had steel in his hide. Cole had learned that well enough. Only trouble was he knew next to nothing about cattle.

Cole followed him to the stable. "What are you doin', Mr. Farrel?"

"I know we're shorthanded. I'll fill the gap."

"With all due respect . . ."

"I know your opinion, Cole. I don't pretend to be proficient, but surely there's work I can do."

Cole leaned on the stall while Mr. Farrel saddled his Arabian stallion. His choice of horse alone showed his lack of knowledge. That high-stepping, long-necked blue blood was no cutting horse and no swimmer, either, by the looks of his breadbasket. He might have a nice smooth stride, but he was skittish and high spirited.

Mr. Farrell tightened the cinch and turned. "I've instructed Will to add horses to the remuda. I'll be covered."

Had Monte read his thoughts? Cole half grinned. Time was when he could have taken twice as many head with seasoned men, but the country was filling up, and folks were testy about cattle driving through their land. Even along the old trails nesters had fenced in claims and farmers were planting crops. They didn't take kindly to Texas Longhorns spreading the fever among their stock, and it could get ugly.

Mr. Farrel was a decent horseman and a good shot, even with his hands scarred up from the fire. But that wasn't his concern.

"Mr. Farrel, I'm not real sure how the men . . ."

"You're the trail boss, Cole. I'm not here to make trouble, just to get the job done. Besides, I want to see for myself what comes to market."

"You lookin' to buy?"

"We'll see what we fetch for the herd."

Cole took off his hat and scratched his fingers through his hair, then shrugged. "I'm ridin' point, and I got the other four ridin' swing and flank. You'll have to ride drag and eat dust all the way."

Mr. Farrel nodded. "I'll manage wherever you put me."

Cole could hardly stop him. Though Mr. Farrel seemed willing to subordinate, Cole knew where his pay came from. He went out and took up Scotch's reins. Abbie stood on the porch. Her belly protruded in her skirts, but the rest of her was slender as always.

How did she feel about her husband going along? She gave nothing away as Mr. Farrel led the stallion to the steps. She leaned down, and he kissed her cheek. They'd no doubt said their passionate good-byes inside.

Cole kicked the dirt with his boot. "Mount up." He swung into the saddle, whistled, and they started. They met Curtis with the herd, then drifted them awhile before lining them out.

Riding point, he chose the path and set the pace. He'd push it hard the first few days to trail break the herd, get them away from the home range, and make them lay down at night. Then they'd take it on gently. This was all second nature. He could hardly remember a time he hadn't known what he knew.

He glanced over his shoulder to see the herd stringing out four or five abreast behind the lead steer. Already the natural leader had taken his place. Cole would keep just ahead of the stronger, rangier cattle while the weak and lazy ones dragged behind.

Mr. Farrel's job was to keep the stragglers moving. Cole couldn't see him through the brown dust cloud, but he figured he was there gutting through it. He'd never mistake Mr. Farrel's fine manners for weakness again.

••••••••

Monte adjusted the kerchief over his mouth and nose. He felt worse for Sirocco than himself, though the stallion kept his pace without complaint. The Arabian was not a cowhorse. It was a mistake to bring him. Monte hoped it was not the first of a string of mistakes.

Cole hadn't exaggerated about the dust, but by weaving to the edges of the herd he could find respite from the choking cloud. It was no worse than the slow suffocation he felt most days now. His attempt to find financing with the Denver banks had proved as futile as he expected.

Too many ranchers were in his predicament. No one would loan without collateral. As much as he disdained the man, at least he had an established relationship with Driscoll. He might be a hard man, but he was honest. And he'd banked all he had on that honesty when he had at last turned over the Lucky Star deed as collateral on the loan.

He didn't want to think about it. He hadn't slept for two nights afterward. But what choice had he? The mining stocks had fallen to a fraction of his investment. He needed the horses and could ill afford the ones they'd lost in the blizzard. In his defense, Driscoll had been considerate and professional. He had allowed provision for prepayment against the principal of the loan. And Monte hoped with this drive to put some of that behind him.

He looked up to see Cole circling back, whistling and waving his hat to keep the cattle at a trot. Monte guessed it was as much to show the men to keep the pace. He passed around between Monte and the chuck wagon, which trailed far enough back to be out of the dust, then headed on up the line.

They pushed hard until the sun was high overhead, then Cole again circled and gave word to spread the cattle out to graze. They would change horses and eat, then move on. Monte urged the stragglers off the dusty trail onto the range alongside, and the fractious animals bawled and balked, then began to feed. He slid from the saddle and slapped the dust from his pants with his hat, then put Sirocco in John's hands and joined the others at the chuck wagon.

By the time they had the cattle settled, Charlie had set up, started a fire, and had coffee on. Though the June heat beat down, Monte swigged the coffee from the tin cup to wash the dirt from his throat. Even his teeth were gritty. But he sat cross-legged on the ground with the others and took the plate of beef and beans Charlie offered.

"Ain't what you're used to, Mr. Farrel, but it's better than some blokes get."

"Thank you, Charlie. Hunger makes for good seasoning." He caught Cole's eye and nodded.

Cole dropped beside him. "Think I'll have you ride flank this stretch, Mr. Farrel. Young Ben can be dragman and keep an eye on the fat Bessies."

"Whatever you say, Cole."

"So are you gonna tell me what you've in mind for the market?"

"I want a look at some faster growing, beefier breeds."

Cole squinted at the herd scattered over the prairie. "You won't find any as hearty as the Longhorn, nor as suited to the range."

"I don't suppose I will. But I don't have the luxury of eight to ten years for a marketable steer. I need an animal I can turn over quickly, a good breeder with more meat than hide."

Monte ran the johnnycake through the bean sauce on his plate. "Times are changing, Cole. I think the days of the open range are ending. The trouble with Gifford and the blizzard showed us that. I've a mind to fence what we can and risk winter feeding of a better breed."

Cole rubbed his jaw. "I've thought on that myself, though it goes against the grain. I've had a lot of years ridin' herd on Longhorns. Don't know as I'm suited for any other breed."

"I won't make the change without your go-ahead."

"I figured you had it in mind when you said take 'em all."

"Well, as we've hardly any calves after the blizzard kill, it seemed now was the time."

"Cain't rightly argue that." Cole scraped the rest of his beans into his mouth and followed it with the final chunk of johnny-cake. "We'll have us a look in Dodge."

"I'll trust your judgment."

"Ain't likely we'll get much by way of numbers."

"Whatever we get will be a start."

◆◆◆◆◆◆◆

With her hand resting on her belly, Abbie watched until the dust died down in the distance. Monte had said it could take a good three weeks to drive the cattle into Dodge City, Kansas, and the same back if they got new animals, and provided they had good weather and no delays. Cole wouldn't rush the stock or they'd lose meat and not bring as good a price.

That Monte was going himself showed just how desperate this drive was. The entire herd. *Oh, Lord.* Had she known how badly her misjudgment would hurt Monte, she'd have spit in Kendal's face . . . and Mr. Driscoll's, as well.

Monte had only confided in her his latest dealing because she so vehemently argued against his going on the drive. How could he have thought to seek a loan from that man after . . . Her chest ached. He must be desperate indeed to have considered it. Thank God he turned Driscoll down.

She turned as Jenny pressed into her legs. "Is Uncle Monte gone?"

"Yes."

"And Cole?"

"Cole too." Abbie felt the child tremble.

"Why can't we go?"

Abbie squatted down till her belly pressed her thighs. "It's a very long way and hard, hard work."

Jenny's hands came to Abbie's shoulders. The brown of her eyes seemed to deepen. "Are they coming back?"

Abbie stroked a hand over the smooth, soft cheek. "Yes, Jenny.

They'll be back." She pulled the child close.

Jenny wrapped her arms around her neck. "Promise?"

"I promise." Abbie said it with more cheer than she felt. How many times had people disappeared from Jenny's life? Her father and mama, her mammy. Monte was just starting to break through, and the child adored Cole. Abbie hadn't thought how their leaving would frighten Jenny.

"Let's do something special. Where shall we go?"

"The mission. I want to play with Katie."

It surprised Abbie how close Jenny and Katie had become. For such an inauspicious start, they had developed a deep devotion. "All right. Run up and have Zena change your shoes and stockings. I'll get the buggy."

She and Jenny drove out beneath a sky hazy with wisps of white strung across its expanse. But the sun was warm, and for once there was no wind.

Glenna's homestead was a single wood-frame room with a loft. The door Alan had built was split so that the bottom half could keep the children in while the top allowed the breeze. Abbie knocked on the bottom half, and Glenna turned from the fireplace where she was scraping out the ashes.

She smiled. "Come in, Abbie. Have ye brought Jenny along?"

"I have."

Katie dropped the board she was holding to receive the ashes, sending dust everywhere, and scrambled up.

"Katie Lynn! Oh, never mind. Run along."

The girls scampered out with Danny tagging behind. Baby Delia tried to gain the door on all fours, but Abbie caught her and set her safely on her bottom.

"I'll help you there." Abbie stooped to retrieve the board Katie dropped and held it in place.

"You'll soil your hands and your skirt."

Abbie swallowed Glenna's unintended insult. "It works better with two of us." She held the edges of the board while Glenna piled the ashes on.

"There, now. I'll just run it to the field where Alan's workin', then make us a cup."

"I'll start the fire."

Glenna raised her brows but said nothing. Abbie had a fresh blaze of scrub oak and cedar going when she returned. Glenna poured water from the bucket into the heavy iron pot and swung it over the fire. "I have to confess I thought I'd find ye still scrapin' for a spark. Nora said you have all your work done for ye."

Abbie felt her face flush. She could almost hear Nora saying it with her singsong voice. *"Aye, and she lives in a fine manor house the like of which I won't enter."* She sat on the three-legged stool by the hearth. "We have servants who help, but that doesn't mean I do nothing. I spent two years in a tent house smaller than this helping Mama cook over a fire pit outside. That was in the mining camp at Auraria."

She flicked a flake of ash from her skirt. "Then we moved to the homestead and lived in a soddy until Pa built the frame house my folks live in still. I've worked every day of my life in the house, in the garden, and at the mission teaching the children."

Glenna sat across from her. "Ye canna blame Nora. She sees everything with a dark eye now."

"Why?"

"I should let her share the grief in her own time. It's enough you know it's not only you that feels her wrath."

"Do you mean Davy?"

"Aye, and others. She puts on a cheery face, but she canna change her heart. It's not your Monte she hates, but others like him."

"How does she even know what he's like? She never laid eyes on him."

"Aye, she did. She saw him in town two weeks ago. Father O'Brien was talkin' with your da, and he introduced your Monte around. She said he was a handsome man with a lordly air." She poured and handed her a cup of tea.

"My husband is a gentleman. Why does that make him an enemy?"

"Because in Ireland the gentlemen are the enemy."

Abbie dropped her forehead to her fingertips. "I don't understand."

"You wouldn't unless you'd lived it."

Abbie sipped. So Nora had met Monte and said nothing of it. What made a woman so bitter she could hate without cause a man like Monte?

Glenna stood. "I'd better take a look at the children. They've been quiet too long."

Abbie followed Glenna out. She saw Katie and Danny parading behind Jenny along the edge of the field where Alan worked the plow, their arms outstretched, feet skipping. Jenny loved nothing better than follow-the-leader, especially when she was the leader. But true to form, Katie stepped out of line and declared herself leader, then hopped down the slope with her hands on her head.

Jenny frowned, but Danny was already making awkward hops after his sister, and she did not want to be last in line. Abbie smiled into her cup. Poor Jenny. She was more like Auntie Abbie than her own mama. She leaned against the wall and finished the tea, then looked across the land at the chapel and mission house.

Should she go tell Nora hello? Somehow she was drawn to the fiery-haired woman in spite of her ill feelings for Monte. Maybe when Nora came to trust her, she could make her see that wealth and breeding did not always corrupt. Whatever her experience in Ireland, things were different here.

"Would you mind if I left Jenny for a bit and ran over to see Nora?"

"I was hopin' you'd ask that."

Abbie pulled herself into the buggy. She was getting ponderous when it came to wagons and buggies. She'd be glad when the next two and a half months were past and the baby delivered. A wave of anticipation washed over her with a rush. Monte's child. How could anything bother her when she carried Monte's child?

The sun was hot, and sweat moistened her upper lip as she stopped the buggy outside the mission house and found Nora peeling potatoes on the step. At her feet the chickens pecked at the peels.

"Hello, Abbie."

"Fine day for sitting outside."

"If I stayed in the kitchen I'd not need to boil the potatoes. They'd just roast beside me."

"Father Thomas always opened the front and back doors to make a draft. But even so he worked up a sweat."

"It's the dry heat. There's never a mist. Either the rain pours down like a flood, or the wind carries dust. There's no softness here."

Abbie remembered Frances's impressions. No fervent defense of the territory's charms would change another's homesick longings. Abbie eased herself to the step beside Nora. "Hand me the long knife. I'll slice as you peel."

Nora took the knife from the step and presented it handle forward. She made no comment, and Abbie wondered if Nora's words about her not working had been more slander than actual belief. Either way, Abbie put it aside. She would not bear a grudge where she could help it.

How strange to have spent the last year proving she was refined, only to have Nora find her too much so. She almost laughed. Would she never be what others expected? Was that her thorn from the Lord?

She took the spud Nora handed her. "Jenny's playing with Katie. It's amazing how they've worked out their animosity."

"Children heal quickly."

"That's true. And I think we underestimate the power of those friendships. Blake and I . . ."

"Yes?"

"We were constant companions, and, well, we were very close."

"Would you have married him if he'd not been killed?"

"No. I loved Monte."

Monte's name hung in the air. Nora shooed a chicken who pecked at her foot. "I've enough potatoes now. I'll set them to boil." She stood with the bowl. "Will ya have a cup of tea?"

"No thanks. I had one at Glenna's. And I should take Jenny home. Monte and Cole have taken the herd to Kansas, every last cow, steer, and calf, along with some of the Dunbars' stock, as well. They'll be gone some while, and I promised Monte I'd not wander far or late."

"Thank you for coming."

Nora's eyes warmed for a moment, and Abbie almost felt the closeness they'd shared before Nora learned about Monte. Then it was gone, and Nora turned inside.

◆◆◆◆◆◆◆

Monte rolled into the blanket on the hard ground. Not for any money would he admit how bone weary he felt. With sundown, they'd circled the herd, closing them in tighter and tighter until they lay down and settled. Now Breck and Matt took the first watch, riding slowly around the herd singing low and mournfully. It might comfort the cattle, but it only made Monte think how he could be home with Abbie.

Even his eyelids felt crusted with dust. Whatever Cole saw to be so cheerful about was beyond him. The work was grueling and, at its best, unsatisfying. But . . . this was his hope: to unload the herd profitably and choose a new breed. Perhaps Cole could have handled it, but with so much resting on this success, he'd needed to be present. If only the ground weren't so hard.

He woke to Cole's shaking him, surprised by the fatigue that kept him from springing awake as he might have. He felt the honor, however, as the others received Cole's boot, something more than a gentle nudge and less than a kick in the hindquarters. He could swear Cole enjoyed it, too.

"Here you are, Mr. Farrel."

Monte sat up and took the cup of coffee Charlie offered.

"I'll whip up some tucker 'fore you've had time to say howdy to yer stomach."

"Quit jawin', Charlie, and git at it." Cole drew down the brim of his black Stetson and stalked off.

Charlie winked at Cole's back. "He wakes meaner than a

spring grizzly. Leastwise he means us to think so."

Monte stood and stretched the kinks from his limbs. Oh yes, he felt each one, bone and sinew, another reason to have stayed with Abbie. Didn't he pay the men to do this? That thought was as sore as he. Would he have the means to pay them much longer?

After packing in Charlie's "tucker" with the best of them, he mounted. Awaiting Cole's orders kept him humble. He'd like to say he'd ride on ahead and meet them in Dodge, but his own pride wouldn't allow it.

There was challenge in Cole's eyes. Good-humored, but challenge nonetheless. And he wasn't about to let some cocky Texan have the best of a true South Carolina rebel.

"I'll have you ride swing today, Mr. Farrel. We'll see what you do with the front side of a herd. Just in case you need to make a run for it, why don't you leave yer fancy stallion with Will and take a real horse."

"When it comes to running, I'd wager Sirocco against any horse here, your Scotch included."

Cole grinned a rascal's grin. "I reckon that depends. Give them a track and you'd be right. But if that long-legged pedigree has ever outrun a frenzied herd, I'll eat my hat." He swung around and started them off, men and beasts alike.

Monte stroked Sirocco's neck. "Never mind, you fine son of the desert. Cows aren't all they're cracked up to be."

Astride a solid bay named Blackjack, Monte managed his side of the herd as they drifted the cattle the first two hours of daylight, then lined them out and drove. Cole must have bones of steel, the way he set the pace and circled tirelessly—ruthlessly, Monte's backside answered.

He noticed a cow weaving outward to the side of the line and increased his pace to shoo her back. She rubbed her head against the steer beside and slightly forward of her. He shouldered her in, but she butted him back. Monte slapped the rope on Blackjack's flank and the horse shot forward.

Whatever had gotten into the cow, he'd need to contain her if he didn't want her irritating her companions into bolting. He drew alongside, and the cow raised her head and gave a long bawl-ing *maaaoo*. Monte swung the end of the rope in a circular motion as he'd seen the others do. She took notice of him with her head turned, then butted through the gap behind the steer.

"Go on, now. Back in line." He swung the rope again, this time catching the ground enough to kick up dust and make it snap.

Her dun hide flinched, and again she moaned, but she wouldn't turn back. She came close enough for him to prod her with his boot in the stirrup. His horse held steady as Monte swat-ted the rope on the cow's flank. "Go on, now."

He smelled the dust kicked up by Cole's mount. The man must have eyes in the back of his head. Monte turned, expecting Cole's scowl or at least his insolent half grin. What he saw was downright amusement. Monte spread his hands, annoyed. "She's turned stubborn. You'll have to rope her in."

"That ain't stubborn. She's givin' you the big-eyed howdy."

"The what?"

"You must have a way with the ladies. You've charmed her into season."

Monte frowned. "Well, tell her I'm married." The last thing he needed was this joked around the fire. And Cole was just ornery enough to do it.

Cole laughed. "Yes, sir, but I cain't promise she'll listen. Fe-males got a mind of their own. Sometimes they'll pick out the rangiest bull when a full-blooded specimen is there for the takin'."

Monte got the point directly. Cole had come a long way if he could tease him about Abbie. He drew up in the saddle. "I'll ride point while you sweet-talk her."

"That's fine by me, long as you keep us headin' to Kansas." Cole grinned.

"I think I know that much."

"I reckon you do."

Monte heard his laughter as he urged Blackjack ahead. The cow bawled. Charmed her, indeed. That man had gall.

Sixteen

From two miles out, Dodge City lived up to its reputation as a noisy, rowdy cow town. Cole felt his pulse increase. Yessiree, Dodge was one rollicking place. He checked the loads in the gun at his hip. Not that he expected trouble of that sort. The law in Dodge was up to whatever shenanigans any of his tribe could dish out.

But if the cattle got spooked, it'd take more than hat waving and whips to get 'em back in line. And he knew well enough the sheriff in Dodge would not take kindly to their running a herd through the streets. It would take all Mr. Farrel's fine words to ease that one.

He glanced at Mr. Farrel beside him. He'd weathered the trip admirably, and even proved useful. After nearly four weeks in the saddle, he hardly looked the gentleman rancher at all. Cole grinned. "Well, Mr. Farrel, we're bringin' 'em in."

"We are indeed."

"We'll reach the stockyards before we hit town, corral the herd, and have us a drink."

"I don't think that word has ever held quite the same meaning."

"Likely forty pounds of dust has made it down yer gullet."

"At the least."

Cole laughed. "Well, sir, Dodge is the place to wet yer whistle."

"The sooner we dispense with these boneheaded bovines, the better."

Cole whistled and gave the signal for the men to draw the herd in tighter. They were in sight of the acres of fencing that made up the stockyards west of town. It had been a relatively uneventful drive, and he wanted to keep it that way. No panic or scattering, no stampeding through town, just a nice, easy finish to a long, dry ride.

When the herd was contained, the men took off with new energy. The half month's pay he'd put in their pockets would not stay there long. Cole clapped Mr. Farrel on the shoulder. "Much as I hate to say it, you're not such a bad cowboy after all."

"Much as I hate to say it, if I never see the bony backside of a steer again, it'll be too soon."

Cole laughed. It felt good. He felt good. There was nothing like reaching the end of the trail, bringing the herd in, and gettin' clapped on the back for a job well done. The sun was sinking into the thick Kansas sky, and flies swarmed their heads as they corralled the herd and left them.

They rode into town and went into the first decent-looking saloon on the street. No good taking a man like Mr. Farrel into some of these places, not with Abbie waiting at home. And he certainly wouldn't be looking for a faro game or poker table. They took a stool at the bar and Cole ordered them both a tall, frothy mug. Nothing chased the dust from the trail better, whether Mr. Farrel took to it or not.

Mr. Farrel cupped the mug and shook his head. "I don't know how you do it."

"Do what?"

"Hold up in the saddle. You must have a steel hide to keep it up at your age."

"I ain't as old as you think I am."

Mr. Farrel sucked the foam from his mug. "How old are you, Cole?"

"Thirty-two."

Mr. Farrel put the mug down hard.

Cole chuckled. "Yeah, I know. You thought I was old enough to be Abbie's pa."

"I don't believe you."

"I've been on the backside of a herd since I was twelve years old, while you was bein' dressed and fed by all them servants."

Mr. Farrel winced. "You don't mince your words, do you."

"Ain't no point." He drank deep. "We know where we stand. But I will hand it to you, you and yer mount both. You're tougher than you look."

"And you're not as hard as you appear. You're a good man, Cole."

"Well, don't let it out. I gotta keep an edge on the men somehow."

Mr. Farrel raised his mug, and Cole met it with his. He shared the smile, then drained his glass. With all the dust he'd eaten, it would likely make mud in his innards.

After a wash and a shave he left Mr. Farrel soaking at the bathhouse and went to find them a room. The others could fend for themselves. They'd no doubt spend the night clean through gambling away their earnings and drinking just enough to make the losing painless.

He settled on a relatively quiet hostelry with better than average food and clean rooms. Likely Mr. Farrel was used to staying in finer establishments than Dodge boasted, but at least this place shouldn't have drunks shooting it up.

◆◆◆◆◆◆◆

Monte felt as though he could soak for days and never clean off all the grime of the trail. The next time Abbie said stay home, he'd listen. He closed his eyes and sank deeper into the steaming tub. *Abbie*. Was there ever a finer thought to fill a man's mind? He jolted suddenly.

Was it possible Cole was only four years his senior? He seemed so rugged and . . . seasoned and experienced. In his thoughts he'd added years to Cole's age, guessed him at least sixteen years older than Abbie. Had he known only a decade separated them, he'd have worried more than he had, when Cole set his eye on her.

Did Abbie know? Did she care? What foolishness was this? He'd put aside his jealousy of Cole. He trusted him completely and, moreover, he liked him. Monte ran a soapy hand over his face.

But the truth was, no female had ever kindled the flames of jealousy as Abbie had, through no fault of her own. And as his respect for Cole Jasper grew, he realized how lucky he was that Abbie had not accepted Cole's proposal. He was a man who could have made her forget her first love.

The bath attendant came in with a fresh bucket of hot water. Monte took it full on the head and exulted in the luxury. What pleasure there was in cleanliness. But before he shriveled up completely, he ought to get out. He toweled himself dry and put on the clothes he'd kept tightly wrapped in the chuck wagon. Though slightly wrinkled, they were remarkably free of dust.

He was surprised to find Cole outside the door likewise washed and shaved, except for the thick mustache he'd grown back after disguising himself to rescue Abbie from the rustler. Monte felt a twinge. He took a long look at the man.

His skin was creased beside the eyes, his jaw sharp, and his cheeks slightly hollowed and wind-burned. His eyes held years of experience, but his physique was strong and straight. He was a swaggishly handsome man. Why didn't he choose himself a wife and get on with it?

"Got us a room. You mind sharing?"

"I don't mind. The less we spend on incidentals, the better."

"Well, it ain't the cheapest, but trust me, it's worth it."

Monte wanted to ask how Cole knew, but refrained. It was just different experiences. Cole would be just as lost in Charleston, or any fine city for that matter. He wouldn't know the first thing about situations that were second nature to Monte. But somehow, he didn't think Cole would care. What made a man so singular of purpose, so . . . self-confident?

He didn't think Cole looked to heaven. He'd never gotten that impression. Cole's confidence was in himself, his abilities. Monte shook his head. Hadn't he had that same confidence when things were going well, when he had all he needed and more? Was his worth based on his achievements, to come and go on the tides of fortune?

What did Cole have? A hard bunk on a ranch that belonged to another. Long days' work and no companions but the men he bullied. No one to love, no one to love him, yet he seemed doggedly self-contained. Maybe a man like Cole didn't need God. But no. No such man ever lived, whether an ornery cuss like Cole ever admitted it or not.

Moths swarmed the streetlamp at the corner where they turned. The town was as well kept as Cole described. The lawmen didn't allow horseplay of the sort that shot out lights and wreaked havoc in the streets. They went inside the gray two-story hostelry and climbed the stairs.

Cole stepped aside at the door, and Monte entered the room first. He eyed the water stain beneath the single narrow window and the sawdust trailed onto the rough plank floor. The linen looked fresh, though. The room was not fancy but suitable.

"Choose yer cot, cuz once my head hits, I ain't movin'."

Monte put his bag on the far cot, and Cole sprawled on the other. Within minutes, he slept. Monte stripped to his long johns and stretched out. The cot felt like heaven after the ground, but he was surprisingly wakeful.

Would they accomplish what they needed? Could he sell the herd for enough to start a new breed? Could he pay back the loan? He passed a hand over his eyes. *Lord, it's in your hands.* He turned to his side and welcomed the fitful sleep that followed.

◆◆◆◆◆◆◆

Monte woke to the dawning light and rose immediately. He was eager to see to business. Cole still breathed deeply in the same position in which he'd landed. Monte washed at the basin, dressed, and stepped up to Cole's cot. He put a hand to his shoulder. With a snarl, Cole had a gun barrel to his chest before he'd half shaken him.

"Good grief, Cole! Do you always wake up like that?"

Cole holstered the gun. He swung his legs over to the floor

and sat up, then ran a hand through the blond waves and shook his head. "I guess somethin' stays alert when I'm in a strange place."

Alert? Reflexes like that were not bred of alacrity. They spoke of downright self-preservation. Had Cole once cause to fear for his life? "Well, the morning's drawing on, and I want to be about our business."

Cole reached for his hat. "Soon's I have a cup of coffee and a smoke, I'll be ready."

"I was considering breakfast myself."

"I'll meet you downstairs."

●●●●●●●

With steak and eggs and home fries weighting their bellies, Monte and Cole set out for the market. Beef buyers were thick, but finding someone to take a herd, half of which was not at marketable weight, was another thing. Monte was glad for Cole's connections. If anyone could do it, Cole Jasper could.

Monte spent his time looking for purchase possibilities. He was fairly settled on Herefords, but he wanted Cole's go-ahead. After all, Cole was the one who would be working the herd, and the expertise he packed into his four extra years was worth hearing.

Cole came toward him with a definite swagger to his step. "We're in luck. Couple of guys are headin' up Montana way to start them a ranch. They've been waitin' on a herd up from Texas, but I convinced 'em to take ours instead."

"How did you do that?"

"Seein' how ours traveled half the distance on good grazing alongside the Arkansas, and as how they're accustomed to wintering in the snow." He spread his hands. "Got a decent price for 'em if you're of a mind."

Monte nodded. "Let's have a talk with the gentlemen."

As they wound through the stockyard maze, Cole lowered the brim of his hat against the glare and swarming flies. "How'd you fare?"

"What do you think of Herefords, Cole?"

"I knew you were gonna say that."

Monte quirked an eyebrow.

"I reckon they're the best choice, much as I hate the stodgy Bessies."

"Then we're settled. Now all that remains is the financing. You get us the best dollar on our herd, and I'll get us the best herd for the dollar." They shook hands and grinned. They might be two very different men, but they'd found a common ground that suited Monte fine. He could do worse than Cole Jasper for his head man—and friend.

✦✦✦✦✦✦✦

Monte rode beside Cole as they brought in the three hundred Herefords and two Guernsey milk cows. The sale of his herd and the loan money had gone far enough. He felt more optimistic than he had in a long, long time.

With the Herefords he would start a new herd. With the Guernseys he hoped to make peace with Abbie's Irish friend . . . for Abbie's sake. She had said nothing directly, but he'd seen her hurt and knew she was torn.

Nora Flynn had made no effort to hide her contempt when they'd met in town. It was an unusual feeling to be so disdained. But even if his offering did no good, the children needed milk. The Lord had looked out for them unloading the Longhorns with the Montana ranchers, and he would share the blessing.

They drove the Herefords into the north pasture where they would contain them until a fence could be run around the majority of his land, all but the acres that would be planted for feed. Those acres would need irrigation come spring, and digging the trenches would keep the men busy until the ground froze; that, and branding and marking the new animals.

The men had already headed for the bunkhouse when Monte slid from the bay's back and made his weary way up the stairs and in the door. James took his hat, and Monte brushed the dust from his clothes. "Is Abbie in?"

"Yessuh. She in the—"

But the library door had already been flung open and Abbie rushed down the hall. He caught her in his arms. "Abbie . . . good heavens!" He clasped his hands around her belly. "Has it only been six weeks?"

She drew herself up. "I ought to shake you, Montgomery Farrel. I feel as big as a horse."

Monte laughed. "Oh, Abbie, how I've missed you." He kissed her. James turned away, but he'd have kissed her anyway, even with all the world watching.

She caught his hands between hers. "Tell me everything."

"I will. In detail. But first let me wash. I can't stand the dust one more minute."

"I'll heat your water, and you can tell me while you wash." Her words heated his blood as he watched her down the hall. Was a woman always more beautiful with child than any other time? She was due to deliver in three weeks, but still her step was spry, if her gait somewhat awkward. He was home, and tonight he'd feel Abbie in his arms, even if he could no more than hold her.

✦✦✦✦✦✦✦

Abbie exulted in the strength of Monte's arms around her. Eight weeks on the trail had toughened him. His scarred palms were callused, his lips dry and chapped. But the tenderness of his embrace had not diminished. He was home, and her heart could not be more full.

Though he teased, she could see the delight in his eyes when he beheld the growth of the baby. Soon their child would be born. She imagined his pride when he took the baby in his arms for the first time. She could hardly contain the joy.

And how kind he'd been to remember the milk cow and bring not one but two. How like him that was. She had not said another word after he explained their plight, but he had sacrificed to help where he saw the need. She would take the cows to Nora the very next day and tell her Monte had provided them. What a good man he was.

Stretching over, she kissed his lips, and he smiled in his sleep. "Mmmm."

"I love you, Monte."

He tightened his grasp and murmured, "And I love you."

◆◆◆◆◆◆◆

Abbie had invited Monte to take the cows himself, but he declined. Of course he wouldn't put Nora on the spot; he was too much the gentleman. Nora could make up her mind without his presence forcing the issue. So Abbie took Jenny along and pulled the Guernsey milk cows behind the buggy.

They made slow progress, but as she now felt every jolt and jar, she could not have traveled much faster. The sun had baked the crown of her head through the straw hat by the time the mission came in sight, but by the look of the clouds encroaching, the ride back would be cool if not wet. She pulled up outside the mission house and ponderously climbed down.

Jenny had already scampered to the ground and run in search of the playmates almost certain to be in Nora's care. Abbie untied the cows and led them to the step. She knocked loudly on the door, knowing the sound must likely carry to the kitchen or the yard behind.

Father O'Brien opened the door and stared at the two mild-eyed cows before him.

Abbie smiled. "Father O'Brien, these milk cows are a gift from my husband. He brought them back from Dodge City, Kansas, with his new herd." She glanced past his shoulder at Nora staring darkly. "They'll provide good milk for the children."

"And a mighty blessin' indeed." Father O'Brien stepped out and looked the animals over. He ran a hand along their flanks. "A peaceable pair, they seem."

"They're very gentle. I milked them myself this morning, but they'll be ready again come evening. The production is a little low from the drive, but I'm certain it will build up in no time." She glanced again at Nora, who now stood in the doorway, and Father O'Brien turned.

"What do say you, Nora darlin'? Is this not a blessin' from God to have milk for the little 'uns?"

"It is a boon, Father. We thank you, Abbie."

Abbie drew herself up. "It was Monte's doing. My part was only telling him the need." She watched the emotions fight inside Nora, but she would not back down. This was Monte's kindness, and he deserved the gratitude.

Nora looked to Father O'Brien but saw that he'd not speak for her. "You'll give him our thanks, then," she finally said.

"I will. Or you're welcome to give it yourself." She saw the flicker of remorse in Nora's eyes. Thunder rumbled, and she glanced around for Jenny. "I'd better go if I'm to outrun the storm." She caught Jenny by the hand as she'd come running at the next flash of lightning. "Good-bye," she called, tossing Jenny up to the seat.

"God bless ya, Abbie." Father O'Brien waved as he led the cows to the shed.

Yes, Father. You have . . . with a wonderful, caring husband, a child to come, small Jenny beside me, and maybe, just maybe, a repentant friend.

Seventeen

Monte rode beside Cole in the mellow September evening, one week after bringing home the herd. How good it felt to be master of his property. The shaggy brown-and-white Herefords dotted the range that had been fenced to contain them. The fences would be extended as the herd grew. He had already filed for government land he'd previously used free. It would strap them, but with times changing, he must lay his claim early.

As he rode back toward his spread from the Dunbar ranch, he shielded his eyes against the westering glare and stared across the range at a large animal moving unnaturally. He pointed. "What do you make of that, Cole? Our Durham bull?"

Cole squinted beside him. "If it is, he busted a fence."

Monte frowned. "I have plans for that bull. Let's bring him in." He nudged Sirocco and circled wide to the east of the bull's path. Something in how the animal moved bothered him. It was too erratic, too . . .

"Looks like he's got into some loco weed," Cole said.

"Loco weed?"

"Lupine or such. Look how he's frothin'."

Monte frowned. This Durham bull was his hope for building the new herd. With Gifford having butchered his other, he was not about to lose this one, too. "I'll circle in and get his attention while you rope him."

"I cain't hold him alone."

"Once your rope's on, I'll throw mine." *And pray.* "Between us we'll bring him in."

"Mr. Farrel!"

Monte ignored him as the bull started loping. He urged Sirocco over. The bull made a zigzagging path, but he intercepted him. He swung his hat and got a good look at the bull square on when it stopped. Its eyes were crazed. Cole was right. The animal looked loco indeed. Poisoned, but hopefully not past repair.

He had its attention. The great head swayed from side to side, then dodged up and down in swift, jerking motions. Foam flecked its mouth and chest. Sirocco shied. Monte held him steady and reached for the rope that hung at the side of the saddle. It snagged, and he worked it free, keeping his eyes on the bull. Sirocco was tense and skittish.

Monte considered how best to handle it, then swung down from the saddle. The stallion was as unaccustomed to this as he, and he wouldn't risk the horse. He'd be better on his feet. He heard Cole holler, but his whole attention was on the raving beast. Its muscles rippled as the head lowered.

Time suspended and his nerves tensed as Monte looked straight into its face and realized his mistake. *Dear God.* Sirocco bolted and the bull charged.

Cole galloped hard. What possessed Farrel to dismount? He shouted and fired, but the shot grazed off the bull's flank and the animal continued its plunge. It hit Farrel full force, caught him up on its head and shook him like a doll. Cole screamed with all the breath in him.

The bull dropped Farrel and spun, tons of muscle and rage. Its hide twitched as it lowered its head and charged. As one, Cole and Scotch swerved. Cole fired into its skull, once, twice, again. The animal staggered to the side and collapsed even as its weight carried it forward.

Cole jumped down and ran to where Farrel lay, blood frothing from his mouth. Desperate, Cole steeled himself and tore open the blood-soaked shirt. He winced as the fabric pulled away from the torn, mangled flesh of the man's abdomen. His rib bones were bared, snapped off and jagged, and inside—

Cole felt his gorge rise. *No!*

Monte opened his eyes. "Cole." It was more wheeze than voice.

"Yes, sir." Cole kept his terror from showing, but the man knew. He had to know.

"Look after Abbie . . . and my child." The blood gurgled in his throat.

There was no point protesting, nor time. "You know I will." His word was all the comfort he could give.

Monte nodded and closed his eyes. "The Lord is my shep—"

Blood bubbled from his nose and lips, then stopped. With a pain like a hammer and anvil in his chest, Cole reached a slow hand to his hat and pulled it from his head. The feeling of loss overwhelmed him. This shouldn't be happening, not here, not now, not like this. Montgomery Farrel was too fine a man to end like this. It wasn't right.

But, then, when was death ever right? He'd seen too much of it to have any rosy impression of peace and joy. Already the blood congealed on Mr. Farrel's chest.

Montgomery Farrel was the closest thing to a friend he'd had. He wasn't sure when that had happened or how it came about, he only knew that Mr. Farrel had brought out the best in him, and the camaraderie they'd shared these last months wasn't near long enough.

He swallowed hard against the knot in his throat. *What of Abbie?* Hadn't she had enough to bear? Cole groaned, gripped his hair with both hands, and pressed his eyes shut. Guilt weighed heavier than grief. Abbie had trusted him, and he'd failed her.

He looked down at the silent face in his lap. He would give anything to be lying in Mr. Farrel's place rather than taking the news to Abbie. How in heaven's name was he going to tell her?

◆◆◆◆◆◆◆

Abbie took one look at James and rushed for the door. She stared down the stairs to the wagon, her heart pounding her ribs. Cole stood between her and the wagon bed, circling his hat in his hands. Why didn't he speak? Why didn't he say something? He must know he was scaring her to death.

"Is it Monte? Is he hurt? Is it bad, Cole?" Her feet wouldn't move as they should. She started for the stairs, but they felt weak and shaky.

"I'm sorry, Abbie. I'm real sorry."

Why was he sorry? Why wouldn't the fool tell her what she needed to know? Why wasn't he running for the doctor? She pushed past him to the wagon. A blanket covered the form in the back . . . covered it entirely.

The breath left her lungs. She reached for the blanket but Cole caught her wrist.

"Let me." His voice was both tender and despairing. He pulled the blanket and freed Monte's face.

Monte's dark lashes lay against the shadows beneath his eyes. His lips were parted but moved not at all. His stillness was not that of sleep or even injured, damaged repose. He was too quiet, too pale. He was dead.

No numbing denial blocked the pain as it had with Blake. Her mind knew with excruciating clarity that Monte was dead. With a high, keening wail she slumped against the wagon side and clutched the child within her. Cole reached out to her, but she shook him free and pulled herself up.

She turned and searched his face. A burning rage filled her. How many times had she trusted him to keep Monte safe? He was the one who knew, his was the experience. How could he let this happen? She yanked the blanket down and stared at Monte's crushed chest. She touched the torn, crusted skin of his abdomen. He was cold. Where was his warmth? She felt his hand, scarred and callused. No gentle caress, no strong grasp, only cold, lifeless fingers.

The horror broke over her like a flood, took her under, dragged her low. She was suffocating. Arms held her, and she heard Pearl's voice in her ear, but the words were lost. Her head pounded again and again. *Monte's dead. Monte's dead. Monte's dead.*

◆◆◆◆◆◆◆

Hours passed, or were they years? Mama came, and Pa. With Pearl they laid out the body, but she sent them away. Her own voice sounded harsh in her ears as she resisted their comfort. No one would touch him. No one but she.

Alone, she washed the blood and gore from his flesh. She dressed him in the gray trousers and white shirt, the black coat he'd worn on their wedding day. Every moment that passed drew him farther and farther away. She felt herself dying with him. Her heart scarcely beat, her breath was no more than a whisper of air through parted lips.

Father O'Brien and Reverend Shields came, and other faces passed through the rooms, too. Doctor Barrow ... Grant ... Clara. They were like specters with no real form or substance. The doctor had her drink something warm and thick, and weariness overcame her.

◆◆◆◆◆◆◆

When she opened her eyes, the sun was bright. She dragged herself from the bed and felt Pearl's arms supporting her. "There, Mizz Abbie. Go slow now, lessen you faint."

Faint? She wasn't given to faints. Hadn't Monte said as much? Hadn't Monte—her legs gave way and she clutched the bedpost.

"It's the medicine the doctor gave you. He wanted you to sleep through till ..."

Abbie forced her eyes to focus on Pearl's face. "Till what?"

"They's gettin' the ground ready."

Abbie closed her eyes. A terrible heaviness weighed her down. She could hardly stand against it, but Monte would not go into the ground without her. Doctor Barrow had no right to order it. Who was he to separate her from the man she loved? Had not death already done that?

She wanted to scream, scream away the deadly shell that closed around her heart. "My clothes."

"Mizz Abbie, the doctor ..."

"My clothes, Pearl." She stood while Pearl pulled the petti-coats and the black linen dress over her head. Someone must have let the waist out in the night. Zena or Pearl or Mama.

The hill was covered with people. They looked like black crows perched beside the headstones on the hill as Abbie approached on James's arm. His elderly hand trembled as he wept, but she stood tearless. The pain went far, far deeper than tears. It was a cavernous hole that would never be filled. More and more of her would fall in until there was nothing left but the pain. The grave gaped, but it was nothing compared to the hole inside.

Reverend Shields spoke. " 'Yea, though I walk through the valley of the shadow of death, I will fear no evil . . . ' "

Her mind felt detached. Around her people cried. Friends and neighbors, acquaintances, those from town, others from much farther, all came to honor Monte. She saw Marcy on Grant's arm, red-faced with weeping. She saw Pa's eyes swim, and Mama's. Little Tucker stood solemn between them.

Where was Jenny? There beside Zena, safe and cared for. Across the crowd she saw Cole, hat in hand, head bowed. He looked . . . diminished. She turned away and let her gaze come at last to the coffin. Not the pine box that had held Blake but a fine mahogany coffin from the undertaker. Who had made the arrangements?

"We know that this life is but a shade, a passing moment in the span of eternity. Montgomery Farrel knew and loved the ways of the Lord God Almighty. He trusted his soul to the eternal destiny laid out for him from the beginning of time. He was a man of vision, of compassion, integrity, and honor."

Honor. *The backbone of all that is just and right and good.* Abbie could almost hear him. *Honor is doing what you must even when your heart is not in it.* He had lived that. Monte had personified honor in every deed, every thought, every decision he made.

"He was a man of subtle temperament, slow to anger and generous with mirth. A man of good humor."

Abbie pictured the smile playing on Monte's lips, the raised eyebrow, the amusement in his eyes. She felt the blackness threaten. The pit of pain ate at her soul. Yes, Monte was surrendered to God. Yes, he walked even now the heavenly streets. But why, why, why?

" 'The LORD gave, and the LORD hath taken away; blessed be the name of the LORD.' " Reverend Shields closed his Bible, and four men took up the ropes. Abbie swayed as they lowered the coffin into the hole. She tightened her grip on James and caught Doctor Barrow's frown. Let him frown. Didn't he know it didn't matter? Nothing mattered.

She reached for the handful of earth, felt it filter through her fingers, heard it strike the wood. He was gone. Monte was no more. Pearl took her other elbow, and between the two old servants she made her way down the slope. Her feet moved of their own volition, propelled perhaps by James and Pearl, perhaps by some muscular function not connected to her mind.

She gained the house, went to her room, and locked the door. She refused, over Pearl's mournful pleas, to admit Doctor Barrow. She refused to admit anyone, not Reverend Shields, not Clara, not Grant nor Pa, not even Mama. She was alone in her grief. No loving arms, no grieving eyes would sustain her. She wanted no one, needed no one, trusted no one. She was alone.

◆◆◆◆◆◆◆

Over the side of the stall, Cole watched Pearl descend on him. "Mistuh Jazzper, I's worried. It's been three days now."

Cole heaved the saddle over the rack. What was three days to a loss like Abbie's? He didn't want to interfere with her grief. God knew she'd had enough to break any lady. She had a right to hurt.

"It's the baby, Mistuh Jazzper."

He rested his hands on the saddle. What did Pearl want with him? Abbie's shocked, condemning look when he'd brought Mr. Farrel home had told him well enough she wanted no part of him. And nothing she could say or think was worse than what he told himself. He had no business letting Mr. Farrel—

"She can't carry that baby with no food and water."

Cole jolted. "No food and water?"

"She been locked in her room three days. She won' let no one in, not even her own mama."

Cole felt like a jackrabbit in a snare, and he'd as soon bite off his own limb as face Abbie. But what was he to do? He stared at the tooled curve of the saddle, then turned. "A'right."

He strode to the house, his stride more confident than his spirit. Zena stood in the hall, wringing her hands. He felt about the same, but he'd make a good show of it for their sakes. He headed up the stairs and tapped the door. "Abbie?"

He hadn't expected an answer. He tried the knob.

"It's locked." Zena twisted her apron. "She done locked herself in."

He hadn't realized they'd all followed him up, even James. The three dark faces implored him, but what could he do? "Open up, Abbie."

Nothing. He stepped back and kicked the door open. Pearl and Zena jumped, but inside, Abbie never flinched. She sat like she was carved in wood. Her face was to the window, but her eyes were blank, hollow, and dark-circled. Shock and dehydration. He'd seen it before in a woman whose husband was shot full of Apache arrows and scalped.

He closed the door behind him. No sense making her a spectacle. He pulled out the chair from her dressing table and straddled it. Guilt and despair churned inside him as the hands on the clock circled the face. She sat there still and mute.

He watched her without a clue what to say. *Sorry about your husband, Abbie. He was the first real friend I had, and I let him die.* He felt her grief invade him. He'd done this to her. He'd failed her. He saw her throat move.

"Why are you here?" Her voice was like wind on dry leaves.

"Cuz I'm the only one ornerier than you."

"Go away."

If she had said it with more life he'd have left, but instead he stood and walked to the window. He stopped in her gaze but couldn't attract it. "I know you want to be alone, but you ain't alone. You got a young'un inside that needs mothering and folks outside needin' you, too."

She said nothing.

How could he break through? The last thing he wanted was to hurt her more, to force the pain to the surface. "I reckon you got a right to hurt, but you don't wanna risk Mr. Farrel's child."

Her eyes flared and met his. That's what he was looking for. If she could fight back . . .

"You gotta think what he'd want, Abbie."

"Don't *you* talk about him."

She said "you" like he was the foulest rattler that slithered the earth. He swallowed the ache and pushed. "I cain't believe he'd want you quittin' like this." He saw her knuckles go white. "He knew you had courage. He'd expect you to carry on."

She stood up sharply, gripping the headboard. "How dare you. You! It's your fault he's dead! You should have helped him, stopped him."

"Don't you think I tried? That bull thrashed him before I—" He staggered back as she flew at him.

Her fists beat his chest. "I trusted you! I hate you! I hate you. I wish it were you the bull—"

"You think I don't know that?" He caught her wrists. "Haven't I wished the same thing?"

"I don't care what you wish! I can't stand the sight of you. I can't—" She cried out, gripped her side, and doubled over.

"Abbie?" He held her arms.

"Don't touch me!" She staggered back to the bed, both hands to her belly.

Cole didn't look twice. He pulled open the door. "Go on in, Pearl. I'll git the doc." If her fury brought on the baby, so be it. He'd take her wrath over them dead eyes any day.

◆◆◆◆◆◆

Abbie fought the waves, crying out and slapping the hands that soothed her. She screamed inside at the injustice. She couldn't have the baby without Monte. She couldn't. She wouldn't! Even as the pains increased, she refused her body's need.

"Don't fight it."

But she would fight! The pain seized her, pressing, crushing. Another hand came to her forehead, with a familiar lavender scent. She opened her eyes. *Mama.* Sobs choked her throat.

"I'm here now, Abbie. It's going to be all right."

No. No, it would never be all right. The pain again. She didn't scream. She wouldn't scream. She wouldn't let them know how it hurt. *Oh, Mama.* The faces faded in and out. Someone put a damp cloth to her lips and she sucked. How long since water had touched her throat?

The pain seared through her again and her body convulsed. Where was Monte? *Monte? Why didn't he come?*

"She's wandering," someone murmured.

"Not long now." The reply was terse. She knew that voice. Doctor Barrow. He'd been with Sharlyn when Monte's son died. *Monte's son. Monte's baby. She'd lose the baby. She knew it. Cole had said . . .*

She convulsed again. Her body was tearing apart, acting without any direction from her mind. She groaned with the terrible tightening that stopped her breath and pushed against it without thought. It passed, and with it her strength. She shook all over.

She was dying. She would die. *Yes.* The thought washed over her. *Yes, she would die. She was tired, so tired. Monte . . .*

But the baby. The pain came so hard she ground her teeth and pushed with everything she had—and felt the release. The baby . . . her baby . . . the cry so weak, then stronger, lusty . . . She opened her eyes. Doctor Barrow held him struggling while Mama wrapped him. He stopped crying, and Abbie's heart plummeted.

Give him to me. No one responded, and she realized she'd made no sound. She tried harder, forcing her voice from the depths of her chest. "I want him."

The room swam. Abbie fought it. She noticed Marcy in the corner, Mama bringing her baby to Marcy . . . "No!"

Mama turned.

"I want him..." She tried to rise and her head spun, but Mama brought the baby to her. Abbie couldn't lift her arms, so Mama laid him at her side.

She spoke softly. "Marcy has milk..."

"No."

Mama bent beside her. "Abbie... you're too weak."

"I'm not."

"You have no milk."

Couldn't Mama see her heart was breaking?

Doctor Barrow laid a hand on Mama's arm. "Feeding can wait. She'll not stay awake long."

Abbie panicked. Not stay awake? If she slept, she'd find the baby gone. She clutched him to her side and fought the exhaustion. How could her body betray her? How could... she jolted awake, then drifted. No! She must... not... sleep....

♦♦♦♦♦♦♦

Abbie woke screaming and thrashing in the face of Buck Hollister's sneer as his men, Conrad, Wilkins, and Briggs, made off with her child. Doctor Barrow caught her shoulders as she clawed him and stared through the darkness, desperate for a glimpse of the baby.

"Calm down, Mrs. Farrel."

"Where is he!"

"Quiet now. Your child's just fine."

A sudden weakness washed over her. "Where is he?"

"In the next room with Mrs. Martin. Sleep and fluids are what you need. The more you get of each, the sooner you'll take charge of your son." He handed her a glass of water.

Abbie drank. Her throat was raw and dry. Her body felt like a hollow husk. It no longer had the baby inside, and she felt thin and weak. She sank back to the pillows and closed her eyes. Yes, she needed sleep. As she drifted off her mind wandered. *Mrs. Martin... which Mrs. Martin? Mama... or... Marcy...*

Eighteen

Abbie forced herself to drink both the milk and the water on her breakfast tray. Under Pearl's watchful eye, she thrust spoonful after spoonful of buttered grits and eggs down her throat. Then washed it down with tea. Surely, surely her milk would come in.

"That's good, Mizz Abbie." Pearl beamed.

"Bring me my son."

"Yessum. But Doctor Barrow, he said—"

"I don't care what Doctor Barrow said. I want my son. I've spent the whole night without him, and I want him now."

Pearl puffed her cheeks. "Yessum." She muttered her way out the door with the tray.

Abbie sat up in bed. If she didn't need to guard every ounce of strength, she'd go for the baby herself. Why had she been so careless? How could she risk herself and her son as she had? No matter. She would stuff herself until she could nourish her child. He was all she had and no one . . .

She glanced up at Marcy with the tiny bundle in her arms. Fear and fury raced through her veins. She saw tears in Marcy's eyes. What right had she to cry? What right had any of them? It was her loss. Hers and her son's. Wordlessly, Abbie reached for the baby.

Marcy eased him into her arms. "Oh, Abbie, he's the most beautiful baby boy I ever saw."

Abbie studied her baby's face. Raw pain ripped her heart. He was so like Monte, dark and fine featured. His limbs and fingers were long and slender. How could she bear it? How could she bear never seeing Monte's joy? Were the angels in heaven singing? Were they rejoicing that this child had come into the world whole and strong, though all around him grieved?

"Abbie, I know you won't believe me, but I'm so very sorry. Monte—"

"Don't. Don't speak his name. I don't want Elliot to hear and know what he's missing."

Marcy swiped at a tear. Her confusion was evident. Abbie didn't care. She didn't care what Marcy or anyone else thought. Elliot Montgomery Farrel would not be marred by the grief that accompanied his birth. He was perfect. The most perfect child ever born, and nothing would spoil that.

"Tell Pa to fetch Father O'Brien. I want my baby baptized."

"Now?"

"Yes, now, Marcy. Right now. This very minute."

She put up her chin. "You needn't snap. Pa's gone home, and it's pouring rain."

Abbie clenched her teeth against the words she wanted to shriek. "Well, send someone. I don't care who." Abbie held the baby close as Marcy left the room. He slept soundly in her arms to the steady pattering of rain, and she dozed in and out of consciousness. She woke at the tap on the door.

Father O'Brien came into the room more solemn faced than she thought possible. His blue eyes held none of their usual Irish twinkle. Even his flaming hair seemed quenched and drab. Of course, it was wet from the rain outside. He set his bag on the table.

Marcy stood in the doorway with Emily in her arms and Grant and Mama beside her. Pearl and James and Zena crowded the hall behind them. Abbie fought the disappointment. It was not as she'd envisioned it, not the joyous welcome into God's kingdom on earth that her son deserved.

Oh, Monte.

Father O'Brien draped his stole over his neck. "Who'll you be havin' for godparents, Abbie?"

She hadn't thought of that. She looked across the room, the cottony numbness starting in her head again. "Grant?" Her voice was pale.

"We'd be honored." He took Emily and put her into Mama's arms, then urged Marcy forward. She looked uncertain, uncomfortable, vulnerable.

"Grant and Marcy will be Elliot's godparents."

"And what name have ya given the child beyond Elliot?"

Abbie swallowed the knot in her throat. "Elliot Montgomery Farrel." Monte had chosen Elliot after his grandfather, and she had added Montgomery.

"A fine, strong name, and one to wear proudly."

Abbie watched dry eyed as Father O'Brien blessed her son with salt and oil and water, then handed him to Grant to bless with the sign of the cross on his forehead, and to Marcy, then back to her. *Elliot Montgomery Farrel. Elliot, meaning faithful to God.*

"Thank you, Father." Her head was starting to spin with weariness.

"I've someone downstairs who wants to see you, but she's not thinkin' you'll admit her."

Abbie watched the reposed features of her son, his tiny lips suckling in his sleep. "Nora?"

"Aye. And she'd've stayed outside in the rain if I'd let her."

"Of course I'll see her." The heaviness settled in her chest. She heard Nora enter and forced her eyes briefly to leave her child. She noticed the others had left, and Nora stood alone before her.

Nora gripped her hands together. "It's sorry that I am, Abbie. Your Monte was a good man, and I'm ashamed I let my grief color my thoughts and actions. He didn't deserve my ire, and I wish I'd come to know him."

Abbie felt the tears form a hard knot in her throat.

"I don't blame you if you turn your back," Nora continued, "but I'm hopin' you'll forgive me. You've been a better friend than I."

Abbie stroked the baby's soft head with her finger.

Nora came forward and sat on the edge of the bed. "I know

how hard it is. My Jaime was a comely man, his hair like jet and his eyes the blue of twilit sky. But he had a fire inside by the name of freedom, and it burned him fierce."

Abbie's head felt leaden as she sat.

"It's the way of the landlords, you see. They don't want us on the land, and if once we can't pay . . ." She spread her hands. "Eviction isn't only humiliatin', it's . . . inhuman. They came to take down the house. That's how they make certain no one will live there again. They pull it down with the ropes until no stones are left standin'."

Abbie listened.

"When they came, no one was at home to warn them that my grandmother slept inside. She was blind and feeble, but alive nonetheless. They had the ropes on the beams before we came in sight. My mother ran. She gained the door callin' out, but they gave word anyway for the horses to pull. Both she and my grandmother were caught in the rubble."

Abbie's lips parted but no words came.

Nora's voice was barely above a whisper. "Jaime, he took a stick to a soldier on the nearest horse." Her voice broke. "What harm could he do, I ask you?" She pressed her hands together until the knuckles turned white. "The soldier hit him with the butt of the rifle. Then they tied him to the wheel of the wagon and whipped the flesh off his back. It took him four hours to die, and he never once knew I held him."

Abbie met Nora's eyes and saw the raw pain. It quickened her own, but she pressed it down.

"I hoped the tellin' would help you understand why I . . . judged your husband poorly. It's no excuse, but it's all I have." She dropped her face to her hands. "And I'm so dreadful sorry for your hurt."

So that was the secret of Nora's grief. And it was dreadful. She had a right to feel bitter, to shut her heart. There was only so much the heart could bear. Abbie clutched Elliot to her chest. She didn't want to dry and wither as Nora had, but already she felt it beginning. Her voice came thinly. "Thank you for telling me."

Nora nodded. "I'll go now. Maybe . . . when you're stronger, you'll have a cup with me."

Abbie swallowed the ache. "I will."

She watched Nora walk out, straight and unbending, wrapped in her grief but refusing to give in to it. Oh yes, they were akin to each other. More so than she had guessed.

She looked down at Elliot, ran her eyes over every tiny feature. He was part of her and part of Monte. He was all she had of the love that had made her whole and alive. She felt the chasm gaping and clung to the warmth of the baby.

Elliot stirred and screwed up his face. He made a small mewing wail, sucked in his breath, and wailed again. Abbie felt a burning in her chest and a rush. She closed her eyes and released a slow breath, then put the baby to her breast.

◆◆◆◆◆◆◆

"You's gwonna spoil that baby. He's got 'im a cradle to sleep in. If you don' put 'im down, he won' never sleep on his own."

Abbie stroked Elliot's cheek. It was no longer hollow after six days of feeding. He was small but strong and alert.

"Let Pearl take 'im, give 'im a nice bath an' . . ."

"No."

"I know you's missin' Mastuh Monte, but—"

"I don't want to hear another word. I told you I don't want his name spoken."

Pearl hung her head. "Ain' right, Mizz Abbie."

"Right, Pearl? What's right about any of this? The only right thing is this baby, and I won't have him growing up knowing what he's missing."

Pearl muttered and shook her head.

"But you're right. It's time I was up."

"Now that ain' what I . . ."

Abbie handed Elliot into her arms and slid out from the covers. "Send Zena. I'll need a corset to get into my clothes."

"Lawd, Mizz Abbie. You ain' goin' out?"

"Unless you'd rather show Mr. Jasper up here to my bedroom . . . again."

Pearl puffed her lips but went for Zena. In less than a breath the young woman was there to help, and Abbie suspected she'd been listening at the door. The corset brought her waist almost to where it had been before Elliot. Abbie supposed that was because he was taking as much from her as she could manage to get in.

She didn't care. She'd give every ounce of strength she had to keep him healthy. It was a miracle he'd received no harm from her foolishness. Doctor Barrow said that's how it worked. She was the one at risk, for the baby took what he needed from her body's reserves.

But that was over now. She would get her strength back. She always did. And she had a ranch to run and decisions to make. She raised her arms for Zena to pull the black crepe dress on. She sat while Zena stroked the brush through her hair. How strange that it now seemed natural to sit there like a dressmaker's doll with other hands doing for her what she could easily do for herself. How much she'd changed as Monte's wife.

Monte. Would she ever not feel weak at the very thought of him? She knew Pearl disapproved of her decision. Didn't they understand she'd die if they spoke of him? How could she go on, raise her son, take each new breath if the pain sucked away her life? The only way was to cover the pit, pretend it was not there waiting to devour her.

Monte would understand. God would understand. Her hand trembled as she reached for the honeysuckle scent and dabbed it to her throat. She remembered Monte dropping his head to breathe it against her skin. It would be easier to simply die, but Cole was right. Monte would expect her to go on. She would not fail him.

She pushed away from the dressing table and stood. Her hair hung loose down her back. Zena hadn't yet twisted it up. It didn't matter. She had a task that wouldn't wait. She swept downstairs. "James, fetch Mr. Jasper. I'll meet him in the study."

She went into the room, Monte's room. For a moment her heart failed her. She could almost see him behind the desk, raising his head to greet her, putting aside his business to stand and take her hands. *Oh, God, I'll die of the pain.*

She turned when Cole tapped the doorframe with a knuckle. A hard knot settled in her stomach, and she walked behind the desk. A barrier, any barrier is what she wanted between them. She could hardly refrain from throwing herself in his face like a wildcat. The very sight of him incensed her.

She cleared her throat. "Mr. Jasper, I'd like you to find employment on another ranch. If you'll tell me what I owe you . . ."

His green eyes held her. "You don't owe me nothin'."

She looked away. "I'd like to square your wages, but I don't know what you were paid." She pulled open the drawer to the desk and searched for a ledger. There. She took out the leatherbound book and opened it across the desk. She flipped the pages to payroll and found Cole's name at the top. Monte had been generous . . . of course. Her chest squeezed and she looked up. Cole was gone.

Cole crossed the yard. His heart felt like a stone in his chest. What did he expect, that she would turn to him in her grief? She'd lost the only man that mattered to her, and she blamed him for that. She sure didn't need him around to remind her, no matter what Mr. Farrel had charged. How could he keep his promise with things as they were?

You'll just have to understand, Mr. Farrel. It's better this way, Cole thought.

He strode to the bunkhouse and gathered his things. It didn't take long. He slung the roll over his back.

Breck stood in the doorway. "Goin' somewhere?"

"Unless Mrs. Farrel says different, you're in charge here."

"How come?"

"I'm movin' on."

"Where to?"

"The next herd, I guess." Cole looked out across the yard, his glance landing briefly on the house, then away.

"Cole..."

"Look after her, will ya, Breck? She's a mighty brave lady, but she's not so strong as she thinks."

"I'll look after her, but Cole..."

"Let it go, Breck. I been here too long a'ready. A man might put down roots if he stays too long in one place. And roots is one thing I never wanted."

Breck stepped back to let him pass. Cole stopped and breathed the autumn air. "Sure is a fine day fer hittin' the road."

"Will you keep in touch?"

"Cain't write, but I might send word somehow time and again."

"Look after yerself."

Cole nodded, then headed to the stable for Scotch. He and that old horse had covered a lot of miles. He had a hankering to sleep under the stars again. Too bad the nights were so cold.

♦♦♦♦♦♦♦

Abbie pushed past Pearl standing in the hall with the coffee tray she'd expected her to call for. "Ain' right, Mizz Abbie. Ain' right you cuttin' him loose. Mistuh Jazzper, he's a good man. He done his best by you an' Mastuh Monte."

Abbie spun, her fury flaming inside. "Take yourself to the kitchen where you belong. If you won't honor my request and refrain from speaking... of him... then you and James may find employment elsewhere, as well." She trembled. She would have to guard her strength.

Turning, Abbie went upstairs to feed Elliot, then took her coat and bonnet and stalked out to the stable. Will stood, sober and unspeaking, and she guessed he'd parted with Cole. In his own way, Cole had looked after the boy these last years, and she guessed Will was not happy.

"Saddle Zephyr for me, Will." No more buggy riding now that Elliot was born. She took the reins Will handed her and mounted. Zephyr tossed her head, and Abbie turned her, then cantered from the yard. The way to Mama's seemed long and difficult, and an ache filled her lower back by the time she reached the house.

She slumped down from the mare's back and clung to the saddle before straightening and going to the door. It opened at her knock, and she looked down at Tucker. He grinned.

"What are you doing out of school, young man?"

"Mama said I can stay with Jenny."

"I see. Well, I hate to disappoint you, but I've come for Jenny. So you have no excuse now."

His face fell, and he kicked the toe of his boot on the floor. "Can't you teach me again? I don't like Mr. Ernst. He's not fun like you were."

"Well, sometimes you have to do things that aren't fun. Learning is its own reward." She saw that her words meant nothing to him. "Where's Jenny?"

"In the kitchen." He dragged his feet down the hall.

Abbie found Mama and Jenny by the stove stirring the crabapples for jam. "I've come for Jenny."

Mama looked up with wide eyes. "Abbie, you shouldn't be up yet."

"I'm perfectly hale." She stooped to receive the tentative hug Jenny offered, then clung longer than she intended.

Jenny wiggled free. "We're making jam. Want to help?"

"Not today. I have to get back to Elliot."

Jenny pouted. "I want to make jam."

"Well, you can't."

"Abbie." Mama took her arm and led her to a chair.

Abbie sank down weakly.

"Let Jenny stay awhile. Have these weeks with the baby; get your strength back."

Abbie rested her head on her hands. Maybe Mama was right. She certainly had nothing to give. Elliot took what he needed, and his warmth in her arms gave her strength. But what good would she be to Jenny?

She nodded slowly. "Do you want to stay, Jenny?"

The child nodded vigorously. It hurt, but Abbie smiled. Children were so honest. Brutally so. But she did feel relieved to let Mama handle her responsibility awhile longer. Jenny was in good hands, and she . . . she was so tired.

It took all her strength to keep in the saddle back home and then walk to the house. She staggered up the stairs to find Elliot wailing in Zena's arms. She sank to the bed and fed him, then slept through lunch and tea.

◆◆◆◆◆◆◆

The next morning was overcast, and Abbie received without interest the breakfast tray Pearl brought. She felt dull and lethargic, and riding Zephyr had caused her to hemorrhage. If she cared to avoid Doctor Barrow, and she did with all her heart, she must be wiser.

She ate and fed Elliot, then dressed and sat by the window with a book. She scarcely noticed which one, and the words passed beneath her eyes without touching her mind. She saw Monte's Bible on the stand beside the bed, but she could not touch it. It would open the pit, and she would fall.

A horse in the yard caught her ear, and she glanced down and frowned. Mr. Driscoll. What did he want? She stood, waited a moment for the dizziness to pass, then went downstairs. James met her at the foot of the stairs, and Mr. Driscoll stood inside the front door. She would have had him stay outside.

"Mizz Abbie, Mr. Driscoll's here to see you."

"Thank you, James." Abbie stood in the hall. This would be concluded swiftly enough she needn't ask him to sit. "Yes?"

"Mrs. Farrel, may I extend my deepest sympathy on the loss of your husband."

She said nothing. Next to calling him a liar, what could she say?

He cleared his throat. "I've come to make you an offer . . . for the ranch."

"I beg your pardon?"

"I figured you'll be selling, and I—"

"I've no intention whatever of selling the Lucky Star. You may go."

"But, ma'am, surely you realize a woman of your tender years knows nothing about—"

His audacity, to come there as though invited, to presume to advise her. His greed showed in his face. "Get off my land, Mr. Driscoll. If you set foot here again, I'll have my men shoot you."

He went white, then red. "You will sell, Mrs. Farrel. Sooner or later. I already hold the deed." He gripped the doorknob and let himself out.

Abbie leaned against the banister. Was it true? Had Monte turned over the ranch deed to Mr. Driscoll? It wasn't possible. But the loan. How had he secured the loan? Had he given in to Horace Driscoll after refusing once? She recalled him pacing in the night, groaning in his sleep. She knew he was worried, but could it have been as bad as that? She rushed to the study, emptied drawer after drawer.

No, Monte. Not the ranch. Not Elliot's land. She sank to the chair and clutched her head in her hands. *Oh, God, how could he?* She braced herself against the chair back. Grant would look into it. He would advise her. Driscoll was right. She knew nothing of running the ranch. But she would learn. It was all here in Monte's books.

She would gird herself with knowledge and fight Driscoll and anyone else who thought to take advantage of her. She would preserve Monte's heritage for his son. One day Elliot Montgomery Farrel would be master of the Lucky Star, and it was her part to keep it running until then.

Part Two

Nineteen

For he's a jolly good fellow, for he's a jolly good fellow, for he's a jolly good fe-l-low . . . that nobody can deny. As Abbie set the cake on the table before her son, Elliot's blue eyes radiated excitement. He extinguished the four candles with one wet puff.

"You didn't make a wish." Jenny tossed her dark braids over her shoulder. "And it's too late now, because you have to do it before the candles are out."

"I did too wish. I wished—"

"If you tell it, it won't come true."

Elliot looked up at her, and Abbie felt a pang. How like Monte's were some of his expressions. Already his little eyebrows quirked expressively, and he had the natural Farrel grace of motion. His dark hair and straight features were Monte's, and he would be tall one day.

Only his eyes were hers. Their blue so closely matched her own that sometimes she longed for them to go brown like Monte's. But at four years old that wasn't likely. He was a handsome child, drawing people's glances, as did Jenny.

At seven she was as precocious as she'd been at three. Though her tantrums no longer took her to the floor in sobs, she still demanded more than she gave. Yet little Elliot withstood her control. His even temper soothed her, Abbie guessed, and Jenny knew he'd not fall for her pouts. Elliot had a poise and dignity beyond his years.

She looked around the table at the children seated there. Sadie's youngsters, Matthew and Hannah, sat beside Marcy's Emily

Elizabeth and Clara's Dell and little Roger. On the other side were the Irish redheads, Katie, Danny, Colin, Meghan, with eleven-year-old Tucker at the end. Around the children stood the mothers and friends who'd come to make Elliot's day special.

Abbie looked at her sister, Sadie. She'd taken the train from Denver to be there with them. Glenna stood straight and winsome, with Nora beside her. Clara stood with Emmy and Pauline, the mission orphans she'd taken in, who now stood almost as tall as she and a good deal more slender. Clara looked to be carrying twins, though Doctor Barrow doubted it. Marcy leaned on the hutch, her golden hair pulled into a chignon at her neck, and her hand resting where her new baby grew but didn't yet show.

Mama brought the knife, and Abbie put it in Elliot's hand, then helped him cut into the warm marmalade cake. Pearl beamed when his little finger snaked out and swiped the sticky glaze. Abbie sliced the cake, then turned it over to Zena to serve.

She stepped back beside Sadie and feigned exhaustion. "Now that they're eating, we can breathe."

"He's a wonderful boy, Abbie. Monte would be so proud."

Abbie stiffened and turned away. "Pearl, bring the ice cream."

The children cheered when Pearl spooned the frozen cream onto their plates. Abbie doubted Glenna's little ones had ever tasted it, and it was rare enough in this house these days. She'd splurged and had Pearl make ice cream rather than the butter and cheese they sold in town. This one day she refused to scrimp, no matter what toll it took. Elliot would have the best day of his life.

When the children had been washed clean of marmalade and cream, Abbie ushered them all out to the yard. She bent and tied a scarf over Elliot's eyes, then motioned to Will. He was a gangly eighteen and looked even taller with the small pony in tow.

Abbie spun Elliot until he staggered, then pointed him toward the pony and let go. The children erupted in giggles and hoots as he wove forward and collided with the shaggy side of the pony. He pulled off the blindfold and crowed. Abbie had traded a good brood mare for the animal. The man had taken her for a fool, but she didn't regret it one bit.

Will hoisted Elliot to the pony's back and handed him the halter rope, though he kept hold of the headpiece. Elliot sent Abbie a brilliant smile and kicked in his small heels. The pony walked obediently in circles as he directed, but he might have just won the new Kentucky Derby the way he held himself in the saddle. Her heart swelled.

"Mrs. Farrel?"

Abbie turned. "Yes, Breck?"

He took his hat from his head. "Sorry to interrupt you, but . . ." He glanced briefly at the others.

Abbie stepped clear of the crowd and approached him. "What is it, Breck?"

"John Mason. He's come down sick."

Abbie glanced over her shoulder. He must be more than sick if Breck was bringing it to her attention. "Where is he?"

"In the bunkhouse."

"I'll meet you there in a moment." She walked back. "Mama, I have to check on something. Will you see everyone off?"

"Is anything wrong?"

"I'm not sure. John Mason's ill. I may need Doctor Barrow."

"I'll send the others home."

"I think that would be wise." Abbie hurried to the bunkhouse behind the stable. Breck stepped aside for her to enter, and she eyed John Mason thrashing on the bunk. With one look she could tell that he was burning with fever. "When did this start?"

"Some while ago, I reckon. Didn't seem so bad until today."

Abbie stooped beside the bed. "John?" His face was splotchy, and where his shirt fell open she saw rosy spots on his chest. "Go for the doctor, Breck." She rushed back to the house. She didn't bother Pearl or James or Zena. She would keep this to herself until she knew what she was up against.

She hurried into the kitchen and got a clean cloth and bowl. Out in the yard, she filled the bowl with cold water at the pump, then hurried back, sloshing as little as possible. A starling darted to the branch of a cottonwood, then parted its sharp black beak and shrilled.

Abbie passed into the stuffy bunk room. Kneeling beside John Mason, she swabbed his forehead with the cloth. He mumbled, but didn't seem to recognize her. "It's all right, John. The doctor's on his way."

She wiped her forehead with her sleeve, stood, and opened the door and windows. The August sun burned in the sky with no clouds in sight. No wonder John Mason was burning up. She hoped it was nothing serious, but he looked bad—as sick as she had ever seen someone since Sharlyn. And Sharlyn had died.

He thrashed continuously, curling up and holding his abdomen. Was it his appendix? Clara's husband Marty had an attack last year, and Doctor Barrow had taken it out. But Clara had said nothing about pink splotches. She bathed his brow again, then turned when Mama's shadow filled the door.

"I've sent everyone home but Sadie. How is he?"

"He doesn't look good."

"Let me see." Mama came close. She let out a slow breath. "I'm no doctor, but I've seen this before."

"What is it?"

"Typhoid. It swept the Auraria mining camp when you were small. Do you remember?"

Abbie frowned. It seemed she did recall a bad sickness that had kept her and Sadie and Grant from playing outside the tent. Hadn't Blake's sister...? "Is that what Mariah had?"

"Yes. She recovered, but the fever ... turned her mind."

"That's why she's the way she is."

Mama nodded.

Abbie tried to picture Mariah without her nervous tension and bewilderment. She would have been about Jenny's age when the typhoid struck. Sudden fear chilled her. She glanced down at John Mason. He wasn't much older than she, and in his distress looked younger yet. But he'd been a faithful hand, working as hard for her under Breck as he had for Monte. "I wish the doctor would hurry."

She heard a horse in the yard and went to the door, but Breck rode up alone. He swung down and removed his hat. "Doc can't

200

come. He's got three cases of typhoid in town and a handful more scattered around. He said we best bring John Mason to him."

Abbie brushed her fingers through her hair. "Well, hitch up the wagon, then. Where are the others?"

"Matt and Curtis are on the range. We got the beef herd separated to ship out next week. Skeeter's ridin' fences—"

A thump on the wall made them both turn, and Breck rushed to the end of the bunkhouse. Abbie hurried behind him and saw Skeeter crumpled on the ground. From the smell, he'd soiled himself, and his eyes were bright with fever. Abbie gripped the edge of the wall. What horrible thing could so decimate a man?

"Get the wagon, Breck. We'll take them both."

Mama touched her arm. "Maybe I'd better take the children home with me."

Abbie felt a tremor. Could she bear to send Elliot away even for a time? She looked down at Skeeter. What choice did she have? Elliot was too fond of running down to the bunkhouse with Jenny, and she wouldn't risk . . . no, she couldn't even think of it. "I'll have Zena get them ready."

As Breck went for the wagon, she and Mama headed for the house. Sadie waited in the parlor with Matthew and Hannah, who played blindman's bluff with Jenny and Elliot. Abbie leaned close to her sister and whispered. Sadie's lips parted with concern, but Abbie squeezed her shoulder. She didn't want to alarm the children.

"You'd best stay with Mama, too. I'm sorry." And she was. Sadie's visits were too far between to miss one. Abbie hardly knew her niece and nephew. But it couldn't be helped. The children must be safeguarded, and Sadie, as well.

"Maybe I should go back to Denver." Sadie steadied Hannah, who bumped into her knee blindly, then turned, arms outstretched, and groped in the other direction.

Mama sighed. "As much as I hate to say it, you probably ought to take the first train out."

Mama spoke too softly to be overheard, but Abbie caught Elliot watching. He was altogether too perceptive.

She bent and swept him into her arms. "How would you and Jenny like to stay with Grandma and Grandpa for awhile? It would be a grand adventure for your birthday."

"How long would we stay, Aunt Abbie?" Jenny clasped her hands behind her back and swung her skirts.

"I'm not sure right now."

"I'll stay with Mama." Elliot wrapped his arms around her neck.

She closed her eyes and rubbed her cheek against his soft hair. Already the ache was starting. "Jenny will need a young man to look after her, Elliot."

"I'll look after myself. I like adventures." Jenny's taunt was more effective than Abbie's request.

"I like adventures, too." Elliot released her neck and frowned.

"You're afraid of adventures because you're little." Jenny's eyes had a teasing glint.

"I'm big. I'm four now." Elliot's cheeks flushed.

Abbie cupped his face. "And you're just the one to accompany Jenny. Your pony will go with you."

His eyes widened. "I can take Ralph?"

"Ralph?" How had the child come to that for a pony's name? "I don't think Ralph would miss the adventure for anything."

"Of course, I'll bring Snowdrop." Jenny slid her arm around Abbie's waist with her most manipulating smile.

Abbie glanced at Mama, who nodded permission to send along the small mare that Jenny rode.

Jenny beamed her triumph. "I'd better go pack at once. I'll bring Amanda and my animals." She used her grown-up tone as though packing her toys was of utmost importance.

Abbie smiled. "Pack Elliot's train." Her quick mention of the train stifled her son's longing for animals like Jenny's. For whatever reason, Elliot coveted the little animals Cole had carved for Jenny, but she hoarded them like treasure. Abbie sighed.

When Zena had the children ready, Abbie lifted Elliot into Mama's buggy. She fought the panic rising inside. It was unnatural, she knew. Four years was too long to still fear having him out of her sight. She'd been very careful not to let it show, but she suspected he sensed it. She must let him go now; his life could depend on it.

She gave Jenny a hug, though Jenny had less need of it than she, then helped her into the carriage. Will tied the mare and pony behind. Sadie waited while Matthew and Hannah climbed in, then took her place beside them. "Maybe you should leave, too, Abbie."

Abbie glanced at Breck bringing up the wagon. She could go. She could be with Elliot. She wouldn't have to be separated. Breck took off his hat and wiped his forehead with his sleeve. He waited respectfully while she decided.

"I'm needed here." She stepped back and waved with more cheer than she felt. If Elliot once suspected the pain in her heart, he'd never go. She forced herself to smile as the buggies pulled out. They were only going to Mama's. They would be with Pa. He'd keep them safe. They'd be fine. But would she?

Breck had Skeeter and John in the wagon bed, with enough padding under their heads to take care of most of the bumps. "Curtis helped me load 'em in. He's denyin' it, but he don't look too good, either."

Abbie pulled herself up to the wagon seat. "Maybe it's just the heat."

"Maybe." Breck took up the reins.

Abbie was glad for the wide brim of her hat. The sun was relentless as it sank toward the mountains. The men in the wagon bed moaned, and that sound scared her more than the rest of it. Seeing strong men like Skeeter and young men like John brought low enough to writhe was not encouraging.

They stopped the wagon in front of the clinic. Doctor Barrow came outside, looked into the bed, and nodded. "Take them to the town hall. We're setting up an infirmary."

"An infirmary?" Abbie climbed down. "Are there as many cases as that?"

Doctor Barrow took off his spectacles and wiped them on his shirt. "We found that drifter—the one you folks took in for a piece. He died just east of town. Seems he made the rounds to a number of homesteads and took a good many meals."

Abbie recalled the stranger who'd taken shelter with them for a couple days. He'd looked ill and hard on his luck. Breck had given him an odd job or two in exchange for food and a bunk. He'd even ridden out on the fall roundup and worked with the cook in the chuck wagon. "He died of typhoid?"

The doctor nodded. "And the worst of it is he camped awhile upstream on Monument Creek. Anyone who's drawn water from there . . ." He spread his hands.

"Is there a serum or . . ."

"I wish there were. Right now the best we can do is quarantine the patients."

Breck shifted in the seat. "Is there someone at the hall to help me unload these men?"

"The marshal's there with Ethan Thomas. I'll be coming myself as soon as I've gathered my things."

Abbie helped Doctor Barrow carry the crates of medicines and cloths. These would help ease the discomfort, but only the victim's constitutions would determine who lived and who . . . She stood in the door, looked at the cots and blankets set out across the floor, and fought the anger. Death was too fierce an enemy.

Breck joined her. "I'll get you home now."

"They'll need help here."

He looked back over his shoulder. "I reckon they will. But you got young'uns to think of."

"I've sent them with Mama."

"I saw. But you don't want to be exposed. You're all the parent they got."

Doctor Barrow passed by and barked gruffly. "Go on, now."

Abbie went out. She was silent all the way to the ranch. Pearl was boiling a massive pot of onions, and the whole house smelled of it.

"What are you doing, Pearl?"

"Onions keep the sickness away."

Abbie ran her hand over her forehead. One hour in that oniony steam would keep anything away. She sank to the chair. "It's typhoid, Pearl."

"I know. I got me a look at them in the wagon. John Mason, he in a bad way."

"They both are."

"You was wise to send the chillen away."

Wise, yes. But her heart ached. Elliot had filled her days since Monte . . . She rested her forehead on her palm. The house seemed oppressively quiet—no pattering feet, no chattering voices. She would even welcome a spat. She straightened. "I'm going to bathe. Will you boil water?"

"Yessum. And you takes this onion in with you."

Abbie glanced from Pearl to the onion and back. "I will not bathe with an onion." She raised a hand when Pearl opened her broad mouth to argue. "I don't care what it does, I'll not have it." She went to the back room and slid the large tub to the center of the floor.

Going out to the pump for water was a pleasure, and she thanked God that they drew water from the well and not the stream.

◆◆◆◆◆◆◆

Abbie tossed and twisted. She listened for his voice, for the sound of his soft breathing. She groped in the darkness. He had to be there, he had to; if she could just . . . *Oh, Monte, I've lost your son. I tried to keep him safe . . . I tried . . .* She threw the covers off and sat up in bed, shaking.

She'd go mad. Three nights of dreams that left her panicked; she couldn't take anymore. She had to bring Elliot back. . . . What was she saying? What was she thinking? Would she risk him to stop her nightmares? What if he caught it? What if his mind turned as Mariah's had? What if he . . . No!

She dropped her face to her hands. With both Skeeter and John Mason coming down sick, who knew how badly contaminated the ranch was? At least at Mama's he was safe, he and Jenny both, she reminded herself, feeling a twinge of guilt that her fear for Jenny was not equal to what she felt for Elliot.

She would go and see them tomorrow. She would hold Elliot as long as he allowed her. She would . . . What if she carried it there? Doctor Barrow said typhoid was transmitted through contaminated water or food . . . or contact. She had doctored John Mason, who even now clung to life by a thread. How could she be certain she was not infected?

She lay back in the bed. She could not go to Elliot, and she felt as though part of herself was tearing away. It was like losing Monte all over again. Why, why, why? She heard Mama's soft voice. *"You must not allow yourself to become unnaturally attached to the child."* How could she not? He was all she had . . . of Monte.

She closed her eyes. *Why, God? Why must I be separated from my son, too? Was it not enough to take Monte? Are you never satisfied?*

She shuddered with the blasphemous thoughts and recalled Reverend Shields' words. " *'The* LORD *gave, and the* LORD *hath taken away; blessed be the name of the* LORD.' " At the time she had hardly heard him speak, but somehow the words had been blazoned on her heart.

They had driven everything she'd done these last four years. She'd filled her days trying to appease the God who could take from her anything He liked. Part of her knew that was not the way of a loving God, but the pain inside said otherwise.

It was easier now to drive the hurt away. She had Elliot and Jenny . . . and the ranch. She had not missed a single payment on the loan in four years. That was thanks in part to Grant's arranging for lower payments over more time. She felt a supreme satisfaction every time she handed over the payment to Mr. Driscoll's greedy hand. She would pay back every cent without fail.

She drew a long, slow breath. She'd talk to Pa in town tomorrow. He would tell her how the children were faring. He would tell her if Elliot missed her as she did him. Oh, Elliot. For his sake she hoped not, but the message would be a thorned rose if Pa said no. She stared into the darkness until her eyes closed on their own.

Twenty

Abbie opened the door the next morning to Breck standing hat in hand. "Oh no, Breck. Not someone else."

"I'm real sorry, Mrs. Farrel. John Mason passed on in the night."

It was as though he'd kicked her. John Mason? The young, blushing cowboy . . . gone? Had he breathed out his last moments while she fretted over separation from her son? Why had she not dropped to her knees and prayed for him? Was she so absorbed in her own pain that she had not even thought of his suffering?

"And Skeeter?"

"He's bad."

"Have Will saddle Zephyr."

"Mrs. Farrel, you ain't thinkin' . . ."

"I am going to the infirmary."

"It ain't no good, Mrs. Farrel. Doc's got people workin' round the clock. Ain't nothin' no one can do that ain't bein' done."

Abbie dropped her hands to her sides. "I can't just stay here and wait for the men to die." But she knew Breck was right. She had a responsibility to Pearl and James and Zena, to the other men still working, and most of all to the children. She looked past the outbuildings to the land resting in the summer heat. What was she to do? Carry on? "What about the herd?"

"Matt and Curtis and I'll get 'em to the train and send 'em off. They're scheduled to go tomorrow."

"Can you manage shorthanded?"

"Ain't that many head. Five hundred steers. We can manage."

Five hundred thirteen to be exact. Not that many, but enough to bring the money she desperately needed. Beef prices were down, but if she could pay only interest on the loan today and make up the principal with the sale, she'd have some breathing room at last. If Mr. Driscoll balked . . . She wouldn't think about that. She had considered asking Pa or Grant to help, but times had been thin for Pa, and Grant was hard put to keep Marcy as she demanded. Abbie doubted either could cover for her without hardship.

"I won't go to the infirmary, but I must see Mr. Driscoll. Please have Will ready Zephyr."

"Yes, ma'am." He replaced his hat.

She watched him cross the yard and thanked God under her breath that he at least was spared from the typhoid. She could not have done it these last years without Breck. She wondered sometimes why he stayed on with her when he could earn more at the other ranches, especially whenever someone new set up headquarters. They offered top dollar to seasoned hands who'd help them get up and running.

But Breck and the others had stayed. Even John Mason. *Father forgive me for failing him, and please help the others.*

She tied on her hat as Will led Zephyr to the steps. "Thank you, Will. Please ask Breck—"

"Will!" Breck staggered around the side of the stable dragging a man by the shoulders. "Give me a hand here."

Abbie ran with Will. The man Breck held was Curtis. He struggled to his feet, thrust himself away from Breck and ran behind the stable. The sounds of his intestinal distress reached them in the yard.

Abbie cringed. "Get the wagon, Will. Fill it with blankets."

She heard Curtis arguing with Breck. "I ain't goin' to no infirmary. It's comin' too fast an' furious."

"You got no choice. It don't matter if you mess yourself. You gotta see what Doc can do."

"Doc can't do nothin'. Look at John Mason."

"You gotta go anyway. Anyone who's got it is quarantined.

Think of Mrs. Farrel." Breck came around the side with Curtis slumped against him. The stench was foul.

Abbie stared with dismay at Curtis Potts. His eyes were haunted, his strong face screwed with pain. He collapsed in the wagon bed that Will backed toward them, then curled like a baby and groaned. That left Breck and Matt. *Dear God, preserve them.*

"Keep Zephyr, Will. I'll ride in the wagon with Breck."

Breck stepped between her and the wagon. "No, ma'am. You take yer own horse."

She shook her head. Breck was starting to sound like Cole. The thought felt sour inside her. "I'll thank you to remember who's in charge here."

"I know who's in charge, but I got my orders."

"Your orders?" She stared at him, and he flinched. "Whose orders?"

"Look, ma'am, I didn't mean—"

"Oh yes, you did. Who's giving you orders, Breck?"

"It ain't like that."

She swallowed against the sudden dryness in her throat. "Suppose you tell me what it is like?"

He circled his hat in his hands. "It's just . . . Cole said look after you. He sends up extra money to . . ."

Abbie's breath came in a sharp burst. *Cole!* So that was why the men had stayed. Cole bribed them. All this time she thought they respected her, accepted working for her, had loyalty, integrity . . . She took hold of the pommel and mounted, then turned Zephyr's head and pressed with her knees.

The wind whipped her hair into her face, but she urged Zephyr to more speed. *How dare he?* The audacity . . . She felt like a dry well. She'd accomplished nothing. Extra money. How had Breck used it? To keep the men, surely, but how else? Had he shored up her deficiencies?

How could Cole have extra money? What could he do to earn enough to send some away? How? . . . Angry tears threatened, but she forced them away. Zephyr tired, and Abbie reined in to a walk. She felt more betrayed than she had since . . .

Oh, God, you knew. You let me creep on thinking I could stand. When all the while Cole Jasper . . .

She drew a long, shaky breath. She had to compose herself to face Oscar Driscoll. She would do it. She would not allow Breck's confession to make her stumble. She would stand if it took losing every man in her employ. She'd run the ranch alone if that's what it took. She pulled up before the bank, dismounted, and smoothed her hair. Then drawing herself up, she went inside.

Mr. Driscoll met her himself at the counter. "Mrs. Farrel. It's always a pleasure when you grace this establishment."

"Thank you, Mr. Driscoll. May I see you in your office?"

"Of course." He pushed open the gate, then followed her into the small, but plush space behind the clerk's cage. He motioned her to sit. "I'm sorry I've nothing to offer you."

He always said that, and she wondered if it hadn't a double meaning. "That's quite all right. I've a request to make." She was certain she didn't imagine the glint in his eyes. She took out the interest payment and set it on his desk. "May I pay only the interest on the loan this month? I've a beef herd ready to ship that will bring in the rest by next month."

He cleared his throat and took his chair behind the desk. "Well, I must say I'm not surprised. I understand you've had several men succumb to the typhoid."

News traveled fast. But then she supposed Mr. Driscoll made it his business to know others' misfortune, anything he might turn to his advantage. "As I said, the sale of the beef—"

"Yes, yes, yes. Well, of course. How could I refuse your request under such circumstances as those you're facing? However, there is something you should know. Have you been yet to the railroad office?"

"No, why?"

"Well, it seems no trains will be coming along this spur as long as the town is quarantined."

"The town is quarantined?"

"So far as the railroad is concerned. They'll take no one in or out, and they'll not carry any livestock from the area at all."

Abbie sank back in her chair. "But . . ."

"I'm sorry, Mrs. Farrel. You look pale. May I offer . . . a spot of sherry?"

Abbie gripped the arms of the chair and straightened. "No, thank you. Forgive me, but I'll verify this news, then decide what's to be done. Thank you for granting my request."

"Uh, yes, but under the circumstances . . ."

"You'll have payment from the sale."

"But how will you make the sale if you cannot transport the cattle?"

She smiled tightly. "I'll find a way."

Once outside, Abbie felt her stomach knot. How? What way? Oscar Driscoll had known about the railroad when he granted her request. Had he only agreed because he thought there could be no sale and she would default on the loan?

He had been fair thus far, but she knew he only waited for her to slip once. He was honest, but not compassionate. Hadn't he capitalized on her ignorance in the dealing with Kendal, then held Monte responsible? Didn't he hold her to the letter of his agreement with her late husband regardless of her difficulty? She was certain he had only agreed so readily now because he believed she couldn't make the sale.

She looked down the street and saw their wagon outside the infirmary. So Breck had arrived with Curtis. Only just. He came back out with Ethan Thomas and together they hauled Curtis inside. She forced away thoughts of Breck's betrayal. After all, what grounds had he to refuse Cole's money? Cole was the one to blame. Cole Jasper. Did he think he could pay for Monte's death?

Abbie shrank away from the memory. She'd spent four years purging the scene from her mind. Monte in the wagon, Cole . . . The look on his face had told her everything. She'd rather die than look in that face again and see his pity.

Well, she couldn't undo any of it now. She had a more critical problem—five hundred head of cattle to drive to Kansas. Breck would have to find men, but where? All who'd been on the roundup were at risk of typhoid contagion.

She walked the length of the street to the infirmary. Had Breck heard yet of the railroad's ban? She climbed the steps and looked in the door. The room was filled with the sick, and there were women and children among them now.

Abbie saw Reverend Shields beside a cot and across the room was Father O'Brien. Had it spread to the Irish homesteaders? No, it was Ferdy Gaines he sat beside, speaking low. Was he offering the comfort of the afterlife? Reverend Shields leaned forward and closed the eyes of the man beside him. She couldn't tell whom it was. The stench and overwhelming misery caught in her throat.

"Mrs. Farrel." Breck took her arm, pushed the door open, and tugged her out with him. He cleared his throat. "I apologize for earlier." His voice sounded weary.

She didn't want to discuss what he'd told her. "Breck, we have a problem."

"I reckon you mean the railroad." He let go of her arm at the foot of the steps.

"We need to make that sale. I've no choice in that. We'll have to drive the cattle ourselves, but we'll need men."

"Mrs. Farrel . . ." Breck sagged against the wagon, and she noticed the sweat beading his forehead.

"Breck? No . . ."

"Get Cole. He'll help ya. He's madder'n a hornet that I told ya, but . . ." He gripped the side of the wagon and winced.

"What are you talking about?" She caught his arm. "Let me help you inside."

"I can make it alone. Cole—"

"Don't be ridiculous. Where would I ever find him? He's left the state for all I know."

Breck doubled over. "He's back . . . at the Red Slipper right now." He stumbled to the pillar and caught hold, then climbed the stairs and went in.

Abbie stared after him. Had every one of her men been infected? All because of the drifter. What was his name anyway? A man passing through, bringing death in his wake. *Oh, Lord.*

Should she even think of the cattle, of the ranch, of anything but the suffering of those inside?

She pictured Mr. Driscoll's face. He didn't care who suffered. He'd expect payment even if every one of her men died. If she missed next month's payment with this month's principal added on, he'd take the ranch. She had to get the herd to Kansas, but how? Cole? She shook her head. No. She'd drag them there herself before she turned to him.

Abbie suddenly felt the immensity of the task. She couldn't save the ranch. She'd fought and scraped and kept her head up, no matter what. Even when they lost forty of the cattle to disease, even when a brush fire had taken a dozen more, she'd fought back. She'd built up the herd little by little. And now after four years, she had enough to make a good sale.

"Why, Lord?"

The sky held gray rumbling clouds but no answer. She glanced down the street. The Red Slipper stood just past the hotel and Peterson's hardware. Beyond that, the bank. She closed her eyes, imagining Driscoll's look of feigned dismay. "*So very sorry to evict you. . . .*" What had Nora said? Evictions are not humiliating, they're inhuman.

No. Mr. Driscoll would not pull down the walls. He coveted the house and property for himself. Where would she go? Back with Mama? To Grant and Marcy? She shuddered. They'd made a tentative peace, but not enough to live under the same roof. Mr. Driscoll thought she should consider any number of bachelors or widowers. What business did a young lady have running a ranch? Especially a ranch he wanted.

Her anger quickened. Well, he wouldn't have it. And if she had to abase herself to Cole Jasper to save the Lucky Star . . . She groaned silently, then trudged forward. The sand on the board-walk gritted under her shoes as she approached the swinging doors. The banjo and piano could be heard in the street.

Didn't they know people were dying? Who could frolic inside a place like that when men and women lay dying down the road? Apparently Cole Jasper could. She pushed the doors open and went in. The smell of whiskey and tobacco caught in her nostrils, and her heel slipped on a hawk of brown spittle in the sawdust.

She searched the smoky haze and saw Cole standing at the bar with Lil Brandon hanging on his arm. Abbie knew the woman's name, though she didn't recall how. She'd come in with the train and made herself popular with the men. She fairly purred at Cole's side now, and he seemed none too reluctant.

The sight of him made her blood burn. It churned the memories until she nearly choked. She couldn't do it. She turned back, but . . . if not Cole, who? Slowly she approached the bar. Lil saw her first, and no wonder. Cole was busy admiring the fingers Lil laid over his. He was certainly living up to her expectations.

"You lost, lady?" Lil twanged.

Cole turned. She could read nothing in his face but a hint of surprise. He looked harder but no older. The same unruly blond curls, roughly cropped, with the thick mustache and a couple days' growth of whiskers on his tanned chin, a dusty kerchief, flannel shirt . . . He held her steadily with his green eyes but said nothing.

She summoned up her courage. "I'm looking to hire someone to drive my herd to Kansas. I have five hundred head of marketable beef."

He narrowed his eyes, then turned away. "I ain't fer hire."

Abbie felt the blood rush to her face. Did he mean to make her beg? "I'll give you ten percent of the sale . . . fifteen percent."

He looked back with a flicker of . . . anger?

She realized she still owed him the wages he'd refused to collect when she'd sent him away. "Name your price. If it's within my means—"

"I don't want your money, Mrs. Farrel." He moved his hand out from under Lil's and stood alone, contained, self-sufficient.

Abbie felt the thrust of his ire as he stared her down. Breck was wrong. It couldn't be Cole who'd sent the money. He was meaner and cockier than ever. Who did Cole Jasper think he was? She spun.

"If it's a favor you're askin', I'd consider it."

So that was it. He wanted her to grovel, cry out her need. He was striking back, and she was vulnerable. Abbie felt the fury crawl her spine like a live thing. She should keep walking, shake the dust of Cole Jasper from her shoes, and walk out the door. But then what? She thought of Elliot and Jenny.

Her throat was tight and dry as she turned back. Lil looked as though she'd swallowed lye, and Abbie guessed she didn't appreciate the interruption. Abbie forced her voice to sound frank and disinterested. "Very well, I'm asking."

Cole reached for his hat, put it on, and tipped it to Lil. Then he turned to Abbie. "After you."

Abbie couldn't get outside fast enough. His insolence burned her. She hadn't expected him to come right away, hadn't expected . . . To her dismay she realized she was shaking. Well, what did she expect? It was too much! John Mason dead, Skeeter and Curtis sick, and now Breck . . . then Cole and his money . . .

The thought put steel in her spine. If she made what she should from this sale, she'd pay back every cent he'd squirreled by her to Breck. She imagined stuffing it into his fist and showing him the door. What if he wouldn't take it? What if he expected something else? What could he possibly want from her—an apology? An easing of his conscience? Abbie whirled and unintentionally smacked into his chest, then jumped back as though scalded.

"Pardon me." Cole's tone was brazen, but he didn't smile.

"If you won't accept pay, what's in this for you?"

He hooked his thumbs into his belt. "You got a job needs doin'; I'm doin' it."

"Why?"

He looked over his shoulder, then back. "As I recall, you asked."

"I don't want you to think—I mean, this is a job only, nothing more. Normally I'd pay . . ." She stared at the ground, at his boots, at the boardwalk, across the street.

"I ain't sure what you're goin' on about, but if you're concerned at my motives, you can rest easy. I ain't lookin' to marry a widow."

Abbie felt the breath leave her chest. How could he? *Oh, Lord, I can't do this.* The hatred boiled up and overwhelmed her. She looked straight into Cole's eyes. "I'm sorry I bothered you, Cole Jasper. It was a momentary lapse in my good judgment. Please, don't let me keep you from your . . . entertainment." She spun and stalked to her horse, wishing Zephyr had wings. Halfway to the ranch, she dismounted, ran as hard as her own legs would go, then screamed and screamed to the wind.

Cole stood in the street, watching her go, then took off his hat and ran his fingers through his hair. He hadn't intended to provoke her like that, but the feel of her against his chest had churned emotions he thought long dead. One thing was certain: her opinion of him hadn't changed. He drew a heavy breath.

Mr. Farrel, I wonder if you realized what you was askin'.

He replaced his hat and crossed the street to Scotch. He'd find out from Breck what they were up against and get the job done. It wouldn't be easy. But he had made a promise. And he meant to keep his word.

◆◆◆◆◆◆◆

Abbie walked the boundary of the south range, Zephyr's reins in hand. The beef herd was separated and waiting, ready to cover her debts for some time to come, but she had no way to get them to market. Could she take them herself?

She'd watched the men on occasion. She could rope a horse but lacked the strength to haul in a steer. She could snap a whip and whistle and shout. If it were just a matter of keeping them moving . . . What was she thinking? She didn't even know where to go.

She may as well face it. She'd thrown away her chance to drive the herd to market. What now? She could beg from Pa and Grant, no matter what the cost to them. Between them they might cover the debt for a month or two. By then Breck and the others would be over the typhoid. But what if they didn't recover? What if she had to start over with men she didn't know, didn't trust?

How could she keep the ranch going? Must she lose that next? *Why, Lord? Haven't I tried? Haven't I listened and worked and served? Must I have nothing left?* No, she couldn't think like that. She had the children. It struck terror in her soul to think she'd offended God with her questions. What if He required the children, as well?

She would die. It appalled her how often she thought of that. But it was true nonetheless. If anything happened to Elliot and Jenny, she would have nothing to keep the breath in her body. Not even the land spoke to her anymore. It had become too much of a struggle.

Maybe she should let it go, take the money Mr. Driscoll offered . . . and what? The blackness of her mood sank to her feet and they dragged in the buff-colored grasses. She smelled the sage and felt the breeze. It had an early autumn feel to it. The season was changing, and so was her life.

She felt a pain as real as any fleshly hurt. What if she let the ranch go? She could find a position teaching, enough to support herself and the children. She'd keep whatever she made on the sale for Elliot, his inheritance from . . .

Oh, Monte. You must understand. I can't do it alone. I can't do it without you. I'm not even sure I want to. What is the Lucky Star without you? Barren land too stubborn to yield anything but trouble.

Abbie kicked at a yucca—the all but indestructible plant known as the Spanish Bayonet, or soapweed to the Indians. The yuccas would be there generation after generation. *Lord, show me the way. I'm tired and confused.*

Courage.

The word seemed to emanate from her spirit. Abbie closed her eyes and stood with the breeze in her face. Courage. So she couldn't quit. Somewhere inside, she'd known it. But where she would find the strength, only God knew. *God knew.* Did she believe that? She had to. She'd go stark raving mad if she didn't.

Twenty-One

Abbie was hardly surprised when Cole knocked on the door early the next morning. He was too stubborn to let it go, but he looked as though he'd slept as badly as she. Good. She hoped his insolence choked him.

He tipped his hat up. "I cain't find Breck. Thought you might know where he's off to."

She stilled her anger. "He's in the infirmary."

Cole frowned. "He's got the typhoid?"

"That's right."

He released a sharp breath. "Who do you got for the drive?"

"What concern is that of yours?"

He leaned against the door frame, his hips slack and his mouth a stubborn line. "I told you I'd drive yer cattle. Now, who you got?"

She relented. If Cole was God's answer, she'd bear the cross. "So far Matt Weston's not come down with symptoms."

"And?"

"He's the only one."

"You tellin' me I got one cowboy to drive the herd to Kansas?"

"How many do you need?"

"Fer five hundred head? Two with experience, plus a chuck wagon and wrangler."

"You'll have them," Abbie asserted with more confidence than she felt.

He eyed her dubiously, then hooked his thumbs in his belt. "A'right. I need some money."

"I thought you said you didn't want my money." She sounded as smug as she felt.

"We need supplies."

Now she felt as foolish as she'd sounded. "Oh. Get whatever you need and tell Mr. Simms I'll square with him after the sale."

"Right. You boil up bedding fer four men, have it rolled and ready. I got my own."

"Boil it?"

"If it's been slept on with typhoid."

Abbie shuddered. When Cole left, she found Pearl in the kitchen. "Pearl, pack up whatever James will need to cook with on the trail."

"What you talkin' 'bout? James don' cook."

"We're driving the cattle to Kansas. And he's the cook."

Pearl brought her hands to her hips. "An' what you s'pose you is?"

"Wrangler, I guess. Will and Matt are the cowboys."

"Mistuh Jazzper, he not gonna like this."

"Mister Jasper's not in charge. I am." Abbie untied her apron. "Now, you gather pots and utensils and tell Zena to make bedrolls for four." She was not about to use the men's bedrolls from the bunkhouse. She had enough fresh blankets at hand in the house.

Pearl and Zena would have to see to the animals and all other details in their absence. She sent Will to help Matt ready the herd and prepare the remuda. When Cole came back with the supplies, she'd have everything laid out and ready. Then he'd hardly be able to argue.

When Abbie had seen to all that she could without further direction, she went to her room. Her heart pounded in her chest when she pulled open the wardrobe that held Monte's things. They smelled fresh in the cedar lining. She sagged against the door. She had not opened it since she'd packed them all in there. But she could hardly go on the trail in skirts and petticoats.

With trembling hands she pulled out beige trousers. Monte had been slender enough for a man, but the waist . . . She would cinch it with a belt. Abbie held the sleeve of the fine linen shirt to her cheek. *Oh, Monte.* She stripped to her chemise and pulled the shirt over, then rolled and tied the cuffs with ribbon.

She cinched the pants and pulled her boots over the rolled cuffs, then stood, strangely comforted by Monte's trappings. His scent was destroyed by the cedar smell, but the clothes had touched his skin. She viewed herself in the mirror. She looked like a boy—well, not entirely. But a vest would help with that. She used the green velvet vest from her riding habit. It was fitted and shapely, but it would do.

With a tap on the door, Zena came in and gasped.

Abbie turned. "Here." She handed her a note. "Take this to Mama's." She'd thought better of going in person. She'd never be able to leave Elliot so long if she laid eyes on him for a moment, especially if he was upset by it. Her chest constricted, but she fought it. Mama would see to him and Jenny.

"And this letter is to be delivered to Mr. Driscoll at the bank. It explains my decision and contains another month's interest payment. See that it's in his hands today."

Zena nodded mutely.

Directly after lunch, Abbie put her wide-brimmed hat on her head and tied it at the throat. Pearl puffed her lips and muttered, but she knew better than to argue. Abbie went into the yard when she heard the wagon rumbling in. Cole would have already seen the stacked items to be loaded. He gave her a slow look down, then leaped from the seat. "I see the stuff. You got the men?"

She'd fed the men and given their assignments. "Matt's on the herd. Will's roped in the remuda. He may not be experienced on a drive, but he's worked with the men and he can learn." They could all learn.

Pearl came out with another armload of things for the chuck wagon. She muttered low as she tucked them in among the food-stuffs Cole had already arranged in the wagon bed next to the firewood and tools. James stood hat in hand, looking from one to another of them as though hopeful he would receive a last-minute reprieve.

Cole leaned against the wagon. "So where are the men?"

"James will cook, and I—"

"No way you're ridin' this trail."

Abbie jutted her chin. "I can catch and care for the horses, saddle and unsaddle. I can chop wood and snap a whip if I have to. You said you need a wrangler; here I am."

Cole swore.

Abbie stared, then clamped her mouth shut. If he wanted to show how rough he could be, she'd show how little she cared. "Now, then. This isn't a crack-of-dawn start, but we can cover some miles before sundown."

Cole shook his head, opened his mouth to argue, then clenched his hands and held one finger to her nose. "Get one thing straight. I'm givin' the orders."

She swallowed her retort and nodded curtly.

He shook his head again and unwound Scotch's reins from the hitching post. He was definitely not happy, and she felt little better. Spending the next two months with Cole Jasper would be like bedding down with a rattler, but she'd won, and that gave her a smug satisfaction. Abbie mounted Zephyr and circled around to where Will waited with two dozen horses. He gave her a sly grin, then sobered and joined Cole.

Cole barked orders and they started out, catching up to the herd at the eastern edge of the Lucky Star range. Matt had lowered the fence; they were ready. Cole raised his hand and whistled, and they left the ranch behind. Abbie pulled her kerchief over her mouth as she trailed the line of cattle with the spare horses. She glanced back at James driving the chuck wagon.

Her heart swelled at the sight. They would do it. They would get the cattle to market and make the sale. She felt fleeting gratitude toward Cole Jasper, then reminded herself she'd pay him off at the end. He was necessary at the moment, but she didn't have to be happy about it.

So help me, I'm a bigger fool than I thought. Cole spurred Scotch and set a brisker pace for the cattle than necessary. He'd have the trail broke by tomorrow if he kept it up, but at the moment the thought of pushing the swagger out of Abbie Farrel was incentive enough. He circled round, hollering and snapping the whip.

He ought to use it on her hide for good measure. He passed the remuda without comment, cut in front of the wagon, and started back up the other side. The Herefords hadn't the spunk and muster of the Longhorns, but they were less excitable, too. That didn't mean they wouldn't spook or stampede, but they'd be less inclined to go off at any provocation and wouldn't run so fast and far.

He pushed the pace until they were well away from the home range, cracking his whip and whistling when the cattle lagged. He was riding point with Matt, and across the backs of the animals behind him he saw Will holding his own. *Experienced*. He shook his head.

Abbie Farrel was more than any one man should have to bear. He'd have liked to strangle Breck when he learned he'd told her about the money. He'd hoped to go on providing with her none the wiser. Now he'd have a fight on his hands—as though bustin' broncs and fleecing seasoned gamblers for the extra funds wasn't punishment enough.

Just before sundown he gave word to Matt and Will to throw the herd off the trail to graze and water. Full-bellied, well-watered stock was more prone to rest easy and less likely to spook. Cole searched out a bed ground with good elevation and dry grasses, such as the herd would choose on its own if they were range cattle.

Then he marked their own campsite near a quiet bend of the creek. He'd kept everyone at it hard, as much to wear out the herd as to show Abbie she wasn't as tough as she thought. But watching her dismount, he had a pang of remorse.

She walked stiffly to the wagon, which James had brought to a halt. From the back, she took out stakes and a hammer. At Matt's direction, she strung a rope from the wagon to one stake and then to another, making a triangular corral to hold the horses for the night. This close to home they might be tempted to head for their own pastures. Will helped her get the horses to the water. A few days on the trail, and Matt and Will would be too weary to take on extra work.

Cole shook his head. He'd set a more reasonable pace tomorrow. He strode to the wagon and took the ax from Abbie's hands. "Get some water ready."

She didn't argue. He splintered the log, then set the next one in place until he had enough for a good fire. The night would be cold. That was one reason they shipped cattle in the fall instead of driving them. Water was another. By August and the start of September all the seasonal streambeds would be running low if not dry. But he didn't tell Abbie that. If she thought she could do this, who was he to stop her?

He piled the wood next to the circle of stones James had formed. "Sure hope you cook better'n I do."

"I don' cook at all, Mistuh Jazzper. Mizz Abbie, she say throw it in the pan an' get it hot. I say throw what in?"

"Sheez. What happened to Charlie?"

"His heart give out last year. Mizz Abbie, she feed de men at de house now."

Cole kicked a log back to the pile and stalked to the wagon. Abbie was stirring batter in a bowl.

"What're you doin'?"

She answered without looking. "Making cornbread."

"So you're cook and wrangler?"

"If need be."

"You won't make it one week keepin' that up."

She flashed her eyes at him. "Try me."

They sat around the fire and ate beef and cornbread and beans that tasted better than anything Charlie had ever forked up, and he'd been one of the best chuck-wagon cooks around. Cole glowered. He scraped his plate clean and set it on the stones by the fire.

"Find a saddle, men. Let's close 'em in." He remounted with Matt and Will and began circling the herd tighter and tighter. The muleys naturally hung back until the horned steers had lain down. They'd be the first up, too, a self-protective instinct amidst a crowd of sharp-horned partners.

When they had the herd bunched in and lying down, Cole nodded to Matt. "You got first watch, Matt. Wake me at midnight." He dismounted.

Abbie took the mare's reins. "What about me?"

"What about you?"

"When is my watch? I expect to do my part."

He kicked the dirt and looked out across the open land. If she didn't beat all. "A'right. I'll wake you at two."

She led the horse to the corral and unfastened the saddle. Cole watched her heave it off and carry it to the row of saddles by the wagon. She put a hand to her lower back, then straightened and made her way to the bedding she'd spread between the wagon and the fire. James was already snoring a short distance away.

He turned and dumped his own bedroll on the ground. He sat down, rolled a cigarette, and lit it. He took a long drag, blew the smoke slowly, and shook his head. *A dern fool and no doubt about it.*

Abbie lay in her blankets in too much pain to sleep. She was accustomed to riding, even riding hard, but not for so many hours at the pace Cole set. She more than suspected he'd done it on purpose. They'd changed horses twice before he made camp, and not all the Lucky Star horseflesh had as smooth a stride as Zephyr. She would harden up, she knew, but that was no consolation at the moment.

She leaned on her elbow and watched Matt slowly circling the herd. He sang softly. She couldn't catch the words, but the tune had a loneliness that echoed her own. She missed Elliot so fiercely it hurt. She gripped her ribs and buried her face in the blanket lest she moan and betray her ache.

Was he snug in his bed dreaming beautiful dreams? Did he miss her? How would she ever bear the weeks without him? It wasn't possible, but she had to do it. Without the sale, they'd lose the ranch. And now that she'd decided to do this, she had to give it everything she had. For Elliot. And Jenny.

But not to have his little arms around her, hear his laughter, watch his every expression. Not to whisper in his ear her love, not to smother him with kisses until his giggling grew to a shriek . . . Abbie clutched herself tightly and moaned. If she got through this she'd never leave him again. Never.

Maybe, maybe if they kept up this pace they'd be there in less time. Without driving a herd back home they could go much faster. The whole trip could be done in . . . five weeks, four? She'd work hard, bear any pain without complaining, if it brought her back to Elliot sooner. Maybe the railroad ban would be lifted and she could take the train home. *Oh yes.* She drifted off imagining the reunion with her son.

♦♦♦♦♦♦♦

Cole stood over Abbie. With her face cradled in her arm and her hair lying loose, she looked so sweet it stabbed somewhere deep. The night's chill didn't seem to reach her flushed cheek, and her eyes were soft with shadow. He stooped, refrained from stroking the hair back from her face, and touched her shoulder instead.

She opened her eyes. They looked foggy for a minute, then fastened on him. "My turn?"

"Look, Abbie, why don't you just sleep . . ."

She sat up and shoved the sleeve that had unrolled back up over her hand. Her fingers were clumsy as she searched out the ribbon and retied it. Then she threw the blanket off and stood up. She shivered and bent for the coat she'd laid beside her bedroll. "I just ride and sing, right?"

"And watch."

"For?"

"Wild things, uneasiness in the herd, anything sudden or loud. Look, you ain't—"

"I can do it." She raised her chin. "So go to sleep already."

"Get Will up at four."

She checked the small clock that hung at her neck and nodded.

"I got you saddled."

"Thank you." She walked stiffly to the horse, and he saw her wince when she climbed up. He could kick himself from here to Kansas.

Cole settled into his blankets but couldn't sleep. Just knowing Abbie was out there circling the herd made him restless. It went against everything he knew. When snatches of her song reached him, he would've liked to block his ears, so badly did he want to get up and relieve her. But she insisted on doing this her way.

He rolled to his side and yanked the blanket over his shoulder. But he was still awake when she bent to waken Will. This was going to be one weary trail.

Twenty-Two

In the dim light, Abbie woke so stiff she thought she'd grown paralyzed overnight. She gritted her teeth and forced her legs to slide out from the blanket. Her back ached from her tailbone to her neck, and muscles she didn't know she had cried out for recognition. She pushed herself up and felt in her shoulders and arms the effect of pulling saddles on and off all day.

She'd be lucky to lift one this morning. She caught Cole watching her from where he crouched by the fire, and smoothed away all signs of discomfort. He was ornery enough to turn back if he thought she couldn't make it. She wouldn't give him that satisfaction. He had the fire going and, by the smell, coffee boiled and bacon frying.

Shame rushed to her cheeks that he'd done her part. She saw James chopping kindling with the small hatchet. With his grizzled head and hunched back he looked too old to be out there. Why hadn't someone wakened her? Abbie tried to stand, but pain shot up her legs. She looked to see if Cole had noticed. She'd be mortified if he had to help her up, but he was pouring a steaming cup of coffee.

Steeling herself, she got to her feet. Once there, walking wasn't so bad. She extended her hands to the fire to chase the chill. Cole handed her the cup and she took it. She sipped the coffee. It was strong and bitter but the warmth felt good.

He tossed his cigarette and crushed it with his boot. "If you want the eggs to be edible, you'd best see to them. I got the bacon ready."

229

She went to the wagon and dug the eggs out of the flour barrel. So far none had cracked. She broke each into the bowl and whisked them. The motion sent pain shooting through her arm, but the stiffness was passing.

She forked the bacon to a plate and poured the eggs into the drippings. With a spoon she turned them until they were plump and moist, then she pulled the skillet from the coals. Will held his plate out without hesitation, and she scooped them on with a smile, then served Matt and Cole, then James and herself.

At the rate Cole shoveled it in, they'd be on the trail in no time. Good. The sooner they were done with this, the better. She refused to think of Elliot waking up without her. Had Mama told him it would be a long, long time before she was back? Or was she letting each day tell its own story?

How were Breck and Skeeter and Curtis? She eyed Matt as she scrubbed up the pan. How was it he'd escaped the typhoid? She wiped the pan dry and hung it on the wall of the wagon. A shadow fell over her washtub, and she looked up at Cole.

"Why don't you ride in the wagon today? Will can take the horses, and Matt and I will handle the herd."

"I'm perfectly capable of riding."

Cole swiped his jaw with the back of his hand, then shrugged. "Suit yerself." He walked away and hollered to the men to saddle up.

"I pack it up, Mizz Abbie." James stuffed the bedrolls into the wagon one by one.

She nodded, wiping her hands on her pants. One thing she hadn't thought to bring was an apron, but likely soon enough she wouldn't care. She roped in Starlight, the four-year-old mare, and saddled her. The minute she was up she realized what a mistake she'd made riding the saddle again, but she was not about to let Cole know.

Abbie whistled between her teeth and moved the horses down with the herd to graze. They trailed along gently for two hours while the animals ate; then Cole and Matt and Will began stringing them out, and once again Cole set a brisk pace, though not, she thought, as brisk as the day before.

If she didn't think about it, the pain in her saddle-weary areas was bearable. At least it kept her from brooding on the inner pain of separation. She should have said good-bye. Jenny especially needed that. She was so afraid of losing the people she loved, and Abbie knew that in her own way Jenny loved her.

It wasn't the warm expressive love Abbie might have wanted. It was love on Jenny's terms. Not like Elliot, who seemed to sense her mood and fill the need with nothing spoken between them. How like Monte he was, warm and affectionate. Her horse stumbled and she cried out, then bit her lip against the jarring pain. Starlight was no Zephyr.

Cole circled around, and Abbie straightened in the saddle. The position put pressure on her inner thighs where the pain was worst, but she maintained it until he was past. He didn't turn her way, but she knew he was watching. Let him think what he liked; she could do this.

At noon they spread the cattle and horses out to graze along the trail. Abbie clung to the side of the wagon while James pulled out the pans and lit the fire. She stirred up hash and corn. In the Dutch oven she soaked dried apple slices in cider and brown sugar and topped them with dumpling batter. She covered the pan and set it in the coals to simmer while the hash heated.

Her coffee was neither strong nor bitter, she noted with pride when she took a sip, and Will and Matt were effusive in their praise of her apple dumplings. Even though the sun was hot, there was an autumn tinge to the air. By evening it would be brisk, and she guessed this night would be colder than last. Well, there were extra blankets should they need them.

They rode again, changing horses once in midafternoon. Freckles, her spirited gelding, had a choppy gait, and riding him was sheer misery until they finally stopped when the sun was no more than a sliver over the distant mountains. Abbie could scarcely remember seeing a sundown that didn't silhouette the rugged peaks, which were now dwarfed by the expanse of empty land between them and her.

Abbie gripped the pommel and prepared to dismount. She willed her leg to come over the saddle and swing down, but it wouldn't obey. She closed her eyes and grit her teeth against the pain, then startled at the grasp on her waist. Cole eased her down, and though the shame of it sent fire to her cheeks, she allowed him. Otherwise she'd spend the night on the gelding's back, and as far as she was concerned, she never wanted to see that horse again.

"Take it slow." He supported her forearm and led her toward the fire ring James was building.

James had loaded the stones in and out of the wagon each time they set up camp where no stones were at hand. As she walked stiffly toward him, she hoped this would not prove too much of a strain on him. She didn't know how old he was, but he'd seemed bent and grizzled the first time she met him at Monte's door.

Cole stopped her four steps short of the blaze. "Stand here a minute."

His command was gentle, and she obeyed. The last thing she wanted was to sit on the hard ground. Besides, if she went down she'd be there for good. He came back from the wagon with a bedroll and set it behind her.

"How can I cook, sitting on that?"

"I'll cook tonight."

"You?"

"I've kept alive, ain't I?" He nudged her down.

The soft roll was immensely better than the hard saddle. She looked up to see Matt tending the horses. Across the camp, Will looked little better than she. He was no doubt every bit as saddle sore and bone tired. She sent him a weak smile, and he returned it. Well, they'd each have a few hours before their watch required them back in the saddle.

Cole's stew was tolerable if a little scorched. A touch of sage and parsley or any seasoning besides his liberal use of pepper would have helped, but she was hungry enough to enjoy it regardless. She washed it down with coffee, though she'd have preferred tea. Why hadn't she thought to bring some? She should have known Cole wouldn't stock it.

She spread out the bedroll where she sat. Since James managed the cleaning up, she may as well take the chance to sleep. In the deepening darkness, while Cole and Matt circled the herd to make them lie down, she knelt and prayed. So many people were heavy on her heart, not least the men fighting the typhoid.

She prayed they'd recover, she prayed the fever would not spread, she prayed for Nora and her friends. And she prayed for Mama and Pa and the children. Her chest squeezed. No. She would not fear for them.

Mama and Pa lived away from town, they pumped their water, and they had not taken the drifter in. Her children were safe. Elliot was safe. She opened her eyes and saw Cole had returned. He was seated cross-legged on the ground, watching from across the fire. He sipped his coffee but didn't turn away.

The intensity of his expression kindled her resentment. She lifted the blanket and slipped beneath. The fire crackled, and tiny flecks of light leaped up and vanished. Her muscles throbbed, but her eyes were heavy and she let them close in blessed oblivion.

Cole frowned. The only way he'd get through eight weeks of this was to put her out of his mind and let her fend for herself. He could do it, too, if he had a mind to. Problem was, he was so starved for just the look of her that he couldn't turn the other way. And when he looked, he'd notice how brave and tenacious she was and get to thinking of all the times she'd surprised him.

Like that time with Buck Hollister and the Comanches. Hearing her tell it the morning after she'd returned safe from capture by outlaws and rescue by Indians had sealed her in his heart. How many years ago was it now? Seven, eight? That she could hardly stand the sight of him didn't change it, except to keep him mindful of what a dern foolish thing it was.

He swirled the coffee in the bottom of his cup, then tossed it to the flames. Morning would come too soon to sit brooding now. He climbed into his blankets, but couldn't get out of his head the feel of her waist in his hands. He scowled. She'd ride in the wagon tomorrow if he had to tie her to the seat.

✦✦✦✦✦✦✦

Abbie woke to the first traces of dawn. Cole was stoking the fire. He laid a piece of log across the top. Did he never sleep? She realized with a start that she'd missed her watch. Had he tried to wake her? No. He'd meant to take her watch. He felt sorry for her.

Her ire brought her fully awake, and she sat up. Cole glanced over. She stood before he could lend a hand. The pain in her muscles was acute but not debilitating. Maybe sleeping through had helped. Maybe she was growing accustomed. She walked to the wagon and took out the pot for coffee.

She dipped it in the water barrel and brought it to the fire. "I'll thank you to wake me next time."

"It don't matter."

"I intend to do my part. Will's as sore as I am, but I imagine you woke him."

"If he takes on a man's job, he oughta do it like a man."

"Then maybe you ought to consider me a man."

From where he squatted, elbows on thighs, he glanced up and held her in his gaze. "That ain't rightly possible."

She turned and stalked to the wagon, returned to lay the greased griddle on the fire rack, then went to the wagon again without a word. With vicious strokes she stirred the batter for the hotcakes. She hoped they choked Cole Jasper.

She left the cleaning up to James and went to water the horses. Will offered to do it, but she refused. She felt battered and stiff and wanted nothing more than to be in her soft bed with Elliot in her arms, but she'd be darned if she'd give in to Cole's opinion. She had the first horse saddled when he joined her at its side.

"Ride the wagon today, Abbie."

"I will not."

"I'm not askin'."

She faced him squarely. "Let's get one thing straight. I don't need you to look after me. We both know how that turns out."

She saw him stiffen, but her vitriol was unleashed and she wanted to sink it deep. "The only back you watch is your own." She watched his jaw tighten. "And another thing. I don't want you slackening the pace. The sooner we're through with this the better."

"You tellin' me how to do my job?"

"If I have to."

"If you want yer herd delivered alive, you'll leave it to me." He took her arm and walked her sharply to the wagon. "You're ridin' here today."

"I'll ride where I please and keep the pace."

"I ain't gonna push these animals now that they're trail broke, and I ain't gonna bury you."

The pain exploded inside her. She looked at him with all the venom that coursed her veins. "Why not, Cole? It's what you do best."

Whatever effect her words had, he kept it from his face. His eyes were mirrors, flatly reflecting her venom. He let go her arm and walked away. The fury left her cold. She felt a hard knot in her stomach and a weariness deeper than her muscles. She looked up at James, who'd taken his place on the wagon seat. His old, dark face was creased with concern. Silently she climbed up beside him.

♦♦♦♦♦♦♦

Selena Martin held Elliot to her chest and rocked. That he missed Abbie was obvious, but then how could it not be so? She'd barely had him out of her sight these four years, and now it was as though she'd gone out of his life. His small sobs stilled as she rocked.

She glanced at Jenny reading by the fire. She'd put on a hard little shell and pretended she didn't care taffy that her auntie was gone. Selena knew different, but the child didn't show it. She kept up her charade with painful dignity.

Jenny talked on and on about the things she had, as though recounting the list would keep them from disappearing. She talked about her dolls and her books and her carved animals. She talked about her mare and the barn cats and even the cattle. But she didn't talk about Abbie, and she didn't cry.

Elliot cried and took comfort here against her chest. Selena sighed. She had read Abbie's note three times before she believed her daughter had actually gone on the cattle drive. Whatever possessed her? Didn't she realize the danger, the hardship, and risk to herself and the children both?

Learning from Pearl that Cole Jasper had returned and was driving the herd for Abbie had assuaged some of the worry. He was a trustworthy, capable man. Still . . . Selena stroked Elliot's cheek. She hoped Abbie knew what she was doing.

Twenty-Three

Cole stood looking out at the darkening sky. The thunderheads were heavy with rain, but that wasn't what concerned him. It was the noise that went along with them. He'd set up camp early, suspecting trouble, and it looked like trouble was indeed rolling their way.

He glanced at Matt and Will sitting by the fire in the fading light of day. It would take all three of them to keep the herd together this night, circling opposite directions so no steer could get loose without being sighted. Even so, stopping five hundred head was no easy task for three men if it came to it.

Abbie dished up plates of beans and biscuits and handed them to the men at the fire. She set Cole's on a rock and walked back to the wagon. He strode over, took it, and went back to watching the storm. It was moving their way, no denying it. He ate the food absently, then returned the plate to the stone.

"No one's sleepin' till this storm is past."

Matt scratched his hand through his tangled brown hair. "I reckoned that."

Abbie came and picked up his plate to wash.

"Abbie, I want you and James to bed down in the wagon." Her lips parted, but he stanched her argument. "It ain't no time to get maidenly. There's a storm comin' that's got this herd jittery, an' I don't want you trampled if they bolt."

"What about the rest of you?"

"We'll be on horseback till it passes."

"Then I'll ride with you. You'd have another hand if I were a man, and I doubt you'd order him to sleep with James."

Two weeks hadn't changed her tune. "If I had another hand, he'd know what to do in a stampede."

She brought up her chin. "So tell me."

"It ain't a matter of tellin'. It's a matter of knowin'. Here." He pressed a hand to his gut.

Abbie turned away and washed the plate, then loaded the supper things into the wagon. The wind gusted and flapped the canvas cover. She flipped the hair from her eyes. He couldn't tell whether her expression was submissive or resistant. She'd built up walls so high, he doubted she was in there at all.

And that suited him fine ... as long as she stayed out of his way. He strode to Scotch and mounted. Matt sent him a questioning look. "I'll tell you when I need ya." He rode out among the grazing herd, sensed their disquiet. It was time to ring them in. He doubted they'd lie down, but at least packed together they'd be inclined to run the same direction.

He took a good look at the lead steer. He'd keep his eye on that one. If he ran, he'd have a contingent. That steer with the white eye-patch was jumpy already. He'd herd him deep inside where he'd feel the others around him. Several of the muleys clustered together away from the rest. They could make a heap of trouble if they'd a mind.

Cole rode back to the fire. "Let's put 'em to bed."

Will and Matt joined him and they circled the herd in. Any skittish ones, he pressed through, keeping the solid steers to the outer edges. As he'd guessed, they kept their feet. He heard rumbling in the sky, but that wasn't the kind of thunder that brought trouble. It was the flashes of lightning and the sudden cracks of thunder that sent a herd careening.

With the three of them, it would be all they could do to keep this a short night. Great drops of rain started and gathered speed until the water ran from his hat brim. He motioned Matt and Will to their positions, and together they circled, singing low in the scant hope they'd soothe the herd. *Ip-e-la-ago, go 'long little doggie, You'll make a beef steer by-an'-by . . .*

The rumbling came again overhead, and Cole tensed. He willed himself to relax. Nothing set the cattle on edge so quick as a nervous cowboy. Scotch held steady. That horse was like his own flesh, though he was growing too old for this kind of business. Cole schooled his mind to focus on the soothing rhythm of horse and song. The rain beat down, and Cole circled, slow and steady, slow and steady.

Abbie watched Cole position himself between the distant herd and the camp. The rain had slackened to a thin drizzle, though the sky hung heavy and ominous. Water ran from his slicker, and his head was bowed, hat pulled low. There was no glow of a cigarette. Instead she heard the wavering tones of a harmonica. She'd not heard him play before. Maybe it was how he soothed the cattle in a storm.

It had a comforting tone, she had to admit, and she recognized the tune, "Wayfaring Stranger." Where had Cole learned the Negro spiritual? She knew it from James's singing while he worked. Once again, she realized how little she knew about Cole Jasper.

And that was just fine. The less she knew the better. Once she had felt close to him, trusted him. Now she knew better. But wasn't she trusting him again? The thought nagged. She trusted his expertise with the cattle. Monte had done as much. But then, Monte had trusted Cole with his life.

The pain gnawed. She had never asked Cole exactly what happened. It was enough that he had failed. She recalled the night Cole brought Monte home beaten by Captain Gifford, felt again her fury that he'd let Monte go in alone. So what that Monte had ordered it. Cole should have known.

Yet he had risked his life to rescue her from the rustler. Time and again he'd been there when she needed him. She didn't want to think about that. She pulled the coat around her shoulders and peered out of the hole in the canvas.

James sat hunched in the other end of the wagon, as uncomfortable as she. Who did Cole think he was, ordering people to do unnatural things? Maidenly indeed. But then he might think nothing of "bedding down" with a strange woman. She recalled his hand under Lil's and frowned.

Lightning streaked the sky and thunder cracked. She could just make out Matt and Will still circling the far edge of the herd in the near darkness. In a gust of wind, she saw Cole raise his head. The harmonica stopped. The storm seemed to hold its breath. Then suddenly lightning slashed down with a queer buzz and split a tree on the low hill behind the herd.

The fireball sprang up, brilliant in the night. Abbie felt the jolt in the ground beneath the wagon. Will's horse reared, then the sudden bawling and trampling drowned out the fresh torrent from the sky. Cole wheeled and fired his gun, spurring Scotch to the side to point the herd. But the cattle kept coming. They would trample him. Again and again he tried to point in, but the force of the rushing animals withstood his effort.

Abbie sat forward and gripped the wet edge of canvas. She watched with fascination and trepidation as Scotch spun and veered sharply, then leaped up a grassy mound and charged ahead of the oncoming rush. Why didn't Cole move aside? He could get out of the way—The sudden realization choked her. He was trying to turn them away from the wagon.

He cut across and fired again and again into the ground just ahead of the steer's hooves. The front steers balked, but others piled on and the lead steers went down beneath a rush of hooves. Cole fired again, riding hard, his gun making firefly flashes.

She smelled the rain, the gun smoke, the herd. She could almost smell the fear. Cole dropped his spent shells and reloaded even as he charged toward the herd. He shot the ground before the oncoming tide. The lead cattle turned aside, and like a wave the others followed, scarcely eighty feet from the wagon.

Abbie felt the vibration of their hooves and loosed her breath. Would they stay turned? Would they scatter? Cole rode hard alongside, shooting and shouting. Matt was with him now, and they rode hard together though their voices were swallowed by the storm.

Lightning flashed and thunder cracked. The pounding of hooves continued as the herd passed out into the night. The rain fell so thickly Abbie could no longer see the rushing animals. Thunder continued in the sky.

"Mistuh Jazzper, he a good man."

Abbie turned to see the whites of James's eyes. What did he expect her to say? She sank wearily down. Yes, Cole had done his job. She shuddered to think of the cattle charging the wagon. She had a clear enough memory of Monte's crushed and trampled buggy when the Longhorns stampeded over it.

Once again Cole had risen to the task of keeping her safe. Why, why had he not done as much for Monte? She wanted to scream, to slap James for his insolence. How dare he suggest Cole was good? What good was he when Monte needed him?

Great gasping sobs seized her at the image of Monte's torn and battered abdomen, his shattered ribs and cold, lifeless flesh. But she staunchly thrust the sobs away, clenched her teeth against the tears. She hated Cole Jasper with as much passion as she'd loved Monte. And if James said one word more, she *would* slap him.

♦♦♦♦♦♦♦

Cole pushed Scotch to stay alongside the herd until he knew all the steers had passed the camp. Each new flash of lightning and crack of thunder renewed the herd's terror and kept them running. Scotch was fagged, but Cole kept on.

If the cattle scattered, they'd lose precious time—time they didn't have. Again and again he pointed in, trying to turn the cattle, force the tide. If he could make the cattle mill, the men would keep them circling until they ran out of steam. But he couldn't do it. He didn't have men enough to stop the flow.

The ground was fast becoming a mire. The cattle would have to slow. If he just kept alongside ... A lightning flash illuminated the jut of rocks, and Cole swerved too late. Scotch screamed as his foreleg caught the edge of rock, and they went down. Cole landed hard on the jagged rocks. Pain shot through his side and head, and his leg was caught beneath the thrashing horse.

Pricks of light danced in Cole's eyes as he pulled himself loose and grabbed the horse's head in his arms. He spoke low, and the horse calmed, though he could see its eyes stayed wide with pain. Slowly he made his way over Scotch. He ran his hands down the bloody foreleg, and his stomach lurched when he felt the bone shift.

He closed his eyes and clenched his teeth, then smoothed his hands over the horse's shoulder. Why Scotch? He should have taken another horse, any other horse. He should have slowed, not pressed so hard. The last of the cattle passed at a lope. They were tiring, some limping. If he'd only held on a few minutes more.

Cole lay for a long time with his head to Scotch's neck, long enough for the herd to make some distance. Then he pulled his hat from the mud running off the rocks and stood. Scotch thrashed, then lay back. That horse would never carry him again. He felt a sick ache in his gut when he pulled the gun from its holster. He drew a long slow breath, then held the barrel to Scotch's head. "I'm sorry, old boy. You been fine." His voice broke as he pulled the trigger.

◆◆◆◆◆◆◆

Abbie stirred from her doze to see Matt riding in. The rain had stopped, though the air still hung heavy, and thunder could be heard a long way off. Dawn would come soon. Quietly, so as not to disturb James, she slipped from the wagon.

There was no stoking the coals. The whole pit was filled with rainwater. But she dug a new hole, took dry kindling from the wagon, and started a blaze in the new fire ring. The men would need something hot to chase the chill. She filled the coffeepot and set it to boil on the grate as Matt stooped beside the fire.

Will rode in and half fell from his horse. He picked himself up and staggered to the fire, where he dropped to the ground and rubbed his shoulder. He looked totally spent.

Abbie handed him a blanket. "Coffee'll be ready in a minute. Where's Cole?"

Matt drained the rain from his hat brim. "Had to put his horse down. I gotta bring him a new mount, but he said to make sure y'all were okay first."

"What happened to Scotch?"

"Broke his leg on some rocks."

Abbie handed Matt a cup of coffee. Will shook his head to the cup she offered and lay down on the wet ground. With a groan he fell asleep. Abbie pulled the blanket over his shoulders. Matt drained his cup and stood wearily. How could he go on?

Abbie straightened. "I'll bring a fresh horse to Cole if you tell me where he is."

"No need. I'll get 'im myself."

In the east the sky lightened to a dull gray. James woke and went about chopping kindling and slicing the slab of bacon. She laid the bacon in the pan to fry and mixed up oats and water to boil.

It was cooked and bubbling before Cole rode in with Matt. In the predawn dim, she could not make out his features, but he moved like he was played out . . . or worse. He dismounted and staggered. Was he injured? A guilty concern stirred inside her.

He had thrown his slicker off, and she saw blood on the side of his shirt and a gash at the back of his head. He slumped against the back of the wagon and lit a cigarette. Abbie dished a plate and carried it to him.

"No thanks." He didn't look at her. "We got work to do."

"You can't do any more without rest and food."

A drop of water fell from his mustache as he drew on the cigarette and blew the smoke out slowly. "I got cattle scattered across Kansas, injured an' lame. I ain't got time to eat."

"Take off your shirt."

He looked at her, unmoving.

"You're bleeding." She kept her voice flat and unemotional.

"Never mind."

Abbie drew herself up. "Cole Jasper, you may not care what condition you're in, but I have cattle to drive, and to do it I need you."

He snorted. "Well, when you put it so kindly . . ." He unbuttoned his shirt and pulled it off.

She saw him wince, but he undid the torn long johns underneath and pulled them down, baring a lean, muscled torso. His side was scraped and bruised, with a gash beneath his ribs that was caked with mud and crusted blood. Whatever he hit had cut through both layers of clothing and a good deal of skin. Abbie glanced up, but he was looking past her.

He tossed the cigarette and ground it out. "I could use a cup of coffee."

"James, get Cole some coffee and find me the medicine box." She took a cloth, went to the fire, and dipped it in the boiling water. By the time she was back at his side it was hot but not scalding. She touched it to his wound and felt him recoil. "I'm sorry."

"Just git it over with."

The dirt was embedded in the skin, but she rubbed as carefully as she could. Fresh blood flowed from the gash. "That'll need to be sewn." She poured a small amount of carbolic acid into the wound, and Cole hissed in his breath sharply. She boiled the needle, then threaded it with gut from the medicine box. Putting it through his flesh nearly turned her stomach, but he bore it stoically.

"Now eat your breakfast while I see to your head."

"It's just a scratch," he protested.

"It's a knot and a cut. Must you be so stubborn?"

He took up the plate and shoveled the oats into his mouth.

Again Abbie wet the cloth and washed the wound. "It's not as bad as the other. I'll just wrap it."

"Be quick about it. I gotta see to them steers."

"You can't do it now. Besides, unless you intend to do it alone, you'll have to wait. Matt and Will are dead to the world."

"I'll rouse 'em."

"No, you won't. This is one time you're taking my orders."

He caught her hand as she wrapped the bandage around his head. "If you want your herd to make it to market, they need doctorin' as much as I do. I already put down one animal. I ain't hankerin' to do others."

Abbie spoke gently. "Just a few hours' rest. Will can't do any more, and I don't think you can, either." She looked into his eyes. They were more gray than green and the whites were shot with red. "Sleep a little. The cattle will fend for themselves."

He released her hand and looked away. "A'right. Wake me in an hour." He turned away.

"Cole . . ."

He paused but didn't turn.

"I'm sorry about Scotch."

He winced when he pulled the bedroll from the wagon. He carried it close to the fire and spread it on the ground. She could have sworn his eyes closed before his head hit.

Abbie rubbed her hands over her face. While the men slept, she'd take advantage of the swollen waters in the creek bed. She took a bar of soap and her honeysuckle rinse and headed for the water. It was cold and fast, but she stripped to her undergarments and waded in, then sank down to her neck.

With a quick breath she plunged her head in, then washed. The weeks in the saddle had left her little opportunity to wash more than her face and hands each morning and night. Even this cold, unfriendly water was welcome. She scrubbed her hair and applied the rinse, then let the current drag the curls one last time.

Climbing up the bank, she squeezed out the excess water and shook her hair down her back. She shivered, then realized she was shaking with more than the cold. Her herd was scattered, her men exhausted, Cole's horse lost. Though they had plenty more in the remuda, she knew Scotch was not just another horse to him.

She recalled the time he'd loaned her Scotch when Shiloh lost a shoe, how he'd come upon her walking the lamed horse on Monte's range and sent her home on Scotch. Then he'd nursed Shiloh's leg and helped cover her dishonest behavior from Monte. Though she had confessed it to Monte herself, Cole had not betrayed her.

Abbie frowned. Seeing him without his shirt and ministering

to his injury had unsettled her more than she wanted to admit. She'd felt blessedly removed from any romantic inclinations. The nine marriage proposals she'd received in the last two years had failed to kindle the remotest desire, yet scrubbing the dirt from the cuts on the man she despised had left her shaking.

What was wrong with her? She pulled on Monte's pants, but they were so dusty and worn she hardly recognized them as his. It jolted her. What if her memory faded, as well? What if she couldn't conjure the look of him in her mind even as she couldn't recognize the pants? She dropped to her knees.

Oh, God, don't let me forget. I don't care how it hurts. Don't let me forget. She'd fallen asleep in the wagon without thinking of Elliot. How could she have gone one night without hurting for him? How could she have felt tenderly for Cole's loss of his horse, when he was the cause of all her pain?

Abbie pulled on the shirt and clenched it tightly. *Monte. There will never be anyone for me but you.* She stayed on her knees, willing the pain to subside, then rolled the shirt sleeves and stood. If it weren't for Will, she'd wake Cole now and send him off. But Will was exhausted by the hard work and long hours. Last night had nearly pushed him to breaking. She knew the look of it. She'd been there herself more than once this trip.

◆◆◆◆◆◆

Cole woke himself and rolled over. The sun was a good way above the horizon, though masked by clouds. It had been well over an hour since he'd dropped off before dawn. He sat up. "Aah." The place Abbie had stitched hurt worse than it had when it happened. He looked down inside his long johns at the bandage. No fresh blood.

He stood and almost whistled for Scotch, then remembered. The glazing of that horse's eyes would be with him a long time. He frowned. Why hadn't Abbie wakened him? He strode over, nudged Will with a boot, then gave Matt the same. "Git up. We got work to do."

He looked up at the clouds. The rain might hold off a short

spell yet, but they'd have wet work ahead. He watched Abbie climb from the wagon. She had his shirt in hand as she approached.

"Here. It's mended."

He took the shirt. "I'd've rather you woke me like I told you to."

"Then I guess we're even." She walked to the line of horses. "When you're dressed we can go."

He looked at the shirt and frowned. The feel of her hands was too fresh in his mind. While she'd doctored him she almost seemed to care. Obviously he was mistaken. He threw on the shirt and buttoned it, then pulled his coat over and hollered, "Move it, ya lazy dogs, 'fore I put lead in yer tails."

Will dragged himself up painfully, and Matt stretched.

Cole scowled. "This ain't a babysittin' picnic. Move it. We got injured cattle to tend." His head throbbed as he stalked to the horses and looked them over. He untied and saddled Violet, the bay mare.

He nodded to Abbie, who had Zephyr saddled and ready. "The first matter of business is to cut out the injured and see to them. Then we'll do a count and look for strays. We'll be lucky to move out by noon."

She nodded. "Then let's not waste any more time."

Now, there was a woman for you. She won't wake you when you say, then accuses you of wasting time. He mounted and spurred the mare. Abbie Farrel was far and away more trouble than any herd put together.

By the time the rain started, they'd cut out twenty-nine steers and treated their injuries the best they could. Charlie had been the one to handle that in the past, but Cole knew enough animal medicine to get by. Three cattle were dead from trampling, and most were sore footed and battered, but in spite of that, they'd come out better than they might have.

Twenty-Four

Reverend Shields read the funeral passage over the three new graves. When would it end, this scourge of the Lord? For so it seemed, like a plague of Egypt taking the strong with the weak. Forty-two graves from the typhoid in three weeks. Some came through, but clearly two out of three would leave this life.

He sighed and closed the Bible with weary hands. Had he done his job? Had he brought these souls to peace and everlasting life? He was thankful for Father O'Brien. The man had an unquenchable strength and compassion. He knelt beside the cots, bathed the disease-racked bodies, spoke of the goodness of the Lord.

Winthrop Shields felt an amazing peace to be sharing this ministry with another, even one such as Father O'Brien with his Irish Catholic ways. They'd gone round and round on their theology, but for all that, he liked the priest immensely. Between them, they might yet reap a harvest for the Lord.

He was not one to disdain deathbed conversions, and the pitiful truth was that when death's door yawned it was an easier thing to say yes to God than when all seemed right with the world. He glanced at Ethan Thomas, standing shovel in hand. As the deaths continued, fewer and fewer were willing to stick their necks out and help with the bodies, live or dead. Some who would volunteer were turned away if they had wives and children at home.

Father O'Brien had given his people strict instructions to keep to themselves until the scourge was past. It was sensible, he said, given the good Lord's willingness to pass them by. But the priest stayed day and night in the infirmary, as did Doctor Barrow and Ethan Thomas.

Ethan had lost a wife and son to cholera before coming west. He'd confided it in a rare moment of tears when young Billy Hamilton went to meet the Lord. Winthrop closed his eyes against the memory. Mrs. Hamilton, so close to bringing new life into the world, had put her firstborn into the ground with agonizing sobs. And now her husband thrashed with the fever.

Reverend Shields raised a prayer of desperation. *How long, oh, Lord, will you keep your face from us?* But did not the everlasting promise transcend this vale of tears? He made his way back to the infirmary and paused at the door. *Oh, Lord, is it wrong to long for a moment's peace, to ache for bodily rest even as my soul thirsts for you?* He climbed one stair and the next, then went inside. Doctor Barrow nearly collided with him.

Now, there was a man walking in exhaustion. Too many depended on him; too many thought he could do the impossible. On his shoulders rested the hopes of the stricken and their loved ones. He seemed to have aged years in the last month. *Give him strength, Father, to carry on. Bless him with the Healer's hands.*

Doctor Barrow gripped Father O'Brien's shoulder where he knelt beside Breck Thompson. "It's over, Father. There are others who need you."

Father O'Brien opened his eyes and slowly rose from his knees. "Sure and it's the Lord they're needin' more than my weak comfort."

Winthrop Shields looked down. Breck Thompson, Skeeter, and John Mason gone, and Curtis still fighting. Mrs. Farrel would have much to face when she returned. He shook his head. She'd not been the same person since Monte's passing. Outwardly, perhaps. Her service to others had remained fervent, but with a desperation it hurt him to see.

God wanted service out of love for Him, not fear. And was it fear that kept her alone? He knew several men had recently asked for her hand, but she had refused them all. He saw her less frequently since Father O'Brien had come and now ministered to her soul in the way she was accustomed.

But on occasion she came to his own little church and heard him preach. And she always greeted him warmly, though he saw the bleakness in her eyes. That was a woman at odds with God, no matter how well she deceived herself. Sometimes he thought it was easier for those who openly raged at the Lord. Their grieving passed. Hers, it seemed, did not.

Had they shared a spiritual like-mindedness, he would court her himself, though he doubted she'd have him. It was ludicrous to think he could succeed where so many failed. He lifted up a prayer for her. *Send her a helpmate, Lord. She needs it more than she knows.*

✦✦✦✦✦✦✦

Joshua Martin sank to his chair at the table in his warm kitchen and eyed Selena at the stove, as slender at fifty-one as she'd been at sixteen. Well, perhaps she'd settled some. Gray streaked her hair like silver veins on brown stone walls, and her hands were no longer supple and smooth. But he loved her fiercely.

Elliot suddenly appeared and jumped into his lap. Joshua squeezed the boy. He'd attended six burials that day, and it was good to feel his grandson's life and energy. One of those put in the ground that afternoon was Breck Thompson, Abbie's head man.

She'd lost three good cowhands, and Curtis hung on by his teeth. How would she keep the ranch now? He puzzled the question without finding a solution. Was it every father's wish to ease his children's burdens? Didn't it seem Abbie'd had more than her share?

If he had the funds to pay off her debts, he would do it in a breath. But though he owned his land clear and editing the newspaper had kept them fed over the years, he had nothing to call savings. He sighed.

"Are you tired, Great Uncle Josh?"

He turned to see Jenny standing at his side. She held herself too stiffly for a little girl. He reached over and tugged her braid. "Yep, I'm tired. But not too tired for a hug from my little grand-niece."

She dutifully hugged his side while Elliot squeezed his neck again for good measure. Tucker leaned on the wall and grinned when Joshua sent him a helpless glance. That boy was turning out fine, and he thanked God again that Abbie had seen fit to put him in their care.

He just might be the one to carry on his work. Tucker loved working at his side on the land, but even more, he was showing an amazing propensity for words. He may be the next editor of the *Rocky Bluffs Chronicle*. But then, the boy was only eleven, and he'd had similar hopes for Grant before his son turned to law.

It had been a worthy choice, too. He clearly excelled in his profession. Even Judge Wilson admitted as much, though having his daughter wed Grant may have colored that opinion. Grant's choice of Marcy Wilson had surprised him less than some of the others. And whereas Abbie still struggled to get along with her, he had a soft spot for the girl.

All in all—he looked around the room—life was good. He had much to be thankful for. None of his loved ones had contracted the fever, though he'd lost some friends. That thought saddened him. Doctor Barrow had an impossible task, God help him. Joshua gave Jenny and Elliot another squeeze, too aware of the frailty of this life.

◆◆◆◆◆◆◆

Doctor Elias Barrow plunged his arms into the steaming bowl and scrubbed to the elbows. At last he felt he could see light at the end of the tunnel. The quarantine had kept the fever from spreading to those who had not contracted the disease directly from the water or the infected man.

Once he had learned the location of the man's camp, his orders that no one use the creek water until the contamination passed had limited the cases far better than he had hoped. And though the infirmary was still packed with sick, few new cases

came in. He believed most of these left would live. They had survived the worst, and now it was a matter of returning strength to
their bodies.

He would not count in his mind the numbers he had lost,
though he kept a tally for his records. He could not focus on that.
Medicine was a chancy calling for one who could not separate his
heart from his work. He looked over the room in the near darkness of the few lamps he kept burning through the night, and
dared to hope.

◆◆◆◆◆◆◆

Horace Driscoll sat at his desk and cracked his knuckles, an
uncouth habit, but one he allowed himself when the bank was
empty. He eyed the ledger before him with decided satisfaction.
It was not that he delighted in the misfortune that was overtaking
so many in the town, but after all, one had to be practical, especially in banking.

Tragedy happened. Typhoid was merely one name for it. And
those like himself who escaped infection had every right, indeed
the responsibility, to carry on. He had the welfare of the town as
well as his own to consider.

He looked down at the page. Those hardest hit by deaths
would be the first to come begging, the proverbial widows and
orphans. He took no pleasure in refusing them, but refuse he
must. He had the integrity of the bank to maintain and his responsibility to his stockholders in the East. That he might personally benefit was only secondary.

His gaze landed on Mrs. Farrel's account. Her property was
the choicest of all. But with three of her men dead and her account delinquent for the first time . . . He scarcely contained the
thought.

No one could accuse him of unfair gain. He was a fair man,
competent and far sighted. But when Mrs. Farrel returned, they
would speak again. And this time she would not dare expel him
from her home. He owned her.

◆◆◆◆◆◆◆

Abbie listened with disbelief to Cole's information. So little? How could she get so little for the herd when they were fine beef stock? Thirteen dollars on the head when they were worth twenty or more?

"We missed the time. The market's glutted. Everyone sold off before us. I found the best price I could."

His words passed over her uselessly. All that work, all that pain, all these weeks away from Elliot and Jenny . . . for what? Could they even make it to spring on what they'd fetch? She dropped her face into her hands.

"I'm sorry, Abbie."

She stiffened. She would not break down in front of Cole. They'd get something, and that was more than she'd have if they hadn't made the drive. She drew a long breath and faced him. "Very well, sell them."

"I can winter them here and try in the spring."

She shook her head. "No, I don't expect that." Nor could she afford it with Driscoll expecting payment. "We'll make the best of what we get. It's just . . ." Her plans for paying off what Cole had sent were foiled. She would not have the satisfaction of settling the score. Nor could she afford to take the train home when they'd need every cent to keep them going until the next sale.

"How long will it take to get home?" Her voice sounded more plaintive than she wanted.

"All depends. Sooner than it took to get here. The horses can make a bit better clip. Reckon it depends on us."

Meaning her. She'd ride in the wagon the whole way if it meant getting home sooner to Elliot. "Then sell the cattle and let's go." Abbie looked down the street. It was hardly the peaceful bustling street of Rocky Bluffs. Dodge City was coarse and loud and dirty. And it smelled.

"We'll stay the night and head out in the mornin'."

"We'll head out now."

He rubbed his jaw. "Abbie, Matt an' Will deserve a night in

town. One night ain't gonna hurt."

Was he saying he wanted a night in town himself? She eyed him briefly. His expression was unreadable, but she clearly remembered his reception of Lil Brandon's attention. He likely intended to have himself a good time tonight. She turned away.

"Walk along with me to make the sale, and then we'll find us some dinner."

"No, thank you. I'll just take a room."

He took her arm and stepped off the walk, taking her briskly along with him. "You may not be hankerin' fer my company, but Dodge City ain't the place fer a lady to spend her hours alone."

Abbie caught up the skirts of the dress she'd changed into before entering town and kept pace beside him. She hadn't the energy to argue. Besides, she took a grim satisfaction thinking she just might spoil his fun, as well. Listening to Cole negotiate, she realized he'd done better for her than she could have hoped. She felt slightly chagrined walking beside him back toward the noisy street.

"There's a tolerable restaurant in that hotel yonder."

"Fine."

"Ain't fancy like some of the others, but there's less . . . activity."

She guessed she knew what he meant by activity. That he was willing to sacrifice touched her not at all. "Fine."

As they sat at the table having placed their orders, Abbie felt distinctly uneasy. For one thing, nearly every eye in the place was on her, and that was understandable since she was the only woman in the room save the one serving tables. She felt regrettably thankful for Cole's presence. "Haven't these men been taught not to stare?"

"I reckon they cain't rightly help it." He raked his eyes over her himself. "It's nice seein' you in a dress again."

She flushed with anger and wished she'd kept the pants on. So much for being thankful.

"Well, Abbie." He raised his glass to her. "Here's to a successful drive."

That his glass held tea instead of whiskey was something, she thought, and raised her own. "Not as successful as I would have liked, but I thank God it's over."

"Nearly. We still gotta get home."

The way he said *home* sent a chill up her spine. Surely he wouldn't expect to stay on. "I think we ought to discuss your wages."

To her surprise, he grinned wryly. "You cain't stand it, can you?"

"Stand what?"

"To have me do somethin' for you."

"No, I can't." She waited while the plates of steak and gravy were served, then looked at him frankly. "I want to pay you."

"I know you do."

"Well?"

"I cain't accept it."

"Why not?"

He took a bite of steak and kept his eyes on the plate. He wiped his mouth with the checkered napkin, then rested his hands on the table. "I don't reckon you want me to talk about it, but I made a promise to Mr. Farrel I mean to keep. A promise to look after you."

Abbie felt herself spiraling down. To hear Cole speak Monte's name . . . to think they had moments together before he . . . Her chest constricted, and she pushed away from the table.

Cole caught her wrist. "Don't go out, Abbie. You may despise me, but at least you know I got no intentions toward you."

She could hardly control her trembling. She stood at the brink with her loss gaping. *God help me.* They were empty words. God didn't help. He only took and took and took. She sank into her seat because her legs wouldn't hold her. The smell of the meat gagged her.

With his eyes fixed on Abbie, Cole released her wrist, then applied himself to his meal. At least he had the decency not to speak again. She fought the dark thoughts and memories, the sudden terror for Elliot. What if something had happened? What if the typhoid had spread? What if he were gone like ... *Monte!* She screamed inside.

Cole reached over and took her hands. "I'm sorry, Abbie. It wasn't my intention to upset you."

His hands were like coals on hers. Seeing that he had finished his food, she pulled away. "I want to go now."

He put his money on the table and stood. He walked her up the stairs with a hand on her elbow, and even that touch seared her. He unlocked her door and handed her the key. "Lock it behind you. I'll be out here if you need me."

She scarcely heard him. She was thankful for the wood of the door between them, and she turned the lock viciously. A promise to Monte. To take care of her? Had Monte turned her over to his betrayer? She dropped her face to her hands.

Monte, how could you? She thought of the love she'd seen in Cole's face when he saved her from the rustler. She thought of the ache in his voice when he'd told her he couldn't leave even though she was married to Monte, that he wasn't sure Monte could take care of her.

Oh, God, had he let Monte die? Had he even caused it, in order to have her? A low wail started in her throat, but she stifled it lest Cole hear. She looked frantically at the window. A narrow balcony ran along outside with stairs to the ground. She would go. She would leave tonight. She knew the way home now.

She would get to the camp where James waited with the wagon. Together they ... no, the wagon was too slow. She'd take a horse, several horses, with James none the wiser. She'd have a whole night's start on Cole. He wouldn't catch her. The others would come on their own.

She pushed open the window. It squeaked dreadfully, but the street was noisier than it had been earlier. Cole would hear nothing. The cold night air struck her, but she squeezed out anyway, crept along the balcony, and went down. She hurried from the alley to the street and started for the livery where she'd left Zephyr when they came in.

If she took the horses Cole and Will and Matt had ridden in, she would not have to brave the camp at all, but how could she get the horses from the livery? Cole had turned them over. Would the man let her take them? She would have to try. She stepped off the boardwalk to the shadows beside the livery.

Before she took another step, a strong arm gripped her waist and pulled her into the dark. A high, foul laugh filled her ear as the hand covered her mouth. "Well, now, what have we here?"

To her horror another voice answered. "Mighty purty. Jist our luck she's alone."

Abbie struggled and thrashed when the man came close and stroked her hair. She could see nothing of their faces, but the men were strong and their intentions obvious. She kicked back at the first one's knee, but he tightened his grip on her waist and crushed the breath from her.

The other grabbed her shoulders. "Come on, lady. We're jist havin' some fun. Give us a kiss." He leaned close enough for her to smell the whiskey on his breath.

She bit the palm across her mouth, and in the moment it was pulled away she screamed. The man shook her hard, then slapped her. She fell, and the weight of the other man came down on her. She raked her nails into his neck. He hollered and jerked back, then struck her again.

Abbie fell back, stunned, as he once again trapped her with his body. Suddenly he was yanked from her, and she heard the crack of bone against bone. He went down heavily, then scrambled up. Were the two of them fighting each other?

She pressed into the wall as the man was sent sprawling. The second one came like a ramrod, head down, and she saw that it was a third man he hit. But the third kept his feet, and her assailant took double fists to the head and stayed where he fell. The one who had caught her ran down the alley into the night. She was pulled to her feet, and she smelled the familiar scent. Cole.

He held her shoulders a long moment. "What in God's name are you doin' out here?" His anger was not cloaked in the least.

Her heart was pounding so hard she could scarcely breathe. She dropped her forehead to his vest, and he pulled her in close.

"Abbie . . ." His voice was hoarse. "Do I gotta hog-tie you?"

She didn't trust herself to speak.

"Come on." He yanked her up to the boardwalk and along its length with his hand firmly on her arm.

The street was as busy and rowdy as it had been in daylight, but she kept her eyes on the ground. How had Cole known? How had he gotten to her? She couldn't ask. It didn't matter. She wanted to cry. She wanted to hide. She wanted anyone but Cole to have come to her aid.

Outside her door he stopped and turned her. "You got anything to say . . . that I might understand?"

She shook her head mutely.

He clenched his jaw and stared down the hall. "I'll have yer word to stay put, or I'll spend the night inside the door and never mind yer reputation."

"I'll stay," she managed, then took the key from her pocket.

He let her in, then pocketed the key himself. "You use that window again, an' I'll let them eat you alive."

She closed the door behind her and fell to the bed exhausted. The shock and ache and relief overcame her, and she slept.

Cole sat outside her door, back to the wood, hat low over his brow. He'd slept in worse positions, but sleep eluded him now. He'd stepped outside for a smoke in time to see her heading off. Why would she try a thing like that? Why did she mean to leave him behind? Had he so upset her, or was it more?

He rubbed the cracked and bleeding knuckles of his right hand, then shook it out and rested it on his thigh. He understood the blame she put on him. Right or wrong, it was a normal feeling. He could tell she wanted nothing to do with him, but up to now she'd depended on his help, if reluctantly. Why all of a sudden would she try to get away from him without his knowing?

All she had to do was tell him to get, and what choice did he have? Was she afraid he'd refuse? He frowned. Was she afraid . . . of him? Why? He drew his knees up. He needed a smoke, and this time he wasn't going outside to do it. He took a paper from his pocket and rolled a cigarette, lit the end, and drew in deeply.

What had he said to upset her? That he had a promise to keep? How could that set her running? Did she think he meant more by it than just ensuring her well-being? Did she think he still hoped . . . no, better not entertain that line of thinking.

He wondered where Matt and Will were. As Matt had taken the boy in hand, he'd probably have to peel them off the floor come morning. But they'd done their job. Now it was just the trip home. Home. And then what?

He drew the tobacco into his lungs. After he got her home, he'd cut loose and go back to drifting. He'd learned better than to stay in any one place. He'd come too close to calling somewhere home. He rubbed a hand over his face and smoothed his mustache. As soon as he saw Abbie safely back, he'd hit the trail.

He rested his head back against the door. He took a drag and blew a slow stream of smoke from his lips. No sound came from the room. Did Abbie sleep? Was she lying there thinking how to be rid of him? Was she shaking still? Was she injured?

He hadn't even checked for injuries, not that she'd have let him. He rubbed the cigarette out on the wood plank floor. She'd see to herself well enough. So far he'd kept his distance. He wouldn't let her fear and trembling change that.

He hunched his shoulder against the door and tipped the hat down over his eyes. He dozed and woke and dozed again, then finally drifted off.

He almost fell in backwards when Abbie pulled the door open the next morning.

"Good heaven's, Cole. Did you spend the night on the floor there?"

"Where'd you think I'd be?" He pulled himself up and frowned. "No, don't answer that." Her smug expression was clear enough. Well, good. Let her think the worst of him. It would make cutting loose that much easier. "You ready?"

"I'd like to wash before we leave."

"Good. I would, too." He scowled at her surprised look, but refused to let her goad him.

She stopped when they reached the head of the stairs and turned. "I owe you my thanks for last night. I suppose now is as good a time as any to say so."

He tipped his hat swaggishly. "At yer service, Abbie. You're most kindly welcome."

She turned and walked down. "Where does one bathe in a cow town?"

"Well, if we'd stayed in one of the fancier hotels, we could bathe there. As it is you'll have to settle for the bathhouse."

"Lead the way."

"Yes, ma'am."

••••••••

Soaking in the dented tub, Abbie lathered her arms. Cole's swagger this morning was enough to make her scream. He probably thought his heroics the night before had given him the upper hand. While it had brought her to her senses, she had no intention of letting him know that.

The thoughts that had plagued her through the night still spun in her head. The feeling of safety and relief in Cole's arms . . . Surely it was nothing more than reflex after the terror of those men. She'd been foolish to think he had willingly caused Monte's death, but that didn't mean she cared for him.

She stood in the tub and poured the pitcher of rinse water over her body, then stepped out. Oh, to be clean was glorious. She refused to think of the men pawing her in the dark. Would she see them this morning, battered and bruised from Cole's beating? She shuddered and pulled on her clothes. The dress was dirty and torn at the waist but it was the only one she'd brought, so she put it back on and went out.

Cole stood in the street. His blond hair curled, and he was clean shaven with his mustache trimmed. In the sunlight, his chiseled cheekbones cut triangular shadows in his face. When he turned her way, her chest lurched. He was so handsome with his green eyes and tanned skin, his angular jaw and . . . What was she thinking? Abbie looked away when he approached.

"Well, now, if you're done . . . I thought you were gonna spend the whole day in there. Almost got us another room."

She put up her chin and started for the livery.

He caught her arm. "I got the horses over yonder. Thought you'd rather not pass that way again."

Cole's thoughtfulness stabbed her. He had no right to consider her feelings as he did. She was not his responsibility, no matter what Monte had charged. The ache heightened as she walked to Zephyr and mounted. As Cole gave her a hand, she noticed the bruised knuckles and a different pang seized her.

Matt and Will joined them at the edge of town, and they rode silently to the camp where James had stayed with the horses. He stood, grinning broadly when they rode up. The fire was burning and he had coffee on. She dismounted and set about making their meal. "We ought to have another bag of flour and cornmeal before we start back."

Cole tipped up his hat. "I planned to pick up some things once I got you out of town."

That was as close as he'd come to saying what trouble she'd caused him. "Cole . . . I do apologize for . . ."

"I'd just like to know why."

She stared at the cornmeal batter in the bowl. What could she say? Her thoughts had been crazy, born of grief and anger and desperate need. What could she tell him without betraying her own mindless fears?

"Yeah. That's what I figured." He walked away.

She almost called him back. She didn't mean to hurt him. Not anymore. But he barked something at the men and strode off.

Twenty-Five

Abbie alternated between riding in the wagon and riding horseback, but she preferred horseback. Sitting beside James in the rickety wagon over the lumpy trail made her restless, and she had toughened up so that riding was not nearly as taxing. Will's horse kept pace with hers.

"I sure do like that Mr. Twain's *Adventures of Tom Sawyer*."

"I'm glad." Her grandfather had sent it fresh off the press the year Colorado became a state. She had given it to Will before reading it herself. "I didn't know you brought it along."

"I hadn't time to read it while we were driving the herd, but these last evenings I've made some headway. It's almost as good as the jumping-frog one."

"I'm glad you're enjoying it, Will." The last evenings around the campfire had been more restful and the men more pleasant. Except for Cole. She looked ahead to where he rode alone. He'd been singularly snappish and cross.

Why didn't he just ride off and go his own way? Surely they could make it now without him, and he obviously couldn't wait to be through with the job. Of course it was his promise that kept him. Who would have thought Cole Jasper could be as stubborn about keeping his word as . . . as Monte had been?

She shook her head, furious that she'd compared them. Monte was a man of honor, of culture, of compassion. Cole Jasper . . . She kneed the mare and caught up to him. "Can't we go any faster? Why must we poke along as though we still had five hundred steers in tow?"

Without a word, he spurred his horse. Surprised, she likewise urged the mare and heard Will and Matt with the remuda behind. They rode swiftly for the better part of an hour. She could feel her horse's chest heaving when Cole reined in. He turned and stopped beside her. "Now we'll rest the horses an' wait fer the wagon."

She looked back. The wagon was nowhere in sight. She sagged in the saddle. Of course James couldn't run the horses pulling the wagon, and the wagon would have come to pieces on this terrain. Why didn't Cole just tell her they couldn't hurry? Why did he have to be so . . . ornery!

She swung down and stalked to the creek with the mare. He was already there with his gelding, Whitesock. He eyed her where she stood, and she squarely returned his gaze.

She raised her chin. "You might have simply told me. All I needed was an explanation."

His look penetrated deep inside her. He walked away without a word. So that was it. He was still smarting that she hadn't told him why she tried to leave. Very well. If he wanted an explanation so badly . . .

Cole heard her come up behind as he walked out across the grassy plain. He kept walking, and she spoke to his back.

"In the first place, Monte had no right to charge you with my care. In the second, I never asked for your help. You had no right to send money without my knowledge to the men I thought were loyal to me. And thirdly—"

He waited.

"I hold you responsible for my husband's death."

He turned. "You think I don't know that? Not that you ever bothered to hear what happened. It might surprise you to know I done my share of grievin' fer Mr. Farrel. But I don't suppose that'd change anything you think or feel."

"Why should it?" Abbie's eyes were like ice, hard and blue.

"It shouldn't, I guess, except you're always on yer knees actin' like a Christian lady."

"As though you would know anything about God's ways."

"You got a right to be how you want. Just seems a person ought not to affect somethin' they ain't. You shouldn't pretend, if you don't believe it."

"What do you mean? Of course I believe." Her face flushed with anger.

"Like heck. You mouth the words, but they don't get no further than yer throat. Yer heart's gone bitter."

"Haven't I the right to be?"

"Maybe you have. But you ain't the only one."

Abbie's eyes narrowed dangerously. "What have you possibly suffered to compare?"

"It don't matter. The point is you're forgettin' one primary commandment. Forgive, that you might be forgiven."

"How dare you judge me."

Cole gripped her arms in frustration. "Maybe I ain't got the right. But I know a thing or two about God's ways."

"You?" She fairly spat it. "You wouldn't know God if He hit you with a bolt of lightning."

Cole stared deeply into her eyes, then released her arms. "Maybe you're right. Maybe I'm deceivin' myself. I thought I knew you, too." He turned away.

"Don't you dare walk away from me."

He stopped, then with a long breath, shook his head and started on. He heard a queer sound from her throat, and a second later she flew at him, her rage giving her strength beyond her stature. He staggered and turned, caught the arms that pummeled him.

Abbie thrashed, freed her hand, and slapped him hard. He took the blow, but caught her arm again and grabbed her close. He held her tight while she screamed and kicked against him. "I hate you! I hate you! I . . ." Her tears came in a rush, and it was worse than anything she could say against him.

Cole dropped his chin to the crown of her head. Her sobs came from a depth that made him wonder if she'd cried at all for the pain inside. He could well believe it was four years of sorrow breaking out now. He felt more helpless than he'd ever been in his life.

What did he know of God's ways? It had been a lot of years since he'd turned his thoughts that way, and they were rusty and unsure. He'd given up looking for God too young. It seemed a man ought to stand on his own. He'd only meant for Abbie to see her way, not for his own thoughts to turn to heaven. But there they were.

God. What do I do? He felt an overwhelming need to comfort but had no idea how. Automatically he stroked her back, her hair. He caught her head between his hands and turned her face up. Awash her eyes were unbelievably blue, her face flushed, her mouth . . .

Cole bent and kissed her, the aching need overwhelming his restraint. He expected another slap for it, but her arms came around his neck and her return kiss was more ardent than he could bear. He didn't dare hope her heart was in it. He pried her fingers loose and set her back. Abbie stared at him, then turned away. She dropped her face to her hands and wept.

God help him, he couldn't take it. He reached a hand to the hair that lay across her neck. Slowly he swept it aside and kissed the place where it sprang from her skin. He breathed in her scent, something sweet and flowery. "How is it you smell good even on the trail?"

"I washed." She sniffed, then tipped her head back as his lips moved across her neck to the hollow beneath her ear.

He turned her in his arms and kissed her mouth gently. Her arms wrapped his waist, and he caught her face between his hands and kissed her hard. She drove his need with her own. Her lips were soft, sweet, willing.

"Abbie . . ." Cole could hardly restrain himself. "Not like this."

She gripped his back and kissed the edge of his jaw.

He closed his eyes and pulled her tight against him. "You got a great emptiness inside, but this won't fill it. Not like this. It ain't right."

"I don't care."

"Yes, you do." He eased her away and looked down into eyes deep with emotion. Looking at her, he thought he'd die of the pain in his chest. Could a man die of loving a woman? "We need to sort this out, Abbie. And I don't think too good with you this close."

She forked her fingers into her hair, resting her forehead on her palm. "I've made a fool of myself."

"No, you ain't. I reckon that cry's been a long time comin'. And as for the rest, that was my doin'." He took her shoulders and made her look at him. "I apologize, Abbie. I had no right."

She clenched her hands, fighting the tears. "I don't know what's wrong with me. One minute I . . . can't stand the sight of you, the next . . ."

"Don't say it. We got a hundred miles to cover yet."

Her eyes met his with new fire. "Cole Jasper, you are the most infuriating man!" She started walking.

"Abbie."

She glanced over her shoulder.

"Don't go far."

Abbie wandered over the Colorado plain. The late October wind was chilly as she left Cole behind. She felt torn apart. What were these feelings she had for him? They couldn't be love. There was no one for her but Monte. God had made them one for the other. They were one. Only . . . he was gone.

That didn't change anything. Monte was her first love, the father of her child. Was she so cheap that the baring of Cole's heart could make her forget what she knew with Monte? Never.

It was only that her own heart cried out to be loved. She was twenty-six years old, and she'd had love for so short a time. Cole desired her, but more than that, he knew her. He knew her pain, her need. He'd suffered with her through the valley, and she sensed a union between them—a union of two souls who'd lived through hell and now hoped to love again. But that couldn't be . . . could it?

She closed her eyes. As always, Cole had seen through her, seen the mockery of her relationship with the Christ she professed. He had provoked her anger, but what he said was true. She shouldn't pretend what she didn't believe. But what did she believe? That if she did one thing wrong God would strike again? Elliot, maybe? Or Jenny?

What had Father Dominic said? *"There on the cross your sin is hung."* Then why did God crush her again and again? She regularly woke in cold sweats fearing to find Elliot stiff and without breath. She guarded Jenny so rigidly the child snuck away just to feel the wind in her face. She couldn't go on living in fear, but how could she stop?

"Forgive, that you might be forgiven." Forgive whom? Cole? She wanted to. Herself? God? Forgive God? The very thought seemed blasphemous. Wasn't it God's right to give and to take? Blessed be the name of the Lord. Yet . . . Abbie staggered and looked up.

She'd gone farther than she should. She turned back. The land lay empty around her. Looking out at its vastness, she dropped to her knees. *Oh, Lord, I don't know if it's right. But I forgive you for taking Monte.* Her tears flowed. *I don't understand why, but I believe your ways are above mine.* She looked into the blackness of her grief, and found that she could face it. *Please God, don't let me live in fear. Please deliver me.*

Abbie stayed on her knees until they ached, but she was hardly aware of the pain as she touched the deeper wounds inside. She remembered Monte's smile, the warmth of his eyes, his gentle, passionate touch. She remembered his hand on her as their child grew inside, his excitement that they had at last conceived. She remembered him lying stiff and cold, his chest torn open, his heart stilled. She wept until the tears were spent, then stayed silent in their wake.

She heard a footstep on the crisp grass before her and opened her eyes to Cole. He reached out and helped her to her feet. "I'm sorry, Abbie. I had no right to knock yer faith. I was wrong."

"You were right. I had lost sight of what I believe."

"I don't know enough about it to say."

"Sometimes the eyes of an unbeliever see more clearly than

those of the people God calls his own." She looked into his face. "Cole . . . tell me how Monte died."

His throat worked, and he ran the back of his hand over his jaw. "I guess you better sit." He dropped cross-legged beside her. "Abbie, I . . . you stop me if you want."

She nodded.

"First let me say yer husband was one of the finest men I ever knew. Gettin' to be a purty fair cowboy, too. But he didn't know the animals like I do. He saw that Durham bull out there walkin' crazy and thought he could bring it in. I tried to tell him otherwise, but fer all his mild manners, he could be a stubborn man."

Abbie smiled slightly.

"He was the boss. There was never any question about that even when he was so green he squeaked. Guess that was his plantation raising. But after the trouble with Gifford and the drive to Kansas, well, he'd surprised me more than once. I figured between us we just might pull it off with that bull."

Cole looked away, and Abbie sensed his sorrow. Did he truly grieve for Monte? She had seen a companionship and ease between them that had been long in coming. Now she sensed more.

Cole drew a long breath. "He moved to cut off the bull's path, and I took the other side. Then he dismounted. I don't know why. I hollered, but he just stood there waitin' to throw the rope, and the bull charged. I spurred Scotch to full gallop, fired off a shot, but there was nothin' I could do from that distance. The bull dropped Mr. Farrel and charged my way. I took it down, but it was too late."

The tears ran silently down her cheeks. *Oh, Monte. Why?* He had risked the fire for Chance, lost his life for a bull. A bull!

Cole's voice grew hoarse. "He hadn't more than a minute, but he asked me to look after you and his child. He was peaceful in that."

Abbie dropped her forehead to the hands folded on her raised knee. It hurt more than she had believed possible. After four years it was like losing him again. *Why, Monte, why? Oh, dear God.* She felt Cole's hand on her shoulder and leaned against his side. He wrapped her shoulders in his arm. They sat in silence.

The sunset rays faded and the air grew cold. Abbie stirred. "I'm sorry, Cole. I blamed you wrongly, and I apologize."

"No need."

She brushed the hair from her eyes. "I'm ready to go back now."

"I reckon that's good as it's gettin' dark. I was willin' to set here all night, but I cain't answer for what the men'd think." He stood and helped her up. He pulled her briefly into his arms. "I don't expect nothin', Abbie. Just so you know."

She walked beside him as the dusk settled. She felt weak and empty. Without the anger to sustain her there was nothing. She was incapable of feeling. Even the thought of reaching Elliot in a few days brought no emotion. What if she'd been rendered unable to love, unable to feel? *I'm nothing but a shell, God. Put what you want inside.*

Twenty-Six

Abbie jostled in the wagon beside James. She could hardly believe they were back in the yard of the Lucky Star. It felt like forever since she'd seen the pale November sunshine on the white walls and pillars of the house. It almost seemed to shine of its own volition. Her home.

Pearl came out and stood on the porch, clutching her hands at her breast and smiling so broadly her cheeks plumped like popovers. Abbie climbed down the moment the wagon lurched to a stop. "Have Pearl help you unload, James. Will, see to the horses and saddle Zephyr for me. Matt, find Breck and . . ."

She saw Pearl's smile die as she shook her head and came down the steps. "Mizz Abbie . . . Mistuh Breck, he die of the typhoid. Mistuh Skeeter, too."

Abbie's breath left her chest. "What?" Not Breck and Skeeter both . . .

"And Mistuh Curtis, he alive but weak like a baby. I been nursin' him myse'f dese last weeks."

Breck dead, and Skeeter and John Mason. It stabbed at the numbness inside. No, she didn't want to feel again, not like this, not more death. She glanced at Cole, whose mouth had set in a firm line. These men had been his friends, his companions.

"It been real bad here," Pearl continued. "De fever took fifty-eight folks."

"Fifty—oh, dear God. Elliot?" The rush of fear was all too familiar.

"The chillen, dey's fine. Dey with yo mama still."

271

Abbie turned. Will had Zephyr bridled, and she swung up bareback and pressed with her knees. The horse surged across the yard and onto the rough. Cole cantered up beside her.

"You don't have to come, Cole."

"How you plannin' to carry two young'uns home?"

She hadn't thought of that. She hadn't thought beyond seeing for herself that they were safe and well. But she couldn't likely go there and leave them behind again. She sent Cole a smile and kicked with her heels. Zephyr shot forward with a burst of speed, and she clung with her thighs, one hand in the gray mane.

Cole kept pace beside her, and they held an easy lope until Pa's homestead came into view. Her heart beating in her chest, she urged Zephyr again. She slid off before the mare came to a full stop in the yard.

"Mama?" Elliot came around the porch and flew into her arms.

Abbie could hardly breathe, so full was her chest with emotion unleashed. She was not incapable of love or feeling. On the contrary, she thought she would burst with it. His soft, dark hair needed cutting, and one cheek was smudged, but he was the most beautiful thing she'd seen in too long.

Jenny pranced over, and Abbie reached an arm to her. They shared a three-way hug, then she noticed Jenny's glance behind her. Abbie stood as Cole dismounted.

"Howdy, Jenny."

She stared up at him frankly. "Do I know you?"

"You likely don't remember. But I remember you. I never forget a purty face."

Abbie felt a guilty pang. "Jenny, this is Cole Jasper, the man who carved your animals."

Elliot's eyes widened as though he'd just seen Father Christmas.

Jenny smiled. "I think I remember."

Cole smiled gently. "It's okay if you don't. You were a real small mite the last time I seen you."

Abbie watched Jenny walk over and take his hand. "Did you bring Aunt Abbie home?"

"Yup."

Elliot wiggled from her arms and reached for Cole's other hand. "Will you make me some animals?"

Cole squatted down. "Well, I ain't sure yet how long I'll be here. But we'll see what I got time to do." He ruffled Elliot's head. "You're a fine boy. You got the look of yer pa."

Abbie stiffened. Of course Cole couldn't know they'd never spoken to Elliot of Monte. Looking at the light in Elliot's eyes from Cole's remark, she wondered if she'd done the right thing.

Having taken care of business, Elliot came back to her. "You were gone too long, Mama."

"Elliot cried, but I didn't." Jenny still held fast to Cole's hand.

Abbie took Elliot up into her arms, and he wrapped her neck tightly. Nothing had ever felt so good. She wished she could savor it alone until her cup was full, but Mama was in the doorway rubbing her hands on her apron.

"Welcome home, Abbie. Cole, how nice to see you again." Mama's voice was warm as new milk and just as wholesome.

Cole took off his hat. "And you, Mrs. Martin."

Abbie knew Mama must be pleased. She had not approved of her sending Cole away. And the warmth in her welcome told him so.

"Won't you come in for coffee?"

Cole rubbed his hand through his hair. "We're trail worn and dusty."

"All the more reason."

Abbie carried Elliot onto the porch and inside.

Jenny proudly dragged Cole to a chair in the kitchen. "I have my own tea set, but it's at home."

"I'd like to see it sometime." Cole said the words without a trace of scorn.

"I'll invite you for tea. Pearl makes scrumptious apple tarts."

"Pearl's a fine cook." He took the cup of coffee. "Thank you, Mrs. Martin."

"Goodness, Cole. You're like family. Please call me Selena."

"Yes, ma'am." He drank. "Now, that hits the spot."

Abbie felt uneasy. With so much unsettled, Mama was being too familiar. And she didn't want Jenny growing attached to Cole again if . . . She caught his glance and smoothed the concern from her face too late. He read her thoughts with ease.

She dropped her gaze to the coffee in her cup. "I'm sorry, Mama. Would you mind if I made some tea? I'm sick to death of coffee."

Mama smiled. "I'd imagine you are after months on the trail. How did you fare?" Mama took the cup and poured the coffee back into the pot, then put tea leaves in the kettle to steep.

"As well as we could, though we didn't fetch the price I wanted." *Or needed*, Abbie added silently. "We went too late."

"Well, the Lord provides."

"I know." She felt Cole's gaze. "Sometimes it would just be nice to know how." She watched Mama strain the tea and took the cup offered. Elliot rested his hands on her leg as she sat. He'd not left her side except to ask Cole for animals. She hoped he'd have time to make something for the child.

What was she thinking? He wouldn't leave again, would he? But if he didn't, what then? They could hardly go back to the way things were, not after the day on the prairie, not after . . . She closed her eyes and sipped. Maybe the steam would hide the flush her thoughts had caused.

Except for not barking orders at her, Cole had maintained his previous demeanor. He had not once referred to their discussion, nor touched her, nor made any move to further his advances. She had caught a gentle look now and then, but beyond that he'd made no show of his feelings.

Perhaps it had been nothing more than a confused response to her grief. Part of her fervently hoped so. She'd come treach-erously close to feelings she feared more than typhoid fever. But what if he left? She smiled down at Elliot, still pressed as closely to her side as possible. She had her son and Jenny and Mama and

Pa. She had Nora and Clara and her other friends. Surely that was enough.

◆◆◆◆◆◆

As Cole rode back to the Lucky Star with Jenny in the saddle with him, he recalled carrying her when her head had scarcely reached to his chest. He'd had to hold tight or she'd slide off the side. She was a slip of a girl now, but there was the same haunted look behind her smile. A look no child her age ought to have.

He wondered if Abbie realized what Jenny felt when she petted Elliot. Not that he wasn't a fine boy. He was so like his pa, though with Abbie's eyes. The ladies would be lining up some years hence. And he could hardly blame Abbie. That baby had likely brought her through as nothing else could.

But Jenny was a queer little thing. Tough on the outside, but not so tough within. She needed someone who preferred a saucy little sprite with big brown eyes and a fetching smile. He wouldn't mind filling the bill if he knew he'd be staying awhile. 'Course, that was up to Abbie, and there was no telling how it would go.

He'd made sure not to pressure her, and though she'd not had a sharp tongue for him recently, neither had she shown any romantic inclination. He knew better than to hope. Maybe he could stay awhile if she asked, but it wouldn't be easy. Here he was again, waiting on a word from Abbie to decide his road. How many years had it been now?

Jenny's head bobbed against his collarbone. "I have my own mare, Snowdrop. Elliot has a pony, but it's small."

"Well, he's a small boy right now. What color's yer horse?"

"White, silly. That's why she's Snowdrop."

Cole chuckled. "Yeah. I shoulda known."

When they reached the yard, he handed Jenny down to Will, who had already taken Elliot from Abbie. He swung down and stood uneasily. These were uncharted waters all right. Will led the horses away as the children ran to greet Zena on the steps.

Abbie approached. "What are your plans, Cole?"

He couldn't read her eyes. Maybe her thoughts were as muddled as his. "Cain't say as I have any."

She looked as skittish as a new foal, not at all the Abbie he knew. That woman had given as good as she got and come back for more. This one looked storm tossed and weary.

He shrugged. "I reckon I can find a place in town to stay. Or if yer needin' help ... with Breck gone an' all ..."

"Oh, Cole, I don't know what to do." Her eyes came up to his, and he realized again just how young she was. "I've hardly made enough on this sale to cover debts until a new beef herd is ready. I've only two men left, and they surely can't handle the ranch themselves ... if they'll even work for my wages without ... extra ..."

She let her breath out sharply and spread her hands. "Maybe I ought to sell after all."

"Then what?"

She dropped her face in her hands. "I don't know."

"From what I hear you got gents lined up wantin' to marry you."

"That's the last thing I want." She spoke into her hands.

So there it was. He looked up at the house, around the yard, the outbuildings, the land. She could get a fair piece for the place, enough to set her well enough. If that's what she wanted. "You got Will."

She looked up. "What?"

"He's a fair cowboy. That'd give you three hands if you don't mind lookin' after yer own stables. You might get a boy to come out twice a week and muck 'em for you."

Her eyes lit. "I know Tucker would. I could spare him a little something."

"I reckon he'd take to it right well. Sounds like all you need now's a good foreman." He quirked the side of his mouth. "I got some experience in the job."

She shook her head. "I couldn't pay you anywhere near what Monte paid. I'm sure you could do better elsewhere."

"I'm sure I could, too. But it's a right pain in the neck tryin' to keep tabs on you from Santa Fe to Cheyenne to El Paso."

She got that coltish look again, and he felt sure she'd tell him to go on anyway. "I . . . don't know, Cole."

"What happened out there on the prairie ain't likely to happen again. You got yer grievin' out, and . . . I'd bunk in the bunkhouse." Her obvious relief sent a pang through his chest, but he ignored it.

"The men take their meals in the house now, since Charlie passed."

"You cover my expenses and feed me on Pearl's cookin', and we'll call it even."

"I wish I could do more."

"When you can, I'll let you."

Abbie smiled, and it took all he had not to pull her into his arms. *A dern fool indeed.*

◆◆◆◆◆◆◆

Abbie almost felt hopeful as she drove the buggy the next morning toward the mission with Jenny on one side and Elliot on the other. Elliot pushed the dark strands from his eyes. ". . . and Tucker fell in with the pig, and Grandpa . . ." Abbie smiled. He hadn't stopped talking from the minute she slapped the reins.

She glanced at Jenny sitting primly beside her. "What's the matter, Jenny?"

"Nothing."

She could feel the child's tension, and reached over to stroke her neck. "You're awfully quiet."

"Elliot's a chatterbox."

"That's not kind, Jenny." And she knew that wasn't what bothered her. "What is it?"

"Katie's getting a new baby."

"I know. Not for a month yet, though."

Jenny turned her serious brown eyes to her. "Are you going to get a baby, too?"

Abbie was amazed how the words hurt. It wasn't as though the thought never occurred to her that she would not have another child, but hearing it spoken so directly . . . She steadied her voice. "No, Jenny. I haven't a husband."

Jenny turned her chin up. "But I thought Cole . . ."

Abbie's heart lurched. She raised her eyebrows in surprise.

Jenny rushed on. "I thought you brought him home to be our pa."

Her pa. How could Cole be her pa? It jolted Abbie somewhere deep. Even if they married, which thankfully Cole had no intention of pursuing, he would not be Jenny's pa unless . . . Was there something deeper Jenny was saying? Did she feel . . . separate?

"Cole is a friend, Jenny."

"Oh. Like me."

Abbie reined in. She turned Jenny toward her. "No, Jenny. You are not a friend. You are family. You're my niece, but you're like my own little girl, and I love you as though you were my own."

Jenny fingered the ruffle on her dress.

"Don't you believe that?"

Jenny shrugged. "I guess. But it's not the same." She looked up. "Could I pretend Cole is my pa?"

Abbie felt her chest quake. "I don't . . . think so, Jenny. One shouldn't pretend things that make people what they're not."

"But we pretend I'm a princess, and I'm not. And Elliot pretends he's a pony. And—"

"Yes, I know. But you see, you're pretending for yourself, not for someone else. Cole might not understand."

"Doesn't he know how to pretend?"

Abbie had a very hard time picturing Cole pretending anything. "I don't think so, Jenny. But Katie does." She took up the reins and slapped them.

"Aunt Abbie?"

"Yes."

"If you got a baby girl . . . would I still be like your own?"

The pain again. "Yes, Jenny. Always."

She had a cup of tea with Glenna, then left the children to play while she drove to see Nora. As she approached the mission house, she saw a rider leaving at a canter. She reined in outside the chapel and led the horse to the trough, then knocked on Nora's door.

"I already told ya no, ya fool lad. Give a girl a minute to think, will ya." Nora flung the door open.

Abbie smiled. "Was that . . ."

"Aye. Davy McConnel's makin' me daft."

"Is he courting you?"

"Aye. He thinks I like the looks of him."

Abbie laughed. "And do you?"

"I'd never tell him if I did." Nora took her arm. "Come an' have a cup. It's a long time ye've been away."

"Seems like forever. I don't think I'll ever sit quite the way I used to."

"I canna believe you drove the cattle yourself, Abbie."

"Not exactly myself. Cole—that is—the men drove the cattle. I mainly saw to the horses and cooked. Poor James nursed his back all night."

Nora handed her the tea. "It's glad I am you're home. And in one piece, as well. But I'm sorry about your workers. What'll you do?"

"I'll manage. The man who used to be foreman for Monte is back. He helped me drive the cattle and said he'd stay on a bit." She tried not to reveal anything but the bare facts of Cole's business with her. The rest was too muddled, too precarious.

Nora nodded. "I don't know how you do it. It's hard enough takin' care of Father O'Brien comin' in at all hours from visitin' the sick and what not."

Abbie tried not to imagine taking care of Cole, but the memory of his cut and bleeding side, his stoic face, his wry smile . . .

Nora waved her hand. "I'd not like to be responsible for too many men at once."

"I imagine you could handle Davy." Abbie gave her an impish smile. "He's the mild McConnel."

"Mild is he? More like mule headed if ye ask me." But she flushed.

"Oh, Nora, I am glad. Four years is a long time for him to still be paying attention. He's a good man."

"Don't be thinkin' ye hear weddin' bells. You're a fine one to talk. What's it up to now? Nine proposals, last I heard."

Abbie stared into her cup. "That's different."

"Not to my thinkin'."

"How was your harvest?"

"Oh fine, an' the weather's been nice an' Father O'Brien's rheumatism isn't near as bad here in the dry, but that's not what we were discussin'."

Abbie smiled. "I knew when you came that we were alike. Four years has turned us into peas in a pod."

Nora laughed. "And a pair of hard, dry ones we are. What if I up an' marry Davy? Where'll that leave you?"

"Has he asked?"

"Aye. Fourteen times a day lately. He's found so many ways to say it, he could put them in a book."

"I never considered Davy McConnel a man of words."

"I suppose any man pushed far enough can find a thing or two to say."

Abbie smiled and sighed. "I suppose so." Monte had been a man of words. He was so well read, knowledgeable about so much. He enjoyed discoursing. How she missed their discussions, their arguments even, the way he'd raise his eyebrow to concede a point. She would never have that again.

Nora sipped her tea. "It's never the same, is it? If I keep waitin' for Davy to be Jaime, I'll die on the vine. I know that here." She tapped her head. "But I'm afraid."

"Of what?"

Nora shrugged. "Maybe comparin' 'em. Maybe . . . forgettin'."

Abbie's throat tightened. "I have a picture of Monte. We had it made in Charleston. I look at it every day to keep him in my mind."

Nora's finger dragged over her cup. "Maybe . . . it's time ya put it away."

✦✦✦✦✦✦✦

Abbie lay awake. Time to put it away . . . to forget? No. To go on? How? *Lord, I can't see my way. I don't know your will. Help me.* She looked at the picture in the shadows. It had taken months after Monte's death for her to look at it, and only the fear of forgetting had brought it out.

But once she had, she kept it where she could see it. High enough to be out of Elliot's reach, but never out of her own. *Oh, Monte.* There was a shadow in his eyes from the loss of Frances, but his smile was there. The photographer had wanted a serious pose, but she insisted he smile.

Her arguing had amused him enough to manage it. Her own picture in the hinged frame beside his was prim, but Monte had sworn he saw a naughty streak in her expression. She clasped her hands at her throat and looked to the ceiling. Too many thoughts, too many memories. She could never tuck them all away. She closed her eyes.

But maybe there was room to live, as well. She had much to live for. The children, the ranch, the men who worked it loyally, and the servants who were more family than not. She might never again love a man as she had loved Monte, but her heart was full nonetheless.

Elliot's kisses were soft on her cheek. Jenny had shown an affection deepened by the sharing of her fears and Abbie's assurance of her love. And there was no arguing Cole's place in her heart, though she couldn't yet probe its depth. He was willing to stay, and that was enough.

She felt grateful beyond words for her blessings. Whatever tomorrow held, whatever fears, whatever grief, God's grace would see her through. Whatever His purpose for her life, He was mighty enough to accomplish the work He had begun. Warm drowsiness stole over and lured her deeper.

"Mama."

She opened her eyes to the white-gowned, tousle-haired boy beside her bed.

His small hand snaked into hers. "I thought you might be afraid."

Abbie translated and raised the covers to admit her little son. As he snuggled into her warmth, wiggling and burrowing, she wrapped him in her arms. "I'm so blessed to have a fine, strong man to care for me." She kissed his soft head and smiled.

But the words conjured another face, rugged and mustached; green eyes that could ignite with sulfurous flames or hold such aching tenderness they melted her knees; arms strong and capable; hands as adept with rope and gun as they were gentle on her cheek. She felt a quickening inside, a tentative searching. Maybe . . . in God's time . . . maybe . . .

Acknowledgments

All thanks and praise to my Lord and Savior,
for whom and through whom all things are accomplished.

And thanks to the people on earth He has provided
to love and support me through this work.

To Him be the glory and honor forever.